The Wish Lists

By JM Spade

Jess,
Thank you for
being such an
inspirational friend!
♡ JMSpade

Publisher: Independently published (October 16, 2019)

ISBN-10: 1694114090
ISBN-13: 978-1694114099

For more information, email: jmspade@mail.com

Acknowledgements:

I want to thank my family and friends for their support as I worked to finally craft my first novel. I have always dreamed of writing my own book and this dream has finally become a reality.

Of course, I want to thank <u>all</u> of my parents. Without them, I wouldn't be the person I am today.

I want to specifically thank:
- ☐ Kimberly Applebey
- ☐ Mary Jane Clark
- ☐ Melannie Canard
- ☐ my work wife, Marcía Ramsey
- ☐ Amber Blett
- ☐ Renee Uitto

who helped me with suggestions, inspiration, and organizing my endless stream of ideas.

I want to thank Leilani Ruesink for encouraging my creativity and love of writing from a very early age.

I want to thank my husband and daughters who sacrificed their time with me while I wrote. I appreciate their love and support in all things I do.

Ultimate thanks be to God.
Love always, J.M.

Chapter 1: How I Got Here

I was in my thirties when I decided to go to nursing school. It took me that long to figure out what I was meant to do with my life. Many times during clinicals, I asked myself if I could have done it when I was younger, but the answer was always no. I was confident that if I had gone into nursing right out of high school, my nursing career wouldn't have gone the same way. I wasn't the same person then as I am now. Either way, I'd have been a fresh-faced new grad entering the nursing world.

The difference is what *I* get out of it. How I react to patients, how they impact *me,* and how much I have to give to *them*. No doubt about it, my nursing career would *not* be the same if I'd have gone to nursing school earlier in life. Of course, I didn't know all of this when I started. But at the end of the first year, I was 100% confident that this was how it was meant to be all along.

After high school, I traveled the world using my dad's checkbook. I had bucked the trend of college and flown by the seat of my pants. I'd grown up as a "rich kid" and having money for everything I wanted. It was such a thrill to go wherever the wind blew me and answer to no one. I had climbed the 669 steps to the top of the Eiffel tower, watched a real bullfight in Madrid, helped to build a church in Africa, kayaked in New Zealand, and hiked through the Amazon. I did many smaller things along the way like drinking beer in Berlin, riding a gondola in Venice, and watching an opera in Sydney. I made new friends when staying in hostels or couch surfing or sometimes even when sitting next to someone along the way. I felt free from the restraints I'd imagined were holding me back and I had flown like a free bird.

That lasted all of six months before I received a phone call telling me it was time to come back down to Earth. I was being cut off. I had a month to get a job or my credit card would magically stop working. Realistically, that lifestyle wasn't actually sustainable. By my dad's standards, I was wasting my life and needed to come back home to get a job. In hindsight, he was right but I would never have admitted it to him. My dad would later admit that he had allowed me to go on my adventure because it was what he had always wished he could have done. Growing up, my father worked for everything he had. It was my turn to work for what I had.

I had no choice but to return home after his phone call. It's not like I could have spent my entire life traveling the world alone anyway. I'd had plenty of time for self-exploration, but at the end of each day, I was alone. The world seemed cold as I traversed it, watching couples in cafes or families trying to take selfies. My father was right and it was time to come home. The friendships I made were fleeting and my friendships back home were nothing more than sporadic phone calls and postcards. The adventure was breathtaking but would have been better if I'd have had someone to share it with. I'd spread my wings long enough.

Home was a brick mansion at the end of a cul-de-sac in a fancy gated community. A housekeeper ensured that all 10,000 square feet were kept clean and tidy. The kitchen was filled with massive cabinets, granite countertops, and a fully stocked refrigerator. Our house also had a theater, a library, and an office that my dad was almost always found in. Staying up late reading books and doing homework as he worked at his mahogany desk were the memories I held close. The yard included a pool, fountains, and a rose garden. I never saw anyone swimming in the pool these days but it usually had a blown-up flamingo floating aimlessly.

When I was in school, our house had seemed like party central. I always had friends over and my dad was always trying to impress some new client. Fancy dinner parties were something my dad and I enjoyed hosting. My first drink of champagne had come at the young age of thirteen while celebrating the opening of another branch of my dad's company. No one noticed me sneak a bottle under the table and share it with my friend Emma. We drank ourselves silly and slept hard that night.

It had been just Dad and me for a long time. He was my rock. If some boy had broken up with me, my dad was my shoulder to cry on. If my friends were assholes, my dad always had the wisdom to cheer me up. While I didn't want him to be right about coming home, he had never led me astray before. He had let me spread my wings and fly right after high school. He'd never said anything negative about my carefree lifestyle I was living. He would ask me about my adventures and suggest new things and places for me to try.

Dad had married my mother right out of college, and she had gotten pregnant within their first year of marriage. By the time I was five, she was an alcoholic. Sleeping all day and drinking into the wee hours of the night became an everyday occurrence. I hated when she drove me to school and tried my best to leave her alone when I was home.

One December day, she's surprised me by packing my lunch. She had never packed my lunch before. She walked me next door and asked the neighbor to drive me to school. I remember the tear that rolled down her cheek as she kissed me goodbye. At the time, I hadn't understood why she was crying as she sent me to school. When I returned home from school that day, she was gone. I didn't begin to worry until the sun set and she wasn't home yet. Eventually, I stopped waiting and stopped worrying.

The void she left grew smaller year after year, but it was replaced by anger. Sometimes I wonder what she did that was so horrible she couldn't stay. Even now, when I think about abandoning a child, my stomach drops as if I'd just crested the top of the roller coaster.

Despite being ditched by my own mother, I felt I'd adapted well and had become a well-adjusted adult. However, I knew I had what must have been my mother's spirit. Taking personality quizzes and job aptitude tests hadn't seemed like my thing when I was in High School. I had good grades but I had enjoyed socializing and being a "free bird". I had no responsibilities and no restrictions. A job was the last thing I'd thought of. A future had been so far from my mind and I lived day by day.

I had been everyone's friend and had been "too busy" to settle down. Sitting down in front of the computer filling out college applications had felt like being in handcuffs. With no one to make me fill them out, deadlines came and went. My friends received acceptance letters and made plans. The same jealousy I had when their mothers picked them up from school, attended field trips, or helped with classroom parties, reared its ugly head.

Returning home, I ended up finding a job working in a lawyer's office as a secretary. Clients from all over the world were easy to relate to with my experience, but each day I found myself sitting at an oak desk with a computer and telephone from 8:00 a.m. until 5:00 p.m. Sometimes, I'd venture out on an errand and feel fresh air instead of the stuffy office space.

I bought a house a short drive from the office and for the first time, I was living my dad's version of my life. I ate the same lunch every day — peanut butter and jelly on white bread. I gained twenty pounds during the first year. I seemed to have everything I needed, and I was comfortable with this life. It wasn't the exciting exploration of the world I had enjoyed those first few months out of high school, but it

7

worked. The longer time went on, the more I realized that I couldn't have continued my free-bird lifestyle forever. This was adulthood. It was time to settle down and develop my life.

Then one day, the man I worked for was dead on the floor. After years of being his secretary, there he was, laying on the floor not breathing, and I had just stood there and stared at him like an idiot. It took me more than a few minutes to realize that I probably should call the police or something. I was absolutely frozen.

Before I found him like that, I had attempted to transfer a call to him, but he hadn't answered. I knocked on his door but opened it when he hadn't responded to that either. I was going to tell him his wife was on line one and his mistress had called to say she was on her way with lunch. I could hear the phone ringing back telling me that his wife was still holding on line one but I couldn't move.

My eyes scanned the room and saw nothing out of place. I hadn't heard anything abnormal from the room. No calls for help, no loud thumps. His window was closed and his blinds open. His computer sat open to Amazon and his cell phone laid on the desk. The room was eerily quiet. And there he was, dead on the floor.

His mistress arrived at the same time as the police. She had crumpled to the ground as the police officer finally answered her frantic cries asking what happened. His wife never came to the office at all. I was confident they knew about each other and that was confirmed when both women attended his funeral. Of course, the wife sat in the front wearing a slim black dress complete with a black hat and veil. The mistress sat at the back wearing a gray suit jacket and skirt with her hair in a neat bun at the base of her neck. The women were easily twenty years apart in age and both had grief written all over their faces.

At the graveside service, the wife spoke a few words, a poem was read by a grandson, and a hymn was sung quietly. Then, the wife tossed her handful of freshly dug dirt on the top of his casket. People followed suit and then quietly left for the luncheon. As the last of the people left, I saw the wife take a second handful of dirt and walk to the mistress.

I thought she might throw it at her or sprinkle it over her head. Again, I was frozen to the spot watching as a million different scenarios played in my head - all of them vicious. Instead, the wife grabbed the mistresses' hand, pulled it forward, and placed the handful of dirt into her outstretched hand. She then guided her gently toward the lowering casket and encouraged her to toss the dirt.

Once the funeral was over, I realized that I no longer had a job. How can you still work as a secretary for a lawyer when that lawyer is six feet under with a granite stone above his head? I knew that all of his clients would be transferred to another practice and his small, cramped office would be leased to another business. What would I do next? Forty hours a week for years had just dissolved into emptiness. Feeling lost, I went to the only place that I could find answers.

At home, I found my dad resting on the couch in the formal living room. My dad wasn't one to sleep during the day or even to rest on the couch, and I was immediately alarmed. It was a weekday and I wondered what appointments he must be missing and how many phone calls and emails he probably had piled up by this point. I gently woke him and felt a flood of relief when he opened his eyes and smiled at me. After a moment, the smile faded and his eyes flashed panic as he asked me to call him an ambulance because he couldn't feel his legs.

By the end of the day, I had learned that my dad had been treating cancer for the last three months without breathing a word of it to anyone. He felt strongly that he could treat it and continue on with all the things he had always done and therefore, no one needed to know. But now I knew. I also knew I wouldn't let him face this alone. It was in this moment of holding his hand and looking into his tired eyes that the answers had fallen into place for me. I wanted to be the one taking care of him. I wanted to take care of all people. I wanted to become a nurse.

It was a three-year journey from realization to graduation. I busted my ass taking the pre-reqs, applying to every nursing school within an acceptable distance, and then studying like crazy once in the program. It had tested me in ways I didn't know were possible and I grew a strong hatred for nursing care plans.

Dad had been doing well with chemotherapy and had reluctantly taken a passenger seat to running his company. He had hired nursing staff to care for him around the clock, but when I got home from class or clinicals, I forced the nurse to take a break and to let me care for him until I had to study. Sometimes, he would help me study my flashcards until one of us could no longer keep our eyes open. There had been much to learn about nursing and Dad was more than willing to help me learn it. The happiness I saw in his eyes was my driving motivation. He had worked hard for the life I had been living and it pleased him to see I'd found a passion for myself.

I graduated from nursing school on a warm January day. Dad had entered remission and begun working again the previous month. I passed my NCLEX on my first attempt and there were so many paths I could go down that I again felt free. I could do whatever type of nursing I wanted and no one was trying to tell me what to do.

I'd sequestered myself in my room the following Monday morning in an attempt to apply for jobs and find "my destiny." Euphoric, I felt eighteen all over again. The world was at my fingertips. Travel nursing would take me all over the country to experience new places and new things like I had before. The emergency room would keep me on my toes and using all of my nursing skills. Pediatrics would be a world I'd only dabbled in, never having had children of my own. Surgery felt too sterile and structured for my current state of being. Home care, hospice, general medicine, doctor's office, recovery, urgent care, trauma care… The possibilities were endless.

When I typed "nurse" into my search bar, three thousand pages of job postings appeared within two seconds. Browsing the first few pages, I noticed that many of them had things in common. I had to decide *where* I wanted to work and then narrow down *who* exactly I wanted to be taking care of. If I were honest, a list of my priorities was probably a better way to narrow it down. I wanted to find something with a great schedule. I wasn't worried about pay or benefits like most of my classmates had been. I didn't want to have to drive a bunch of places. This eliminated home care and hospice. I wanted to go someplace where I would get experiences.

Applied and accepted, I found myself dressed in scrubs and entering an "eat your young" world that literally made me want to shit my pants. All of that freedom I'd felt was gone the first time I entered the hospital armed with a license. Nursing school was supposed to prepare me for what I was about to do, wasn't it? I watched people walk by with purpose in their steps and there I was with my lunchbox, praying to God that nobody would die on my first day.

I had completed the hospital-wide orientation sessions the week before and today, I was to report directly to my new unit. I'd be spending thirty-six to forty hours a week here. My stomach wanted to expel everything I had eaten for breakfast. Why couldn't I be one of those over-confident women that thought they knew all the answers and signed up for every new opportunity like their life depended on it?

During clinicals, most of the instructors had nothing but positive things to say about me. This was shocking since I'd seen how well some of my classmates handled situations and performed skills while I struggled and took longer to perform the same tasks. There had been that time at clinicals when the instructor had asked me to hang a bag of IV antibiotics and I had excitedly agreed. Before I finished studying the drug information, she began to pepper me with questions. Not allowing me to get a word in to answer the questions completely, she had reprimanded me and sent me away. My classmate hung the bag in my place.

First Month: March

(Part I)

The Palliative Care Unit at McKinley Baptist Hospital, or PCU as the nurses called it, was a 20-bed unit that held patients who had chronic diseases and serious illnesses. I liked that the focus of the PCU was on symptom management and improving the quality of life for the patients. Unlike hospice, some of the patients would continue to receive curative treatment. I knew I'd be dealing with things like cancer, congestive heart failure, chronic obstructive pulmonary disease, dementia, and things like that. I thought the variety might be something I would enjoy, not to mention it sounded like a slower paced environment than an emergency room.

The unit was set up in a square with a large nursing station in the center. A small nutrition room, medication room, breakroom, and a few offices were scattered between patient rooms. From where one sat at the nursing station, you could keep an eye on over half of the patients at any given time. Each room had its own bathroom, television, sleeper sofa, and a glass sliding door that faced the nursing station. There were no smells and no alarms heard as you walked in the hall. The goal of the unit had been to make patients feel comfortable. In the midst of all that, I felt extremely uncomfortable. I reminded myself that I could do this and entered the unit.

I found my preceptor in the breakroom with the rest of the oncoming shift. Her name badge was fastened to her scrub top with a rainbow pin and read "Kristi, RN." She introduced herself saying "I'm Kristi with an 'i'." I smiled and nodded but said nothing. Kristi was tall with short, curly black hair. A sparkly pin held hair out of her face but a stray strand fell across her forehead anyway. Her navy blue scrubs were a size too small for her medium build and her top was very tight across her chest.

"Today, you're going to follow me around. We'll meet people and you can see how things flow. If at any point you have questions, go ahead and ask them - but not in front of a patient! God forbid. I had a gal do that once and it became a big fiasco."

"Got it."

Clearly, I would be spending the day watching Kristi sweet-talk patients into taking their medications and listening to them complain. I followed her into an empty office.

"Now listen," she said as she huddled close to me as if other people in the empty room were going to eavesdrop on our conversation. "301 is a sweet - and I mean sweet - eighty-three-year-old lady who is experiencing an exacerbation of her CHF. She's as sharp as a tack. Her family is really sweet too. She's wearing oxygen by nasal cannula at two liters. If she gets breathing too hard, we give a call to respiratory for a breathing treatment. She takes her pills whole. She's continent but needs the girls to help her walk to the bathroom. I don't want her to trip on cords or get too short of breath, ya know? Any questions on her?"

"Not yet."

"302 is a forty-nine-year-old lady who is waiting for a liver transplant. She also takes her pills whole. She has ascites and gets a paracentesis every week or so. Not sure how long they plan to keep her here. She's already been here for about a month. Just when it seems like she can go home, something happens and she stays. She wears oxygen some days if her belly is filled up, but she got tapped just yesterday so she's feeling pretty good. She's continent also and can take herself to the bathroom, but occasionally she'll call for help if she feels weak."

"Got it."

"Because I have you, we only have two patients today. Usually, we have like five or six. Having only two gives us a chance to go over more stuff as we do it, which I found helps so much more than rushing through it because we have a normal workload."

I nodded my head because I wasn't sure if I was supposed to respond or not. With report completed, we set off to start our day. Kristi walked quickly and I did my best to stay by her side as we made our way to the nursing station. She introduced me to a few other people and then sat down at the computer and browsed our two patient's medication records, showing me a few things as she went.

Once we'd gathered what we needed, we headed to see Sweet Old Lady in 301. She was resting with her eyes closed when we entered the room so we didn't stay. Moving on to the next room, I could hear our patient crying before we even slid the door open. 302 was wide awake and sobbing loudly.

"What's wrong?" Kristi said with compassion as she rushed to the side of the bed. Ms. Liver Transplant was clutching her left side as she sat on the side of the bed, feet dangling on the floor.

"I hurt!" she barked.

"Where do you hurt?" Kristi was calm. Ms. Liver Transplant was frantic.

"Right here!" She pointed to her left side while fat, wet tears streamed from her eyes.

"Okay. On a scale of zero to ten, how bad is it?"

"Ten. Stop asking questions and get me some pain medicine, please!" Ms. Liver Transplant was losing patience.

"Alright, it looks like you're due for some more morphine. We will be right back." Kristi ushered me from the room quickly. She closed the door behind her and took me to our med room to gather more supplies and her morphine.

Kristi gave me a quick orientation to how she checks the orders, showed me how to obtain the meds from the dispenser, and how to enter the pain charting into the system. Upon returning to the room, Kristi remained calm as she scanned the syringe and the ID bracelet and gave Ms. Liver Transplant the injection into her IV. Ms. Liver Transplant was inconsolable at this point. She called Kristi a "bitch" and told her to get out of the room as soon as the IV was clamped.

"Welcome to the PCU," Kristi said sarcastically as the door closed behind us.

The day was moving along fast and Kristi and I had lunch in the breakroom at a table with another nurse named Ashley. Ashley told me *all* about the unit's social dynamics. I wasn't sure that I trusted everything she had to say, but what else did I have to go on? All I knew was that I didn't want to be involved in any "social dynamics." I'd learned fast in nursing school that social dynamics spelled t-r-o-u-b-l-e. Ashley was nice, but I knew we wouldn't be fast friends just from the way she spoke about others.

Once back on the floor, the other set of nurses were scheduled to go to lunch and Kristi and I were to watch Jessica's patients. Kristi took her pager and we went to check on our own patients first. Sweet Old Lady was resting with her eyes closed, her lunch half-eaten on her overbed table. Ms. Liver Transplant was typing frantically on her laptop and talking on her cell phone. When we'd entered the room, she motioned with her hand for us to get out.

Taking a seat at the nurses' station, Kristi logged into the computer to see what tasks, if any, we had to do. Jessica's pager beeped. The display showed that room 320 was asking for pain meds. As we headed in that direction, I thought to myself that using a pager seemed quite archaic for a hospital, but was glad it spelled out messages better than using code as we had done when I was in high school.

When we entered room 320 to assess the pain, my nose immediately turned up at the stench that met us at the door. I felt as if I'd stepped into a port-a-potty sitting in the sun. Looking for the patient, there was a trail of watery, brown stool from the bed to the bathroom. Kristi shot me a look with wide eyes. She peered into the bathroom where the patient sat, stark naked on the toilet.

"Hi. I'm Kristi. I got the message you needed pain medicine. Where does it hurt?" she hesitantly asked.

"My asshole is on fire. I can't make it stop. And I just keep shitting." The patient was in his eighties, frail, and had a head full of long grey hair to match his beard.

"Okay. Let me talk to Jessica and we will see what we can do. I'll send in your PCA."

Kristi informed me that in this scenario, we would have Jessica handle it when she was back from lunch. I was just glad to be out of the room. Back at the nursing station a few minutes later, Jessica returned from lunch and we gave her the information from the patient in 320. She rolled her eyes and headed off in his direction. Kristi and I spent the remainder of my shift going over the computerized charting.

For the record, no one died on my first day. No one coded either. It had seemed like a pretty typical day and certainly seemed like something I could handle. Since I didn't have a medical background, many things were new to me unless I'd experienced them during nursing school. Sometimes, I felt like an idiot. I lacked self confidence, but I was up for the challenge.

As soon as I entered my house that evening, I threw my bag down by the door, kicked off my comfortable white sneakers, and collapsed onto the couch. Objects from my travels all those years ago happily hung all around me on hooks nailed into the walls. A rug I'd bought in India was carefully placed beneath the coffee table. An oversized chair accented the room. From the couch, I could view into the kitchen with its high-end stainless steel appliances and shiny subway tile backsplash. My ranch home was completed with three bedrooms, three full bathrooms, a finished basement, a study, a two-car garage, and a large deck overlooking a large fenced in backyard. Many large windows let in plenty of natural light and views of the field behind my house.

The house was silent and falling asleep on the couch had been easy. Waking myself up and finding the motivation to feed myself dinner had been difficult. I'm not sure if I was exhausted from being on my feet or from the ever-present amount of stimuli at the hospital. The refrigerator contained outdated yogurt, a half-eaten cheesecake, milk, butter, and a jar of grape jelly. I rummaged through the cupboard to find it was nearly as empty as the refrigerator. Chinese food would take an hour to be delivered and I could very well have been back asleep by then so a pizza was en route to my house no more than 15 minutes later.

The rest of the week in the PCU was about as exciting as reading a science book for the second time. While someone else might think it was a wild week, I had been entertained at best. I had watched boring procedures, passing of medications, and dressing changes. I learned how to place orders, chart on the computer, and where to find the best sandwiches when your patient had an early morning need for lunch instead of breakfast.

Unfortunately, my first encounter with an asshole doctor had knocked me back down to Earth. I had called her for a patient with uncontrolled pain and clearly woken her up from a deep sleep. Once she fully understood what I was saying, she rapid fired questions as the instructor had in nursing school. When I couldn't answer fast enough, she called me incompetent, told me to call back when I had the answers, and hung up the phone. I had been defeated and desperately wanted to hide my head in the sand like an ostrich. Kristi called her back with the information and got the orders we needed. I could see the smirk she was suppressing.

Kristi had encouraged me to take the lead with one patient by day three. I had entered the room to see that Sweet Old Lady had pulled out her IV. Upon seeing me, she'd announced God had miraculously healed her CHF and she was ready to go home. While I had only been a nurse for a few days, I struggled to silence the giggles bubbling up inside of me. If this lady didn't let me put that IV back in, the only home she would be going to was the one where God was her neighbor.

On day four, Sweet Old Lady declared she wanted all resuscitation efforts made if something happened to her and was transferred to the cardiac floor two hours later when she began having arrhythmias. The new patient who moved into her room was a younger male with pancreatic cancer. I had assumed that the woman holding his hand was his mother but I had been wrong - it was his cougar girlfriend. And yet, none of this seemed all that strange to me.

Finally, Friday had arrived, and I had prepared myself for another exciting day. Kristi had the day off so I had been paired with Holly. Holly was an older nurse with a mixture of dark brown and grey hair that was tied neatly at the base of her neck and fell to the middle of her back. She was from the south and had a quiet southern accent. Something about her was warm and welcoming.

We had been assigned four patients and all had had an uneventful night per report. Holly seemed ready to hit the floor running and I did my best to keep up with her as she scurried down the hall toward the med room. Soon, we headed down the hall to start med pass. We entered the first room to see a husband holding his wife's hand as she lay resting with her eyes closed. He stood as we entered and moved away from the bed.

"I don't want to be in your way," he quietly stated.

"Sir, no worries. You're more than welcome to sit by and hold her hand," Holly said with a caring tone.

I watched as Holly gently woke the woman and handed her the pills one by one, scanning her ID bracelet and each pill package. I liked watching Holly work. Kristi was wonderful, but it was nice to see a different approach to the same tasks. Once she had a handful, she threw them all into her mouth, took a swig of water, and closed her eyes again. The husband resumed his post next to her bed and placed his hand in hers. Assured that there was nothing the husband needed, Holly and I went on to the next room.

Mr. Pancreatic Cancer was awake and waiting for us when we entered his room. He was pale and ashen. When asked how he was feeling, he had told us he was exhausted and had been unable to sleep through the night. Holly took her time as she listened to his lungs and took a set of vital signs. She then followed the same procedure of scanning his ID bracelet and each of the dozen pills as she handed them to him. He stared at the pills for what seemed like forever and then dropped them onto his lap. Holly quickly grabbed a medicine cup and began to scoop them up. We would have to replace any of the pills that hit the floor and the process for replacing the narcotics was a genuine pain the butt. Luckily, she had been quick enough to catch them before that point. Before handing him the cup with the retrieved pills, she looked at him.

"Do you want these?" her voice spoke with hesitation.

"I'm done taking pills. I'm not sorry. I just can't stomach any more." His words were spoken softly and while I could barely understand what he'd said, but Holly had.

"That's okay. We can try again later," Holly reassured him. "Is there anything else I can do for you while I'm here?"

"Can you help me die?" I froze, but Holly didn't miss a beat.

"No, I can't help you do that. I took an oath to care for you, not to kill you. I want to make you comfortable though. Is there anything I can do to make you more comfortable?"

"Can I have something that will make me sleep? Something that will make me sleep until my time comes?"

"I'll see if there is anything ordered to help you sleep. Have you had breakfast?" I watched as Holly grabbed the phone from his over the bed table and helped him order breakfast. She then smiled and assured him we would be back, and we left.

"Do you get asked that often?" I asked once we had closed the door.

"All the time."

"Do you ever consider helping them?"

"All. The. Time." Holly smiled as she repeated herself. "Listen, the folks here are already dying. Maybe not today or tomorrow, but they are taking a shortcut. Some of them have been admitted many times. They know their fate, and they have no control over anything in their lives. They want to control one thing — the end. I wish I could help them, but morally, I can't do anything more than make them comfortable."

Nothing could have prepared me for our next patient. He had been admitted for deepening depression, increased anxiety, and shortness of breath. A combination of congestive heart failure and chronic obstructive pulmonary disease were the main cause of the shortness of breath, and the constant feeling of being unable to breath. Life circumstances accounted for the depression and anxiety. The night nurse reported he had slept well and maintained a blood oxygen concentration above 90%. Holly and I had assumed that his breathing would be our biggest battle of the day, but we were completely mistaken.

As I opened the sliding glass door and pushed the curtain aside, my eyes grew wide in shock and horror, and I stopped in my tracks. Holly, who had been right behind me, bumped into me. I heard her inhale sharply the moment her eyes saw what mine had. In my lifetime, I could never unsee what I had seen nor would I be able to forget it.

Despite inexperience, adrenaline took my body over and I began to move like a mechanical machine.

First Month: March

(Part II)

Blood was splattered all over the patient's bed. Droplets of blood littered the bedside table. His face had smears and a streak ran through his hair. Several spots were noted on the ceiling tiles and the wall behind the bed. Caught in the act, he dropped the pocket knife and watched as Holly and I rushed towards him. Holly quickly put on gloves, asked me to get another nurse, and applied a wad of blanket to his wrist and another to his thigh in an attempt to stop the bleeding.

Once he was secure in the psychiatric ward, housekeeping was called to clean up his room, which resembled a murder scene from a television show. I'd been working as a licensed nurse for all of two weeks — I wasn't prepared for that! Once the adrenaline wore off, I felt physically drained. Was I cut out for this?

Each evening after work, I had passed out on the couch as soon as I got home. Twice, I hadn't even removed my shoes. I'd had Chinese, pizza, and Indian food delivered rather than cooking. My phone had four unheard voicemails and six missed calls. I hadn't even bothered to check into social media or read emails. I was surprised at this point that my dad hadn't sent someone to check on me. I felt guilty for not checking on him either, but the moment his cancer had gone into remission, he'd resumed his time-consuming responsibility of running a multi-million dollar company. His grown daughter not contacting him in a few days probably hadn't even crossed his mind.

A BMW pulled into my driveway that weekend and a tall, good-looking man emerged carrying a bouquet of lilies. I had met Asher at the grocery store after my second day at the hospital. I had been looking at bananas for quite some time, almost as if I were in a fog when we bumped into each other. After a moment of awkward apologies, he asked if he could take me for coffee or lunch. His boldness caught me off guard and I had accepted before I had time to process the thought. His brown hair was full and combed over, I could see muscles under his white t-shirt, and his selection of groceries practically matched mine. How could I say no?

Noon on Saturday had seemed like a safe bet and I had stupidly given him my phone number and address before I shuffled off, embarrassed, down the opposite isle. My cheeks had flushed when he had asked me out and I was sixteen all over again with butterflies in my stomach. My brain clearly hadn't been working because the idea of "stranger danger" hadn't processed until I was driving home.

By the time Saturday had arrived, I'd forgotten what he looked like other than he had been good-looking. Panic was setting in as noon approached. Who had I agreed to have lunch with? Who picks up women in the grocery store anyway? Don't normal people use online dating sites and apps for that stuff? He could be a serial killer and I had walked right into his charming trap.

As he stepped out of the car, I confirmed that he was tall, dark, and handsome, just as I had remembered. After awkward re-introductions, I put the lilies in a vase of fresh water and we took off on foot for the café down the street. It was perfect weather for a walk, and now that my brain was functioning properly, I wanted to be somewhere near other people.

"What do you do for work?" Asher asked as we took off down the street.

"I'm a nurse. Well, I just graduated from nursing school actually and started my new job this week. I'm not sure that I feel qualified to call myself a nurse yet." I was too hesitant to look at him as I spoke so I watched my feet on the sidewalk instead.

"I think that qualifies you as a nurse." He was watching me intently.

"Thanks. What do you do for work?" The conversation felt kindergarten to me.

"I'm an engineer. I build roads and bridges and stuff like that." Recalling our meeting at the grocery store, I remembered how all of the items in his cart had been placed neatly and in an organized fashion. His profession, in hindsight, wasn't a shocker. "You know, you have very beautiful hands," he said as he blushed.

Interested, I'd looked up. Was this a pick-up line? He had seen the odd look on my face and quickly explained that he had noticed them as I was fumbling for the right set of bananas. He explained that your hands tell a lot about a person.

"Is that so?" I replied quickly. "What do my hands say about me?"

"That you wash your hands a lot." He gently bumped his shoulder into mine and laughed. "And I was right!"

The physical contact sent a jolt of electricity through my body. It left butterflies in my stomach and flushed cheeks. I had to admit, it had been a while since I'd felt that type of spark and I enjoyed it. In fact, once I'd been reminded what it felt like, I craved it. Complimenting my hands was cheesy, but it had worked.

Reaching the cafe, he led me to a small table by a window and pulled out a chair for me. This small gesture brought a smile to my face. The waitress took our drink orders and we began scouting the menu. When the waitress returned with our drinks, we placed our orders and without a pause, Asher picked up the conversation.

"In August, I'll be traveling to Spain for work. Have you ever been there?"

"Have I? Well… Right after high school, there was a period of time that I was… I guess you could call it… wild," I said with a smile and he laughed.

"Wild, eh?"

"Wild. I spent about six months traveling the world, solo."

"Solo? That sounds like a hell of an adventure." He took a drink of his water.

"It was. I spent about a week exploring Spain. It's such a beautiful country."

"What was your favorite place you visited?" he asked with genuine interest.

"Wow, that's a tough one. I loved so many of the places I went." I had to pause and think hard to come up with a favorite. In the end, I was unsuccessful. "How about a top five instead?"

"Sure. Let's hear it."

I made my hand into a microphone as I announced, "In at number five, kayaking in New Zealand."

He laughed, "Wow! I've heard that is breathtaking."

"It was beautiful, but I was scared to death. I'm not a big fan of being out in the ocean on a boat that a whale or shark can easily mistake for prey… I've seen those shows on the Discovery channel! But I never want my fears to hold me back, so I signed up for the tour and off I went."

"I love Shark Week, but I don't think I want to swim with them either." His smile was beautiful. His teeth straight and his mouth turned up slightly on the left side.

"I guess cage diving is off our list of future adventures then."

"Agreed."

"Next is probably Oktoberfest."

"Really? You must be a big fan of beer then?" he said with surprise.

"I wouldn't say I'm a fan. I can drink one here or there. But Oktoberfest is more of an experience. You have to live it. And yes, it includes lots and lots of beer. I loved the atmosphere. Everyone is just having a good time. I love the German people."

"I'm sure you're cute in a dirndl." I blushed as he said this with a mock German accent.

"Maybe you'll find out," I said coyly.

"Oooo. Sounds like a challenge."

"Then there was La Tomatina. It was so much fun!"

"What is La Tomatina?" he asked, trying to mimic my Spanish accent.

I laughed. "La Tomatina is a festival in Buñol, Spain where everyone gets in a big tomato food fight and then goes to the bar! Come to think of it, it's held at the end of August. Where in Spain are you going to work and when? Maybe you can check it out?"

"I'll look into it," he said amused. "You've really have been everywhere, haven't you?"

"Somewhat. I feel like I crammed it all in. I didn't want to miss anything, so I tried to do it all. I was young and free and had just enough money to do as I pleased."

"I can see that. Maybe someday, if things go well, of course, we can go back and do some of these again and take our time?"

"I would like that," I said as I blushed. "My absolute favorite, and something I would do again in a heartbeat, was an African safari."

"You went on an African safari? That is absolutely amazing. That is one of the top things on my bucket list."

"Well, then you'll enjoy it when we go back, right?"

"Absolutely." He reached a hand across the table and took my hand in his. Electrical sparks zapped through my body again.

The waitress had impeccable timing as she delivered our plates to us and scurried off. The conversation was easy with Asher. We talked about travel and our jobs. We talked about our likes and dislikes. It was one of the best first dates I'd been on in a very long time. Walking back to my house, I found myself wishing he didn't have to go home. But after walking me to the door, he gave me a peck on the cheek and told me he would call later before he sprinted off to his car. I stood on the porch and watched him drive down the road.

Monday morning arrived like a speeding car hitting a brick wall — fast and hard. I woke up with a pounding headache and was thankful for the dark roast I'd gotten at the grocery store. I rolled out of bed, showered, dressed, and was driving to work ten minutes later. I combed my thick brown hair in the car and threw it in a high ponytail, applied a little eyeliner in the parking lot, and grabbed a blueberry muffin in the cafeteria on my way to the PCU.

When I got there, I noticed Kristi looked as rough as I felt. I immediately liked her even more. She handed me a paper with our assignment on it, held up her finger to signal she needed a moment, and chugged down the rest of her coffee.

"Last week was a fluke. I must have been excited to have someone new working with me because I am *not* a morning person." Kristi stated matter of factly. "I spent the night wrangling a sick toddler and this morning was *not* kind to me."

"I'm sorry," I managed to reply.

"For what? Having the luxury of sleep?" she bellowed with a smile.

"Uh… I'm not exactly sure, I guess. Trying out this whole new compassion thing. How does it suit me?" I joked sarcastically.

"Oooo, I like it. Very nice." She gave me a fist pound and then off we went to check in with our patients.

Mr. Pancreatic Cancer was ours again, as well as Ms. Liver Transplant. We now had three patients since it was my second week, and now added a woman with end-stage COPD. She was admitted due to the large burn on her face from falling asleep with the cigarette lit in her mouth. Thankfully, she had been smart enough to remove her oxygen when she felt the urge to smoke.

Unfortunately, the son was as hot as an inferno and reminded her of this every chance he got. We called security to come assist us long before mid-morning break. He loudly reminded her that the house could have burned down, but he returned from a bathroom break to see she had found a cigarette hidden somewhere and was attempting to light it. At this point, he lost his cool. Despite his attempts to keep her safe, *he* was escorted from the property and Smoky was given a nicotine patch.

That afternoon, we found discharge orders for Ms. Liver Transplant. I had grown to like her and her family and was saddened that they had made the decision to remove her from the transplant list and go home with hospice. As ridiculous as it sounded, a small part of me felt I had failed her. I had been unable to ease her suffering or make things better in some way. She gave me a tight squeeze around my shoulders and thanked us all for her care as she left the unit. I found it extremely challenging to say anything in reply.

How do you say goodbye to someone who is terminal? It was my first experience with this sort of thing. It seemed so different than saying goodbye to someone who was unconscious and actively dying. This woman walked and talked, yet within a week or two, she would meet her maker. I spent a few minutes pondering all of this as I watched her leave.

My best friend Mary Jane came over for dinner that evening. Mary Jane and I had met while taking a college math class before nursing school. I had taken a seat next to her on the first day of class and we'd instantly connected. By the end of the semester, we were besties. Since

I lacked a mother figure, Mary Jane became the friend who comforted me, guided me, and overall took me under her wing. I loved our friendship. I could say or do anything and she would be there. She was always 100% honest with me. She was exactly what I needed in my life. While I had gone on to nursing school, she had fallen in love and gotten pregnant with twins. As a stay-at-home mother, she found my stories about nurse life unimaginable.

As we shared a pepperoni pizza, we talked about how I was adapting to hospital life. Over a glass - or two - of wine, we talked about my date with Asher, Mary Jane's lack of a sex life, and the stress of having twins. Mary Jane had been recently divorced and was single-parenting her two daughters, Bella and Brooke. Mary Jane had always been the friend who had it all together but as I listened to her talking, I didn't feel like my life was such a mess anymore.

"How's your dad doing these days?" Mary Jane asked.

"He's been doing well. So far, all of his tests have continued to show remission. He's been busy with a new account at work so I haven't seen much of him."

"Ah, I'm glad to hear that!"

"How's Bella's ballet class going?"

"Oh my gosh. She's gotten so good! You should come to one of her recitals. Her class is *so* cute when they dance."

"I would love to if I don't have to work. I'll be starting night shift at some point. That will be an adjustment." I gulped the rest of my wine.

"Ha! You better drink another glass!"

"How's Brooke doing with her sister taking ballet and not her?"

"She's loving all her one-on-one time with me," she laughed.

Mary Jane reached for the wine bottle and attempted to pour me another glass. "If I have another, I'll never make it to work in the morning!"

She finished her own glass, and we picked up our dishes and took them to the kitchen. She was "my person" and I always loved when we had a dinner-and-gab session. Since the divorce, we didn't get to have them nearly as often as before, but I understood. Her ex had become a nightmare and rarely spent time with the girls. When he did, it was only for a few hours and always on a weekday.

Despite refusing another glass of wine, I started off Tuesday with another headache. Wishing I'd have drank the glass after all, I made my way in to work. Kristi had called in saying she had a sick kid so I had been assigned to spend the day with Jessica. Had we met in high school, I'm sure we would have been friends. I couldn't pinpoint what it was about her that I liked so much, but we seemed to instantly hit it off. She handed me a large white pill from a bottle in her bag - Motrin 800mg - and I knew I was going to have a good day.

Our patients for the day included Smoky, Mr. Pancreatic Cancer, a young man with ALS, and an old man with newly diagnosed dementia. During report, Jessica told me the case manager was working to place Mr. Dementia at a local skilled nursing facility with a memory care unit. His wife had been unable to handle his care for a while now but when he fell and broke his hip, she had no choice but to admit the inevitable. Mr. ALS was a veteran who had served time overseas. He had come home, struggled to re-assimilate, started a family with his wife, and then began to notice muscle weakness when at the gym. Many doctors and tests later, he had been diagnosed with ALS. Yesterday, he had begun having shortness of breath and had gone to the emergency room.

Unlike when I was with Kristi, Jessica had gotten her normal share of the patients and the moment report was done, we were off. Four patients kept us busy. Jessica tried her best to let me take the reins, but we slowly fell farther and farther behind until Jessica took control. Just as we had gotten back on track, Smoky had called to use the bathroom. Our aide was nowhere to be found.

Relieved when she saw us, she threw her covers off and swung her feet over the edge of the bed. I followed closely behind her, managing her oxygen tubing so she wouldn't trip, but it didn't matter. She lost her footing and before I had a chance to catch her, she crashed to the floor and cried out in pain. I saw it unfold in slow motion but I wasn't quick enough. Should I have done something different? Had I done something wrong?

My eyes flashed to Jessica in panic, but she was already on the floor reassuring Smoky. For a brief moment in my panic, I questioned my choice of becoming a nurse. Then, I snapped out of it and knelt to the floor to help Jessica assess her. Smoky's right hip had sharp pain and she would scream out in pain anytime we attempted to move her right leg.

After being seen by the doctor, having an x-ray, and receiving a boat-load of narcotics, Smoky was resting with her eyes closed. Jessica was still charting the incident when the alert appeared on the screen with the x-ray results. Our fears were confirmed - right hip fracture. Jessica pressed the "send" button and the report was headed to the attending physician. She pushed away from the computer, took a deep breath, and announced it was time for lunch.

At the end of the day, my feet were aching and I was emotionally drained. I hadn't realized how much energy it took to constantly be watching and assessing every little thing that happened, the sound of the alarms, and the time spent at the computer. I couldn't stop thinking about ways I could have prevented Smoky's fall even though I knew it wasn't my fault.

By the third week, I was on my own and Kristi checked in with me frequently. The charge nurse had given me the same two patients all week and I was finding that I, like Kristi, enjoyed the small talk and getting to know the patients. I stopped seeing the patients as textbook models and began seeing them as live people. People who had jobs, friends, family, and lives outside of their illness. Most of all, families were trusting me to take care of their loved ones and patients depending on me to care for their needs. The immense responsibility was the complete opposite of what I had felt my entire, carefree life and it was exhilarating.

I'd had dinner with Asher again and it had been just as amazing as our first date. Asher had filled me in on the standard childhood-till-now stuff. Growing up with married parents who were born into their wealth, he had been outgoing and a jock all through school. He had spent the years after high school studying at a prestigious Ivy League school that his mother was an alumni at and he had hated every moment of it. Upon graduation, he went on for his Master's degree at a Big Ten school to spite her. He'd had a serious girlfriend while in undergrad but had found her "stuffy". None of the girls he met during grad school had been marriage material.

Finding women in the grocery store had been a new approach, he told me with a grin. At the end of dinner, as he paid the bill, he'd asked to see me again. He had earned a third date and as we stood at my front door, his kiss confirmed this to me. While I thought he was leaning in for another peck on the cheek, I was pleasantly surprised when I felt his lips touch mine.

During my fourth week, I had my first patient die. At ninety, he was alone. He and his wife of fifty years had decided against having children. She had passed away fifteen years ago and he had been very lonely. Together, they had traveled often but now he had nothing but memories. His life had consisted of dementia and a nursing home. The fall that broke his right ankle and lower right femur had left him with constant sharp pain and his failing brain left him trying to understand why he couldn't stand up and walk whenever he wanted to.

He reminded me of the dementia patient we'd placed in a nursing home earlier in the month. I wondered what he had been like before his diagnosis. What he had done for a living, what experiences he'd treasured, or what regrets he had. As I held his hand, I gave him his scheduled dose of Roxanol and watched as he closed his eyes. Not long after, he stopped breathing and I could no longer find a pulse.

Opening the blinds in his room, I let the sunlight pour in. I gently closed the door behind me when I left to call his doctor. His death had come as no surprise and without having a family to contact, the transport team had him in the morgue within the blink of an eye, and housekeeping had his room ready for the next patient a mere two hours later.

This process, while necessary, had felt cold and lonely. What became of the bodies of those without families? Did someone claim them? Who gave them a final resting place? Had he known his death would be like this? I found it hard not to wish I could have done more for this man. Maybe if I'd have been able to learn more about him, his wishes, and his dreams, I could have.

Second Month: April

(Part I)

April signaled the end of orientation on day shift and my switch to "the dark side". When I was younger, I'd stayed out late partying with friends on numerous occasions. I'd always loved sleeping more than parties and had never stayed out too late despite my friend's pleas. The only time I had ever stayed awake all night was a few romantic nights in Paris.

I'd met Alexandre at a café around the corner from my hostel. Medium height, slick blond hair, and bright green eyes. Perfect teeth. French accent. He worked at the cafe, and on my second visit, he'd asked for my phone number. He'd called that afternoon and invited me to dinner. Living in the moment had been my theme, and I'd gladly accepted. Dressed in a peach sundress with my hair long and wavy, I'd met him at the cafe and donned the helmet he'd handed me, and hopped on the back of his motorbike. My arms around his waist as we drove through the streets of Paris had fed my endorphins, and by the time we reached the restaurant, I was convinced he was Prince Charming.

After dinner, he drove through the streets of Paris to a nightclub where we'd spent the entire night dancing, singing at the top of our lungs, and kissing. As the sun began to rise the following morning, we were perched on a stone wall taking it all in and eating croissants. Dropping me back off at the cafe that morning, he asked me to join him again that night and the butterflies in my stomach refused to allow me to say no. I slept all day in anticipation of another amazing night.

The second night, he arrived in skinny jeans and a soft t-shirt that hugged the ripples of his washboard abs. He had embraced me in a hug and softly kissed my neck before whisking me off to a boat. Lights flickered on the Eiffel tower as he held me close. I'd woken up in the morning wrapped in his arms and stark naked. We had gone back to his apartment just before the sun rose and he had placed his hand in the small of my back and passionately kissed me. Leaning against the wall just inside his apartment, his hand landed on my upper thigh. The weight of his body gently pushing me into the wall and the soft touch of his lips as they made their way from my neck to my clavicle sent shivers down my spine. I'd tugged at his shirt as I attempted to peel it off his chest. He'd placed his other hand on my other thigh and slowly moved his hands up my body, undressing me as he went.

Having stripped me of my dress, he grinned and asked, "no panties?"

My dress landed carelessly on the floor as he carried me to his bedroom. I'd unbuckled his pants and he'd shed them quickly. Wearing just his boxer briefs, I could feel his erect penis as it rubbed against my groin as he laid me on his bed. At eighteen, my body was doing things I'd never experienced and I could feel my body demanding more and more. When his mouth met my breast, I had no control over the moan that escaped my lips or the graceful arch of my back.

"Do you want me to stop?" He whispered into my ear as his hands rummaged around my body.

Unable to speak, I leaned in for a kiss and tugged at his boxer briefs. Without saying another word, he removed them and paused staring at my naked body lying on his bed, begging for him to touch it. His fingers moved up my thighs and found a pool of moisture between my legs. Within minutes, my body had been moving in rhythm with his fingers and I found myself breathless. Removing his fingers, he looked into my eyes and in his sexy accent asked if I was ready. Rather than speak, I pulled him into me and felt him enter me. I gasped with a sharp pain, but he continued pushing himself into me.

The pain melted away moments later as I relaxed, and time ticked on as our bodies moved in rhythm together. Noises escaped my mouth that I didn't know I was capable of making as I struggled to take in fresh air and my muscles tensed up reflexively as electric feelings tore through my body. When I didn't think I could handle any more, my body began to relax and contract and I could finally breathe. His sweaty body collapsed on mine and his ragged breathing began to slow.

The experience had been life changing, and I left Paris that evening and never returned any of Alexandre's calls. Those had been the best two nights of my life and I knew I had to move on or risk falling in love. Ending the phone call after accepting the night shift job, I'd immediately found myself reminiscing that sultry night and touching myself right there in my office until I came. Sex with Alexandre had been the most passionate and hottest sex in my life and it was the scale I was hoping my future husband could live up to. Until then, I could turn any man into Alexandre using my mind.

I arrived at the hospital that night still thinking about my only all-nighter, and the smile on my face had continued. The day shift staff had been so kind and I was looking forward to meeting the people I would be working with at night. In the breakroom, I was introduced to the other night shift nurses, and they mostly chose to ignore me as I sat down at the table. I felt invisible. There were three night shift male nurses but it was clear they felt they were part of the "girls". Elizabeth had been assigned to shadow me and help me complete orientation over the next few weeks. Our aide, Bethany, was already rounding on our patients.

The breakroom was a moderate sized room and held a long, rectangular table with enough seating for about twelve people. One end of the room held a kitchenette, complete with a bare refrigerator, sink, and microwave. The opposite wall held a large bank of lockers for staff. There were no windows and the room was flooded with L.E.D. light. When both shifts occupied the room, the air felt stagnant and I almost felt claustrophobic.

After we received report, Elizabeth and I split up our patients and headed off in different directions to get started with our "day". My patients were already in pajamas, complaining of pain, and irritable from being poked and prodded all day. I found myself running in all directions and trying my best to keep pace and prioritize the best I could. The patients were kind and accommodating with me being new, but they had so many needs!

The rhythm of the night shift was completely different than that of the day shift. On day shift, everyone seems to follow a schedule based on meal times. Without meals, night shift was one big free-for-all with patients calling me whenever they felt the wind blow. Every time I sat down to chart, my pager would buzz. By midnight, I was hungry and needed a break.

As I began to approach the nursing station, I heard an alarm coming from my patient's room. Getting closer, I recognized the familiar alarm of an enteral pump piercing an otherwise silent room. I entered the room and the L.E.D. display read "flow error", which I knew meant there was a blockage between the pump and the resident.

First, I looked for a kink anywhere in the tubing and then I checked all the clamps. No luck. The patient was dripping with irritation at the inconvenience of being woken up. I grabbed the syringe hanging from the IV pole and attempted to pull back on the plunger. No movement. I attempted to push the plunger in. Nothing. This plunger wasn't budging.

This was a continuous feed. It couldn't have been stopped very long, so I was confused as to how it could have become blocked in such a short period of time. I began to apply more pressure to the syringe in the hopes of getting it free flowing again. I wasn't having much luck, and my frustration level was rising.

Not that I'd say it out loud, but I didn't have time for this. I tried my best to remain calm and repeat the steps I'd already taken despite the patient watching my every move. Finally, I had to accept defeat and find Elizabeth. Although she was busy with her own list of things to do, she reluctantly dropped everything and followed me back to his room.

Giving me tips and coaching me, I was finally able to unblock the tube - with an explosion of gastric juice and enteral feed peppering my scrubs. I can't exactly explain what happened because it happened so fast. I was initially frozen in my spot as I assessed the damage, but it appeared I was the only one hit with flying liquids. Elizabeth covered her mouth in shock. I quickly hooked the enteral feed back up and hit "run".

Busting out into the hallway, Elizabeth and I erupted in hysterical laughter. Luckily, Bethany walked up just then and I asked her to clean up the resident while I cleaned myself up. Obviously, I didn't need to explain. Eyeing me from head to toe, she giggled and walked off to get fresh linen.

I was pretty sure I'd managed to avoid the juicy mixture from landing on my face. There was no question who the new girl on the unit was as I could see the sneers and hear the whispers as I walked past. Elizabeth guided me to a closet that held scrubs and extra supplies for occasions just like these. As she handed me a freshly laundered set, she smiled.

"What?" I asked, curious about her smile.

"I forgot to tell you… Your patient just returned from an MRI."

My mouth tightened as Elizabeth let the door close behind her, leaving me in the closet alone. MRI. I shook my head with frustration and embarrassment. Elizabeth, and I'm sure all the others, had been fully aware that my patient had gone to MRI and just returned. An hour in MRI would definitely explain how the enteral tube had become blocked, since the pumps did not go with the patients. I had been played.

I changed into baggy, pale blue surgical scrubs and placed my scrubs in a bag in my locker. I wasn't even sure I was still hungry, but Elizabeth encouraged me to take my break and I found my way to the cafeteria to scavenge for something that would bring back my appetite. Between knowing that everyone on the floor was laughing behind my back and having just received a spattering of gastric juices, I wasn't sure if it was even possible.

From across the dining area, I noticed his smile. While I knew he hadn't even seen me, *thank God,* I pretended he was smiling just for me. At this moment, I needed that. His eyes were large and brown, his hair cut short, and he was dressed in blue jean shorts and a grey polo shirt that hugged his biceps. He was handsome. As he sat alone eating what looked like a cold slice of pizza and laughing at his phone, I munched on my salad wearing my oversized borrowed scrubs, wondering why he was in the cafeteria at this hour. Did he work here or was he visiting a loved one? Mystery Man looked up from his phone and looked around the dining area.

The dining area sat just outside the cafeteria on the ground floor. It was filled with round tables and chairs, trash cans, and large plants acting as dividers. The walls rose five stories tall with windows on three sides letting in natural sunlight during the day, but remained black at night. On the right side, each floor had a balcony that overlooked the dining area. The sound echoed and the faint hum of people seemed to be present at all times of the day and night.

Few other people were in the dining area at that time and finally, Mystery Man's eyes locked on mine. I was busted. His smile broadened but I quickly looked down. I grabbed the trash from my sandwich, tossed it in the bin, and took off back to the PCU leaving Mystery Man to watch me walk away.

Back on the floor, I yawned reflexively as I sat at the nursing station. Elizabeth sat down next to me and smiled. She was dark skinned with dark, thick curly hair held back by barrett. She was taller than me and athletic. She had been a nurse for the last ten years and enjoyed working night shift because it allowed her to go to school functions for her three children. I was struggling to stay awake at this point. It was going to take time to adjust to night shift work.

"How was lunch?" Elizabeth asked me with a sly smile.

"Unsatisfying." We looked at each other and laughed.

"You know we were just messing with you earlier, right?"

"Yeah."

I was still upset about earlier, but I didn't want it to ruin my entire night so I tried to brush it off. An alarm sounded overhead as the paging system came to life. The voice was female and soft.

"Code blue, north campus. First floor, room 104. Code blue, north campus. First floor, room 104." Someone, somewhere, was dying.

"I hate hearing those paged. I always wonder if the person has family with them or if their family is at home sleeping. I'd hate to get woken up with that phone call," Elizabeth said.

"Yeah, I can't say I'd like that much either," I agreed.

"What brought you to night shift?"

"It was my only choice?" I said as a question. "Not many jobs available in the day for a brand new nurse."

"What brought you to nursing? It wasn't your first job, was it?"

"No. I was a secretary for a long time for a lawyer. He died unexpectedly. When I went home at the end of the day, I found my dad paralyzed on the couch. Turns out he had cancer. That's when I knew. I wanted to be able to help people like him, so I went to nursing school."

"That makes sense. Is palliative care what you see yourself doing for the rest of your career?"

"I really don't know. How about you?"

"Oh no. I want to get out of the hospital. I'm thinking home care or something. I just want to wait until the kids are older. If I work in home care, I'll be on-call and stuff and I don't want to miss anything."

"That makes sense. That's the great thing about nursing - we can always change directions when the wind blows. I know this sounds cliche and all, but I just feel like something is calling for me to do *more*. I'm still not sure what *more* is, but that's where I'm at."

She just smiled as if she knew exactly what I meant. I had been honest with her. I *didn't* know what I was being called to do exactly, but I felt this gravitational pull every time I stepped into the nursing role. I didn't have all the answers, and I didn't have the slightest clue. I'd spent a lot of time lately contemplating my life and my goals. Deep down, the one thing I *did* know was that I was being called to be a nurse.

The rest of the night was uneventful, and I could barely keep my eyes open as I left the hospital that morning. Every minute of driving in the car felt like another bag of sand being placed on my eyelids. I'd been awake over twenty-four hours. I rolled down my window and took in fresh, chilly air in an attempt to stay awake. Instead, I felt myself fall asleep at a stoplight.

When I opened my eyes, the light was green. I looked both ways and didn't see a single soul anywhere. As I began to accelerate, a white SUV appeared from nowhere in my right peripheral. I didn't have time to hit the horn, to slam on the brakes, or to even scream in fear. The SUV barreled towards me and before I could blink, rammed into my passenger side. I heard the crunching noise as my car was pushed sideways and then rolled twice. It landed upright with a thud on the other side of the intersection.

When the dust settled, I saw the SUV had managed to stay upright and was sitting in the middle of the intersection. The light turned yellow and then red. I wasn't sure which way I'd come from or which way I'd been going. I was completely disoriented. My vision was blurry but I tried as hard as I could to focus.

I immediately began to take an inventory of my body parts. Head, check. Torso, check. Legs, check. It appeared I was mostly in one piece but I could see the blood quietly leaking from a deep gash on my right forearm. Seeing the crimson pool on my thigh, I was immediately irritated at the thought of a ruined pair of scrubs. Considering what had just taken place and the fact that these weren't even my scrubs, it was a ridiculous thought.

Who the hell had ran into me? What had happened? I looked out the shattered window and didn't see a soul. No white SUV. No humans. Just me, an intersection, and a stop light. Had I been dreaming? No, I was confident that I'd actually seen a white SUV ram into my passenger side. I'd see it sitting in the middle of the intersection. Hopefully there had been a witness who would attest to seeing a white SUV.

As soon as the thought of trying to apply a tourniquet to stop the bleeding registered in my head, I passed out. I woke up to a large man breathing heavily and attempting to remove my seatbelt. My head was throbbing like the bass from a dance club. As I looked around, the pain in my head soared and the sudden urge to vomit overtook me.

"Ma'am, what is your name?" The large man asked as he successfully removed my seatbelt.

"Ellie Arthur." I managed to whisper on my third attempt. My throat felt like I'd swallowed sandpaper.

"Where do you hurt?"

"Head. Right arm. Make it stop." I croaked at him. Full sentences were impossible at the moment and it took a lot of concentration to get those six words out.

"Okay. We're going to take good care of you, Ellie. First, we need to place this collar around your neck. It might not be comfortable. Then, my partner and I will get you onto a backboard like you might have seen in the movies. Once we do that, we can take a look at everything going on, get some meds in your system to help with the pain, and get your arm splinted. Does that sound okay?"

"Do I have a choice?" My first full sentence was dripping with sarcasm.

His partner, a short heavy set woman, quickly answered "nope" and helped to get me onto the backboard. While he worked at splinting my right forearm and applying a dressing to the laceration, she started an IV.

"Do you have any allergies?" She asked.

"Allergic to work." She smiled at my answer.

"Do you take any medications?"

"Occasionally but not today."

"Okay then, I'm going to give you something for the pain. It should kick in pretty quick."

She attached a syringe to the end of my IV and pushed the plunger slowly into the syringe. I wasn't sure what it was about her, but I liked her. I don't remember the ride to the hospital as I'd drifted off into a peaceful sleep. Or I'd passed out again, I'm not sure which.

Bright lights crowded my vision in the cold, echoing room when I opened them again. As my eyes adjusted, they fell upon the doctor. I knew he was the doctor by the white coat he wore and the command and control in his voice as he spoke to the other people bustling around the room. Noticing I'd opened my eyes, he came to me and smiled. He had salt and pepper hair, brown eyes, and perfect teeth. He was by definition handsome.

"Hello there. I'm Dr. Hardy. What's your name?"

As my brain fumbled to process information, I decided to call him Dr. McHottie from here forward since I was confident I'd never remember his actual name. I knew what he was doing to me. He was trying to assess my mental status. I knew the drill. I just wished my brain would get on the same page.

I rolled my eyes and said "Ellie Arthur. It's Monday and April but I don't know the exact day right now. I know I'm in the ER and I vaguely remember a white SUV driving into my passenger side. Is the other driver okay?"

"The other driver?" He looked quizingly at me with zero understanding of my question.

"Yeah, the other driver. The person who was driving the white SUV that slammed into my passenger side at the intersection." Irritation laced my statement as he continued to stare.

Looking at a nurse by my feet, he whispered "add a drug screen to the lab work, please."

"I heard that, and I didn't take any drugs." My irritation continued.

"Ellie, there was no other vehicle involved in your crash." He spoke softly as if he was reassuring a child that everything would be okay after scraping their knee on the sidewalk. "It was just you and your car. No white SUV. I thin…."

I cut him off. "I know what I saw. You pull the cameras. I'm sure there were traffic cameras. You watch the footage. I didn't take any drugs. I worked my shift upstairs and just wanted to go home." My tongue was sharp and my blood pressure was rising in anger.

"Let's not worry about that now. We're going to get you to radiology so we can take a look at your arm and do a CT of your head. Do you hurt anywhere else?"

"Apparently, you won't believe what I say anyway."

I was inappropriate, and pissed off. With those words, Dr. McHottie nodded and walked out of the room. Clearly, he didn't want to stay and play and I can't say that I would have done any different. I didn't know exactly why I'd become so angry over not being believed, but I was confident my head was the reason. I just closed my eyes and allowed myself to drift back into sleep.

Cabinets lined the two opposite walls with my stretcher being locked in the middle and toward the far end wall. The cabinets were filled with supplies at the ready to save someone's life. Above me I could see bright lights and a computer monitor. The door stood across from me, open with a curtain blowing gently with each passing person. The room was mostly quiet except for the annoying buzz I could hear in my head. With nothing to do but stare at the boring ceiling tiles, I felt the fingers tingling in my right hand and a sharp pain begin to creep back up.

What seemed like hours later, another doctor entered the room. He was young and fresh faced, a resident I'd assumed. He introduced himself as an orthopedic resident and informed me that besides the concussion I was suffering from, I had broken my radius in my right arm. He had spoken with his attending physician and an OR was being scheduled and I'd be whisked off to surgery within a few hours. He asked if I had any questions. I closed my eyes and pretended to sleep. While I didn't think that constituted consent, I was over the whole "being a patient" thing. Rejected, he let go of a heavy sigh and left the room.

Thankfully, a nurse entered the room immediately after the orthopedic resident had exited because at that exact moment, I vomited. Projectile vomited. Looking at her nametag, I saw her name was Joyce. I knew the exact thoughts running through Joyce's head because they were the same things I thought watching someone upchuck. Oh shit. Why me? Where's the aide? Just my luck. And right on cue, she swooped in with a basin as another wave came over me. She called for assistance from the device hanging around her neck and another nurse entered with a cool washcloth for my forehead. Somehow, the presence of a fellow nurse calmed me and as I looked at Joyce to thank her, I proceeded to vomit down the front of her scrub top.

Joyce didn't say a word as she handed the basin to the other nurse, excused herself, and promptly left the room. She was pissed. As soon as the curtain closed, the nurse holding my basin erupted into laughter. Tears streamed down her cheeks. The laughter was infectious and within moments, I too was laughing.

"Thank you. I needed that."

She began to clean up the room. I could still hear her giggling as she left the room ten minutes later. I was wearing a new gown, had new bed linens, and she'd pushed another round of pain meds. I felt like an ass for puking on Joyce, but it had been unexpected.

Before I had time to think about it, Mary Jane appeared in the doorway, heavily sighed, and rushed to my side giving me a soothing hug.

"I got here as soon as I dropped the kids off at school. Are you alright?" Her hair was pulled back into a messy ponytail, her make-up applied delicately, and she was dressed in black yoga pants with an off the shoulder sweatshirt. I rolled my eyes.

"Of course I am. I'm a steel tank. Nothing a little surgery can't fix, right?" Her eyes landed upon my right arm wrapped with gauze.

Clutching her chest and inhaling deeply, she exclaimed, "Oh my God! What happened?"

"A broken arm. Doctors will put in some rods and I'll actually become a steel tank," I said with a little laugh. "My head has been throbbing and they tell me I have a concussion to top it off. I'm just sick of laying flat on my back and staring up at the ceiling." I paused before saying, "I'm glad you're here."

With this, her lips parted into a big grin. I knew she hated hospitals and everything inside of them. The site of the gauze on my arm probably gave her the creeps. However, when they asked if they could call anyone for me, I knew she was the right person to call. She would, of course, then call my father.

"Always." She gave me another light squeeze and pulled up a chair from near the door.

"Thank you," I whispered.

"Where's your dad?" She asked as she looked around the room.

"I'm not sure. Did you try to call him?"

"Yes, but it went to voicemail."

Mary Jane waited patiently on a blue vinyl couch at the in-patient surgical waiting room holding a circular paging disc. In the OR, I was unconscious as rods and pins were placed in my arm and a beautiful cast was applied. I'd come back to consciousness in the recovery room and immediately felt the stabbing and shooting of the pain in my forearm. My stretcher was parked by a wall and surrounded by three tall curtains. I could hear everything the nurses said as well as the other patients. With the pain meds on board, I was in and out of sleep and after what seemed like forever, Mary Jane was brought back.

"Did you reach my dad?" I asked with a raspy voice.

"How are you feeling? Your cast looks great!" She'd avoided my question completely.

"My dad?" I squawked at her as I noticed her eyes dart around the room. "Stop avoiding the question. I don't understand why you won't just tell me. This wouldn't be the first time he'd been too busy with work to attend something important."

"Oh, Ellie. I wish it were that easy. He just can't be here right now."

I saw the gloss in her eyes as I sighed heavily and closed my eyes. I was still upset with him five hours later, when Mary Jane and I arrived back at my house. I was armed with ice packs and pain medicine and went straight to my bed. Mary Jane announced she had arranged for her kids to stay at their grandparents and would be staying with me as my personal nurse for the night. I felt a wave of relief flood over me. I didn't want to be alone right now. I don't even think I was *allowed* to be alone right now.

"I've heard you talk so much about being a nurse over the last few years that I wanted to give it a shot." She joked with me as she got me settled into bed. "I've read the discharge instructions twice and have a notepad for when I give you your pain medicine. I'm ready."

"You're the best." I said with a smile on my face. I paused before saying, "but are you ready to explain where my dad is?"

Second Month: April

(Part II)

I could see Mary Jane flinch when I asked her where my dad was. I knew her so well and I knew she was withholding information from me. I could see in her eyes that she was frantically searching for the right thing to say. She held my hand before she spoke.

"Ellie, when no one could reach your dad after your accident this morning, police were sent to his house. No one answered the door, but the housekeeper arrived and let them in, your dad was found. He passed away in his bed."

I gasped and began to shake, tears running down my face. I couldn't speak, and Mary Jane swallowed me in a hug. Could things get any worse? Devastated didn't even begin to describe my emotions. The last twenty-four hours had taken a toll on me, and this pushed me over the edge. I just didn't want to believe that my dad was gone. It hadn't been characteristic of him to ignore important calls like "sir, you're daughter has been in a car accident." But the reality was starting to sink in.

Reality was that I was alone. Yes, Mary Jane was still in the room physically, but I was alone. My life had been my father and me for many years, but now it was *just* me. I couldn't stop the flow of tears, the feeling of my heart ripping in two, or a deep pit in my stomach that was growing with each passing thought. My father was dead.

"What am I going to do? What *am* I going to *do*?" I began to repeat this phrase over and over.

"I'm so sorry," Mary Jane said, desperate to say something meaningful, but she was unable to find any words.

There was nothing to be said. I continued to cry until the next round of pain medications knocked me out. I don't know that I would have slept had it not been for them. I couldn't describe my feelings, and I couldn't turn off the movie of memories playing in my head. I hadn't even been able to say goodbye.

The moment his oak casket was lowered into the ground, I had been swarmed by a mob of lawyers. They were cruel, vicious, and careless. They used all these big words that just swirled around in my head. I had just lost the first man I ever loved and they wanted to talk about what was to happen now as if it were only a business transaction. They didn't give me time to grieve or think or even ponder my next steps before they were in my face and telling me what I needed to do.

I wanted them to leave me alone. I had gotten in a car accident, broken my arm, had surgery, and planned a funeral all in the last week. If it hadn't been for Mary Jane, I'd have started using foul language and throwing punches, but she'd intercepted them. I'd finally just shut off my phone completely. I was empty inside and no one would want to talk to me anyway.

Dad had named some friend of his from his company as the executor of his will. I was informed via voicemail that there would be a reading of his will at his company office promptly at 09:00 a.m. on Monday morning. I wanted to pretend that I had so many things that I had to do, but the reality was I had nothing. Absolutely freaking nothing. I was laid up with a broken arm, and still trying to gather my wits from the concussion. I didn't respond to the voicemail.

At 09:00 a.m. on Monday morning, I sat in a little office in a cushy chair prepared to listen to what my dad had done with all of his assets. It was crushing and it felt like all of the weight of the world was sitting on my shoulders. It was miserable. The pressure of the room was about to make my head explode.

"Would you like some water, sweetie?" Gwen had said. "You look exhausted. Have you eaten?"

That was code for "you look like shit." I felt like shit, but I didn't think I looked like shit. Gwen had been my dad's long time receptionist. She was more like a personal assistant - she ran all of his errands and followed every command he barked at her. There were more times than I could count on my two hands that she was the one delivering birthday treats to me at school or attending a field trip at the last minute when my dad "forgot he had a meeting" and couldn't make it. While many girls might think more of this person as "mom", I always thought of her as Gwen. She was the sixty-something woman with long brown hair and big green eyes who was trying too hard to replace someone she never could - my own mother.

"Let's get started, shall we?" Black Suit #1 stated as he stood at the head of the table.

To his right was Black Suit #2 and #3 - all lawyers from his firm. To his left was Gwen, Perry, and myself. Perry was the next-in-line at my dad's company. He sat smug in his grey tweed suit, sure he was going to be running this company like he owned it yet he was pretending to have lost a dear, dear friend. I saw right through his bullshit.

Black Suit #1 shuffled some papers in the briefcase he had laid on the table and placed his half-rimmed spectacles on his face. His brow was furrowed and he appeared very nervous. He had a few beads of sweat forming on his forehead and he continued to shuffle the papers. By all accounts, he was anxious and that made all of us uneasy. What could be said in those papers that would make this confident lawyer so anxious? I looked down at my feet and prayed I wouldn't vomit all over the massive boardroom table.

"So… uh… I've been assigned to… uh… read the will of… uh… Franklin Arthur." Hearing my dad's name made my stomach churn. The urge to vomit became stronger.

Franklin Thomas Arthur had been raised in the deep south by Baptist parents who preached hard work and love of family. Tall and lean, he had gone to a prestigious college and played football. One he'd graduated from college, he moved away from his family in an attempt to make something of himself. He began at the bottom of an up-and-coming business, worked his way to CEO, and eventually bought the company. He had been well respected within business circles.

He had continued his hard work once I was born. His parents had died when I was around middle school age, but I remembered it vividly because he took an entire week off work to focus on family. He had one brother, Barton, but he passed away when I was in high school from a heart attack. He left behind a son, Gregory, who I had only met once or twice. I hadn't seen anyone from the Arthur side of the family show up to the funeral, despite there only being a small handful remaining.

"Wait. Gwen, can I have that glass of water please?" I managed to croak.

The suits across the table looked startled at hearing me speak for the first time since I'd exited the elevator on the fifth floor and approached the boardroom. Gwen looked most surprised and jumped to her feet, scurried out of the room, and returned with a bottle of water. I drank the water while everyone stared at me. Were they waiting for me to finish? I wasn't sure. I sat the bottle on a napkin and looked up at Black Suit #1 and nodded to continue.

"Uh… yes… I've been assigned to read the will of Franklin Arthur. The most recent will was filed with our firm… uh… on January 4th of this year." He seemed to have found some confidence and began to read the standard lawyer language at the beginning of the document.

I kept staring at my feet waiting to hear something that mattered to me. My father had written this exact will in January of this year. That meant that while I was graduating nursing school, he was in his lawyer's office *changing* his will. Curiosity was gnawing at my insides, wondering what it had said before he'd changed it. Questions flooded my mind but my mouth remained closed. Had he changed it for the better or for the worst? Where had my pain pills gone? My arm waxed and waned with a dull ache but my head pulsated with a raging, sharp pain behind my temples.

"Now that I have finished all of that, let's get down to the division of assets." Finally, the part that mattered most to me. I took a deep sigh and focused all my energy on paying attention.

"This shouldn't take us long. Mr. Arthur has chosen to leave all of his assets to his beloved daughter, Ellie M. Arthur."

My mouth fell open as I looked up at black Suit #1, who was staring intently at me. In fact, everyone at the table was staring at me. Shit. Was I supposed to speak? I was frozen to my chair. The room felt like it was spinning and I that urge to vomit was stronger than ever.

"Excuse me?" Perry barked in outrage. "I have busted my ass for this company for over twenty years and he left everything to the girl? What. The. Fuck." He paused before looking directly at me. "Do you even know what this company does? Do you know how many families will be affected by this? You didn't even go to college! You fucking vacationed all over the world and then became a *secretary* of all things." As he enunciated the word secretary, Gwen shot him a hateful look and held her middle finger up in protest.

Perry continued his tirade, "This business has never mattered to you. You father was an idiot for leaving it all to you. You're going to run this place into the ground. You'll ruin his reputation. You'll ruin my reputation. No. No, you won't do this to me. Fuck all of you." He shook his head, excused himself, and as he left, he uttered, "I fucking quit."

Everyone in the room sat silent. Everyone in the room had their eyes directly on me. My father had just died and all anyone cared about was his *stuff*? Every word Perry had hurled at me had felt like a new knife being stabbed into my chest. I took another deep breath and put my head in my hands. I refused to let any of them see me cry. I refused to let Perry break me. I might have partied too hard. I might have not cared about this company. Hell, I might not even know what this company does. But the one thing I knew without a doubt was that I was an Arthur and I wouldn't be beaten. I was strong.

After what seemed like an extremely long time passed, Black suit #3 spoke, "Ms. Arthur, there are many matters we need to discuss. Like how to properly handle the transition of assets from Mr. Arthur's name into yours, how you'd like to proceed with ownership of the company, and sorting out other small details. Are you available next week to meet with us?" Black suit #3 looked at me from across the table. "I know you may be overwhelmed, but we can certainly assist you and answer all of your questions."

I sat silently, my mind racing. Had I really just become a 30-something year old millionaire? Was I really the owner of a Fortune 500 company? Never had I imagined that he'd have left every penny and possession to me. At this point, I was emotionally exhausted.

"I'll have my lawyer contact you."

I didn't trust a single suit in the room. I'd find my own lawyers and they would handle this. I stood and walked out before any of them had a chance to say another word. I needed fresh air.

For the first time in a very long time, I felt lost. Physically, I knew exactly where I was and where I belonged, but emotionally, I was lost and very alone. Laying on the grass at the nearby park, I finally allowed myself to cry. The big, wet tears streaked my face and all of my emotions flooded to the surface and overtook me. Not only was I lost, I was alone.

Despite being only six o'clock in the evening, I pulled on my ratty old pajamas and crawled into my bed. I'd been at the park crying for an hour when I'd been approached by a police officer. Once assuring him I was fine, I'd found my way home. I threw my car keys into the basket by the door, placed my pumps neatly on the mat, and stared at myself in the bathroom mirror before deciding to just go to bed.

My phone vibrated, startling me out of my funk. Caller ID read "Mr. Handsome." He'd tried to call me a few times over the past week and I'd sent them to voicemail and replied with texts saying I was busy and I'd call back, but I hadn't.

"Hello.," I answered, realizing my voice was raspy.

"You're alive!" Asher exclaimed before hesitantly continuing, "Did I wake you?"

"No," I started before he interrupted me.

"To be honest, I wasn't sure if you wanted me to keep trying or if I should have just given up."

"I'm glad you didn't," I smiled. " I'm sorry for not getting back to you sooner. It's been a hell of a few weeks."

"Everything okay?"

"Not really," I said as I felt tears begin to form in my eyes.

"Wanna talk about it?"

"Yes and no," I said with a nervous laugh.

"That's fair."

"I got into a car accident and broke my arm," I said quickly.

"What? Are you serious?"

"Yeah, unfortunately. And my father died."

"Wow. I'm sorry for your loss. You certainly *have* been through the ringer!"

From my first patient dying, to starting night shift, to the car accident, to the death of my father. It all come out in a pile of word vomit mixed in with occasional tears. It was incredibly vulnerable of me to tear down my walls and just unload on Asher, but he'd caught me at an emotionally drained moment and I'd needed someone, anyone, to talk to.

He was incredibly sweet, offering to come right over with ice cream. Mentioning he didn't know my favorite flavor, he'd offered to bring them all. I politely declined and instantly felt a pang of regret. I missed having a male companion and everything about Asher felt right, so why had I told him no?

"Thank you," I said sincerely at the end of the call.

"You're welcome. Get some rest and we can talk again tomorrow." His voice was warm and comforting.

I spent the following morning running errands and tying up loose ends. As the afternoon approached, my arm was aching and I was ready for a nap. I pulled into the driveway and noticed a note card taped to my front door when I got home. My first thoughts were all negative. Had I forgotten to pay the water bill? Was it an electric shut off notice? Maybe it was from someone trying to sell me lawn services. I pulled the note card from the door and ripped it open.

"My life will only get better with you by my side. With love, Asher."

Stepping through the door, I could see that every available surface in my house was covered with a vase of flowers. Roses in white, pink, and red. Carnations of all colors. Orchids, tulips, lilies. Hydrangeas and daisies. My house smelled like a florist, and it was gorgeous. I was smiling ear-to-ear and blushing as I text a simple "thank you" to Asher. How he'd managed to get access to my house was a mystery, but I wasn't complaining.

I spent the rest of the week talking to different Lawyers and trying to find the right team to help me transition everything, and coming up with a game plan. It was going to take a lot of patience and time to get everything settled. Luckily, until my cast came off, I had nothing but time. Throughout the week, I had talked to Asher a little bit each night and we had set a date for the weekend.

When Saturday arrived, I was hugging the porcelain throne and unable to keep any food or fluids down. Rescheduling with Asher hadn't been easy, but I didn't want him to see me like this! Instead, I spent hours talking to him on the phone. I felt like a school girl all over again, never wanting to hang up. I loved the sound of his voice and the way he made me feel.

By Monday, he was at work and I was back to the tedious task of managing the estate and transitioning everything. I had started to make progress by the fourth week. I had decided to hire a team to hire a new CEO and to just maintain ownership. I wasn't suited to run a company. I wanted to get back to helping people and the career I was just beginning. My bank account had grown significantly, my dad's house was on the market, and an estate company had come in and begun evaluating his possessions. It would be a long process, but I was in no hurry.

Leaving yet another meeting with my lawyers, I was feeling drained. While I'd made progress with everything, it was exhausting work and my arm still ached as the bones continued healing. I was tired. Plain and simple, I was mentally and physically tired. I wanted to go home and take a nice, long nap. I'd never had to make as many decisions in my entire life as I had in the past week. I now understood why my father was the way he had been. I also understood that I didn't want to follow in his footsteps.

Third Month: May

(Part I)

Wide awake and hungry, I rummaged through the pantry for lunch and sat down at my laptop to begin my job search. Since the accident, I'd been contacted by human resources at the hospital and told I'd been fired. According to their policy, missing four weeks of work within your first ninety days didn't equal continued employment. It had taken all of my might to not tell her to fuck off before I hung up the phone. People had zero compassion these days.

I began sifting through the job postings once again, laughing occasionally at some. While most of the postings gave a description of the actual job one might perform as well as the type of person who might enjoy it, several contained a bunch of garbled information that read more like a legal document and you had to search for any information pertaining specifically to the job posted. Some of the postings I skipped included the local zoo needing a nurse for the summer, an obstetrics office looking for a triage nurse, and a nurse to teach nursing assistants. I sent resumes to the ones I felt I'd enjoy most, such as a nursing home, a hospice facility, and palliative care unit in another town.

By the time I finished, it was getting late in the afternoon and my stomach was growling. Asher would be arriving soon to pick me up for dinner so I threw on a pair of skinny jeans, a long sleeve cream colored shirt with lace sleeves, and a pair of brown suede boots. I gave my hair a quick curl, pulled half of it back with a barrette, and applied my makeup. When I looked in the mirror, I admitted to myself that I looked fabulous.

Reservations had been made at the posh restaurant downtown that sat on the tenth floor of the newest highrise apartment complex. The elevator doors opened and Asher guided me into the restaurant and gave our information to the hostess. As we were escorted to our seats and the drink orders taken, I looked around the room. The large square room was lined with windows on three sides and overlooked the city. Square tables sat couples and groups who chatted while eating their dinner and drinking expensive-looking wine or champagne. Heavy red drapes decorated the edges of the windows and several large gold chandeliers with dangling crystals hung around the room sending light in every direction. In the center of the room, water cascaded down a stained glass wall used to separate the room into two parts.

The menu contained offerings of fancy chicken dishes, seafood delicacies, and hearty homemade pastas. In the middle was a drink menu with overpriced wine, cocktails, and champagne. Looking across the table, Asher looked as unsure as I did as he browsed the menu. Despite my upbringing, fancy food didn't appeal to me. Anytime I'd gone to a restaurant like this, I'd just eaten an overpriced salad and stopped at McDonalds on my way home later in the evening. I was a simple girl.

I wasn't sure if Asher had brought me here to impress me or if this was his favorite place to grab a bite to eat. But I didn't need fancy restaurants to be impressed. As I studied Asher, I saw the anxiety written across his face. It became clear that this *wasn't* his favorite restaurant. I didn't want to disappoint him, but I also didn't want him to have unnecessary anxiety. Finally, I decided to just be honest.

"Can we get out of here?" I said with a sly smile and a wink.

"I thought you'd never ask!" he said taking the innuendo and throwing a ten dollar bill on the table for our drinks that had yet to arrive.

Just as we reached the exit on the ground floor, it began to lightly rain. Rather than pause, Asher grabbed my hand and lead me out into the rain and down the street, laughing. Feeling the rain on my skin made me feel alive and this spontaneity brought back many positive memories. I wanted unplanned moments, things to go wrong sometimes, and to live in the moment. Watching Asher do just that made my heart skip a beat.

As the rain began to pick up, we ducked into a small café on the corner and found a booth. The café was practically empty but a few diners sat at the counter chatting with the waitress. An elderly man sat in a corner booth toward the back wall, reading a newspaper as he ate french fries. The only other diner was a young woman in the next booth with textbooks scattered around her open laptop.

I grabbed the menu from the middle of the table and flipped it open. Cheap burgers, a variety of sandwiches, and a great selection of fried food. Asher and I caught each other's eyes, smiled, and returned to our menus. When the waitress returned, we ordered two cheeseburger baskets and a large chocolate shake to share. She grinned as she headed back to the counter to pass the order to the cook.

When the food arrived, Asher thanked me as he took the first bite of his cheeseburger. While we ate, we took turns making up potential life stories of strangers walking by on the street. By the time we finished our meal, the rain had stopped and my stomach hurt from laughter. Asher went to the counter to pay the bill and returned with two peppermint candies.

"How would you feel about making another stop before I take you home?" Asher asked with a suspicious smile.

"Okay," I said with hesitation.

"It'll be good. I promise."

When we arrived at our destination, I saw a row of run-down buildings and could hear the music escaping from inside. It was a karaoke bar. Looking at him, his smile reminded me of a young boy presenting his mother with a gift. The cheesy grin made me shake my head as a smile crossed my own face. It was on our first date when I'd joked that my perfect date would include a nightcap at a karaoke bar. I could carry a tune as well as a cow can cluck like a chicken. I hadn't realized he would take me seriously, but I couldn't back out now.

The karaoke bar was jammed between a furniture store and an antiques shop on a quiet street across town. The windows had glowing signs advertising half-off drinks during happy hour and of course, karaoke. Opening the door, the air was heavy and thick with smoke. The place smelled of stale beer and I felt my feet stick slightly to the wooden lacquered floor as we walked toward the bar. It was packed with folks from all walks of life and a robust man was on the stage crooning Celine Dion. His voice was soprano and he was perfectly in tune as he hit a higher note and held it out. The crowd was impressed and began to clap as they stood in ovation.

Asher held my hand tightly as if he would lose me in the crowd if he let go. Reaching the bar, he squeezed in between a tall frat boy flirting with a bartender and an older lady sipping a margarita. He ordered our drinks and patiently waited. After handing the money to the bartender, he handed me a glass and took my hand again as he led me through the crowd to a small table directly in front of the stage.

"What are you going to sing?" he yelled towards me to be heard over the music.

"What?" I hadn't actually thought about singing on stage. I didn't have a song picked out nor had I a clue about what I could even attempt to sing. Until an hour ago, singing karaoke had just been a joke. I clearly hadn't thought it all the way through.

"What are you going to sing?" he leaned in closer and yelled into my ear this time.

"Michael Jackson."

Michael Jackson had been the first artist to pop into my head. He had been the first concert I'd ever attended. When the discman was still the player of choice, I'd bought all his CDs and spent hours with my headphones on laying by the pool. If I was going to get on stage and sing a song for a bunch of strangers, I'd better sing something I knew. A song I'd rehearsed in my bedroom mirror hundreds of times.

"What are *you* going to sing?" I shot back at him.

"Umm… I hadn't thought about it really. What do you want me to sing?"

"I'll think about it."

When it was my turn, I suppressed my fears and insecurities, and took the stage. As I looked out across the crowded bar, I immediately saw him sitting with friends in the middle of the room. His eyes were locked on mine. From where I stood, I could see he was wearing a collared shirt, drinking a beer, and undressing me with his eyes. At least I felt like he was undressing my with his eyes. I took a deep breath and saw Asher take his seat in the front row as the music began.

Squawking like a dying bird, I belted out my best impression of Michael Jackson's "The Way You Make Me Feel." If I was going to sink, I couldn't do it halfheartedly. I had to go all-in. Minutes later when the song ended, he rose from his seat and began to walk through the crowd. Asher stood and clapped as if I had been a Grammy winning artist. I looked down as I climbed the steps on the left side of the stage but when I looked up again, I ran into him.

"Excuse me," I sputtered as I took a step back, completely caught off guard.

"Ellie, right?"

"Yes." His eyes mesmerized me, and I was unable to respond further.

"You did a great job up there. Michael Jackson. Great choice."

"Uh.. Thank you," I stammered.

I could feel the color drain from my face as my brain raced to think of a way to introduce Mystery Man to Asher, who had just approached. Luckily, Mystery Man held out his hand and introduced himself as Jennings. Was Jennings his first name? A last name? Asher shook his hand and then gave me a hug and told me what a great job I'd done, completely blocking this Jennings guy out.

"It was great meeting you," he said to Asher. "Ellie, I'm sure we will see each other again," Jennings said as he laid his hand on my good forearm and locked eyes with me once more.

Who was this mystery man? When I'd first seen him in the hospital cafeteria, I'd thought he was a potential suitor but now I wasn't so sure. Asher hadn't paid any attention to him and didn't ask about him. I was curious what he meant when he said we'd see each other again. Something about him was familiar and reassuring, but at the same time, elusive and mysterious. I watched him walk back to the table with his friends before I turned my attention back to Asher.

"Now that that's off your bucket list, shall we go?" Asher asked.

"You think you're going to get off the hook that easy?"

"I'm hoping to," he countered.

"You are one lucky fella. My arm is starting to ache and I'm ready to get going. However, I'll get you back for this some day, I promise."

"Deal!"

The orthopedic technician pulled a saw out of a drawer and began walking towards me, eyeing my arm. I'd seen a cast removal during nursing school, so I had nothing to be afraid of, but a part of me was still anxious. Something about watching a sharp blade moving towards an important limb activates the fight-or-flight response. Instead of watching, I gazed at the ceiling and began to hum the Michael Jackson song that had been stuck in my head.

With plaster flying, he cut the cast off and for the first time in four weeks, my forearm saw sunlight. My skin was wilted and pale except where the surgical incision had been. The line where the surgeon had cut into my skin was bright pink, straight, and I knew the scar would make for a great story. Seeing the orthopedic physician's assistant, I was cleared of the cast and graduated to a soft split. I'd finally be able to use my arm again — and finally able to start my new job!

My arm ached as I drove home sporting a black soft splint. I knew a few Motrin would solve it and that it would be this way for a while. However, nothing was going to stop me from starting my new job. I had worked my ass off in nursing school, and had only a small taste of it before the accident. Of course, I could just take more time off, kick up my feet, and do nothing, but that just wasn't me. I wanted to be out in the world, interacting, and doing something positive.

Shortly after I submitted the applications a few weeks ago, I'd received interviews with two of the three jobs. Ultimately, I'd decided to accept the job at Rolling Hills Hospice Home. Rolling Hills is a 20-bed hospice home, much like the PCU. It was newer and beautifully built. Rooms were private and contained many windows. Comfortable seating areas converted to beds for family members wishing to stay overnight with their dying loved ones. The death of my first patient had shown me that I was built for this type of work. I could hold someone's hand as they passed away and then move on to the next room and provide excellent care. What mattered to me was that they passed away with dignity and with comfort.

Unlike when I'd started my first day at the hospital, I was confident walking into Rolling Hills that first day. Meeting my first patient with my preceptor, Cora, I was greeted by a room full of family. The patient laid quietly on her hospital bed with pillows surrounding her while her family sat in folding chairs around her bed. The social worker was at the foot of her bed leading a discussion about finances with all of them. Cora ensured the patient had everything she needed, and we quietly closed the door while they resumed their meeting.

Our second patient was crocheting a scarf when we entered her room. Cora introduced me and the patient shook my hand, but quickly went back to her crochet hook. Cora took a set of vital signs and asked about her pain level. She was a pleasant woman and didn't say much.

"Have you had breakfast?" Cora asked the patient.

"No, I don't really have an appetite." The patient spoke softly and kept on crocheting.

"If you get hungry, please let us know, and we will get you something to eat."

"Thank you. I will do that."

Cora quietly closed the door, and we walked back to a nursing office. At Rolling Hills, there wasn't a lot of activity in the halls. It was quiet and comforting. Nurses were either in patient rooms or in the nursing lounge to reduce noise. Each nurse carried a phone to communicate with the patients. A soft melody played throughout the building and at times you could hear the birds chirping. Windows built into the ceiling provided plenty of natural light throughout the hallways and rooms.

Cora was in her fifties, married, and had three grown children and four grandchildren. At five feet ten inches, she met my definition of tall. Some felt this made her intimidating, but I found her to be warm and friendly. She had been nursing for nearly thirty years and her experience showed. We spent all morning and most of the afternoon reviewing the paperwork, policies, and procedures.

About once an hour, we would check in with our patients and attend to any needs they had. Watching her interact with the patients was soothing. It was more than just what she said to them, it was her soft body language and her reassuring tone. As a preceptor, she was patient and easy to talk to. She offered thorough explanations with each question I asked and seemed to have a never ending bag of tricks. I understood exactly why she was the designated preceptor for all new nurses. In fact, throughout the day she seemed to be the go-to nurse for any questions other nurses had as well.

When the day was finished, I thanked Cora and left. I'd see her again in the morning and honestly, I was looking forward to it. She had so much to teach me, but I was already positive that I'd taken the right job for me. Some people avoid death, but something about it was reassuring to me. I'd already dealt with enough loss, but helping others through it gave me hope. At least it was something like that.

Unlike after my first shift at the PCU, I went home and rearranged the living room furniture. I was energized and feeling inspired. Maybe the accident had been a blessing in disguise. As the thought crossed my mind, I felt the familiar ache return to my forearm. I left the furniture as it was and headed to the kitchen to make some dinner. I probably shouldn't have been pushing heavy furniture on my own when my forearm was barely healed.

Asher called around bedtime and I found myself talking with him on the phone like a schoolgirl. Butterflies in full flight, we talked about all kinds of things. My first day at the new job, his parent's upcoming trip to France, high school glory days… You name it, we talked about it. When I couldn't keep my eyes open any longer, he told me to close them, and he softly wished me a good night. But neither of us hung up.

When I woke up the following morning, he was still on the line. Lazily, I looked at the clock and I screamed "shit" when I saw that it was thirty minutes past the time my alarm would have gone off. I could hear Asher on the other end fumbling around and uttering "shit" as he noticed the time. Without a word, I ended the call. There was no time for a shower or breakfast today.

The road to Rolling Hills was a dead end. I thought it was quite the metaphor to be honest, placing a hospice facility at the end of a dead end street. The large brick building was outlined in white trim and beautiful, brightly colored flower beds sat along its base. The yard held a variety of trees, bird feeders, and wind chimes. The entrance doors had stained-glass on each side and a large welcome desk sat in the middle of the foyer with tall plants on each end. Everything was open, bright, and pleasant.

I flung the door to the nursing lounge open five minutes before the start of my shift. Cora was waiting for me while I put my lunch in the refrigerator, tightened my pony tail, and attached my name badge. I peeked at the clock to see I was right on time when I stood before her, ready to go like a soldier in basic training reporting for duty. She didn't say a word, but softly chuckled.

Third Month: May

(Part II)

Randall was in his sixties and was dying of pancreatic cancer. He was experiencing a lot of pain, but tried his best to smile through it or ask for meds. Per Cora, his wife arrived each morning at ten and left at four. Throughout the day, one of his four children always made time for a visit before hurrying off to fetch a child, attend a meeting, or make a quick trip to the grocery store. Today, his daughter Delilah was sitting next to him on the couch in his room while his wife was perched on the recliner reading a magazine.

"Good morning, Randall. How are you feeling today?" asked Cora.

"I'm doing as well as can be expected. You've met my daughter, Delilah, haven't you?"

"I believe I have. Is there anything you need at the moment?"

"Ha! A new pancreas?" He grinned and laughed.

"I'll see what I can find in the storage closet down the hall. I'll let you know if I find one." He laughed.

He instinctively offered his arm when I grabbed the blood pressure cuff. I noticed his arm was black and blue. Noticing my eyes evaluating his arm, he shrugged. His daughter asked what his blood pressure was when I took the cuff off and seemed relieved when I reported it was 110/62.

"Keep up the good work, Dad. At this rate, you'll be able to make Jonah's graduation party this weekend!" Delilah smiled as he patted her leg.

"We'll see. Lots to figure out before then," he reassured her.

"Is there anything we can do to help?" I asked, the new-nurse-positivity glowing on my skin.

Looking startled, Randall looked up at me and said, "What do you mean?"

"Is there anything we can do to help get you to the graduation party? Or help you figure everything out?" I offered as Cora smiled sweetly.

"That is so sweet. Thank you, but unless you find that new pancreas in the storage closet, I don't think there is anything you can do at this point. I appreciate the offer more than you know," Randall said.

"Dad, why don't you try to get some rest. I'm going to head home but I'll be back tomorrow." She kissed him on the forehead.

Delilah walked with us to the door and stopped us just as she closed the door behind her.

"Had my dad been more anxious than usual the last few days?"

"Not that I've noticed," Cora responded.

"I'm not sure if he should even go to Jonah's graduation party. I think it might be too hard on him, physically and emotionally."

"What do you mean?" I questioned.

"Dad and Jonah were extremely close and spent many hours rebuilding a 1964 Corvette Sting Ray. Dad always told Jonah that if he worked hard and graduated with a 4.0, he would give him the car at graduation."

"Wow," I said.

"Yeah, but that's the problem." Delilah sighed heavily. "My mom and dad have hit financially hard times and the car is being auctioned off tomorrow in order to pay the bills."

Delilah continued that Jonah had not only graduated with the required 4.0 grade point average, he had completed a year of college level courses. Attending the graduation party would be a sour reminder for everyone involved just how cruel life can actually be. However, she also understood how important having Randall present would be for Jonah, car or no car.

I apologized to Delilah for mentioning it, but she assured me that it was okay. She had explained to Jonah the circumstances and as a smart kid, he understood. In addition to the pancreatic cancer killing Randall, his heart was broken. Delilah talked openly about the relationship Jonah and Randall shared and I realized that it was therapeutic for her to talk about the situation.

We had learned in nursing school all about therapeutic nurse-patient relationships, but this was honestly my first time experiencing it. Unfortunately, I was wrong when I thought that nursing meant always being able to fix the problems and make people healthy and happy again. I could help Randall deal with the pain from his cancer, but I couldn't stop the pain in his heart from the disappointment he felt he was causing. Randall's emotional pain was unfixable by modern medicine.

This was something I hadn't encountered yet and I wasn't sure how to handle it. Something about Randall's story was gnawing at me. Was it just because I'd made a personal connection? Was it because it was something I couldn't fix? My gut was screaming at me but it was speaking a language I didn't understand.

A nurse on my med-surg clinical rotation had once told me to always expect the unexpected when it came to nursing, that I wouldn't be able to fix everything or everyone, and sometimes I would have to admit defeat. Sometimes, she'd said, I would take work home with me. A patient or a situation would affect me in some way and I'd be forever changed. She was right about it all. What bothered me most was the *why*. Why was Randall's story affecting me like this? I'd never seen myself as overly emotional, but when the soft tear rolled down my cheek as I drove home, I realized that I was changing!

After pulling in the driveway, I walked to the mailbox and grabbed the stack of mail. Since my father had passed away, I found that my mailbox was always full. I should have rented a post office box rather than forwarding all his mail to my home. Usually, the stack contained advertisements, coupons, newsletters, requests for donations, and bills. It was the invitations to parties that made me laugh the most. Clearly my father hadn't meant much to some of these people if they were still sending him invitations and were completely unaware that he had passed away. Real good friends, I thought.

Today, the mailbox held a letter from the medical examiner's office and I quickly tore into it. Despite thinking I already had the answers, I had been waiting for this. Finally, my dad's autopsy results had been finalized. As I'd long suspected but didn't want to believe, my dad's body had been riddled with cancer and his heart had given out. His final cause of death was natural causes. A heart attack. I neatly folded the letter and placed it back in the envelope and shoved it in the middle of the stack and walked in the house.

Refusing to let my emotions drown me, I pushed Randall and my father from my mind. I changed out of my scrubs and headed for the kitchen to make spaghetti for dinner. My cravings for carbohydrates were a clear indication that I couldn't just push my emotions away. If I wasn't careful, my emotional eating would start a whole new set of problems. I had to find a better outlet!

Maybe I needed a hobby. I sat down on the couch with my overflowing bowl of pasta and watched mindless television. A few reruns of a home makeover show, a reality competition, and a Criminal Minds marathon. Finally, it was a respectable time for sleep and I made my way to the bedroom. I fell asleep easily but was restless. I continued to have flashbacks to my auto accident. A car slamming into the side of me, a man walking up to my window, and me looking at my broken arm. It was like watching the entire event happen to someone else —

from another viewpoint. Waking up, I rubbed my arm and then sat bolt upright.

My mind had been seducing me all day, but it had finally relaxed enough to allow the solution to reveal itself. How I'd gone from reliving my accident to this, I wasn't sure. Revelation achieved, I made notes on my phone for the morning and allowed myself to fall deeply asleep and did not dream of the accident again.

In the morning, I made a few phone calls before I showered and dressed for work. I read the newspaper, drank coffee, and ate a bowl of cereal. These were things I usually reserved for a day off, but today, I felt deserved it. A good night of sleep and a clear mind had been something I'd been missing for the last few months. Lately, I felt my mind swimming in decisions I hadn't been ready to make, but today, I was crystal clear.

Pulling into the parking lot, I saw the ambulance pulling away from the building. Someone had passed away. Most of our patients had entered the building and it was our job to make them as comfortable as possible until their "number was called." While death was scary to so many people, knowing that our patients left this world as comfortable as possible and feeling loved put me at ease.

Sobbing family members met me at the door. Seeing me, Delilah rushed to hug me. We held each other for a moment before we broke away. Assuming her father had passed away, my heart ached for her. It had been too soon since the passing of my own father. Offering her condolences felt like a slap in the face and very insincere, but I did it anyway. She assured me that everything would be okay in the end and returned to her family. I, on the other hand, continued to feel at peace and walked to the nursing lounge with a soft smile on my face.

The crisp air hit my face when I walked into Rolling Hills the following Monday. The air conditioning inside was a tundra compared to the hot, wet air outside. My arms prickled and a cool shiver went down my spine. I shrugged it off as I headed for the nursing lounge. My first few days had been a roller coaster of emotions, but I felt confident heading into my second week.

The nursing lounge had a giant dry erase board covering the top half of one wall. It was used to list the patients, their diagnosis, their current nurse, and any pertinent information. Glancing at the board, I recognized some of the patient names and was thankful I would be spending the day with Cora again. Once everyone had arrived, the off-going shift gave report.

I took the last drink of my coffee and gathered up my stethoscope and pen. Cora smiled at me and placed a set of keys into my free hand. Apparently, I was in charge today and Cora was actually following *me* this time. I wasn't sure if I was nervous or excited. I displayed a confident smile and headed for the door.

Metastatic cancer was slowly taking over the body of my ninety-year old patient in room 16 and a recent stroke had paralyzed half the body of my sixty-two year old patient in room 17. I had never met either of them before, but I'd heard about them from the other nurses when they had admitted on the same day the previous week. Both had been described as kind, patient people with bad circumstances bringing them to us.

In room 16, I saw a frail elderly man sitting on the side of his bed talking animatedly to no one. He kept asking for the fictitious person to bring him his shoes because he needed to get the newspaper from the porch before the neighbor stole it. Afraid of what he might say to me or do in his current delusional state, I approached with caution.

"Good morning, sir."

Startled, he looked up and asked me to fetch his shoes for him.

"Where are you headed?"

"To get the paper off the front porch before that bastard neighbor steals it again," he stated matter-of-factly.

"May I take your blood pressure before you go to get the newspaper?"

"I suppose." He relaxed slightly and held out his arm.

"102/71. Good. Now what do your shoes look like?"

"Are you my nurse?"

"Yes."

"Why are *you* looking for my shoes?"

"I'm sorry. I thought you wanted to go to the porch for the newspaper."

"Why on Earth would I do that? Ah, nevermind. Listen, I have a few things I need for you to get me from the store. Can you do that or do I need to call my bastard neighbor to get them?"

Smiling, I asked for his list. He pulled out a wrinkled piece of lined notebook paper from the back pocket of his blue jeans and handed it to me. Scratched onto the paper was the following list: toothpaste, toothbrush, razon, deodorant, crossword puzzle book, Danielle Steele novel, three bananas, and a strawberry rhubarb pie.

"Is this all you need?" I asked with a soft voice.

"Yeah, my mouth feels dry and sticky. I'm not sure when I last brushed these fake teeth the dentist made me. I'm bored out of my mind in this damn room. And I'm going to be hungry."

I held back a laugh. "When do you need the items by?"

"Oh, today or tomorrow will be okay. Think you can get all those items alright?"

"Of course. It won't be a problem."

"You're a lifesaver, dear."

While I had been getting the grocery list, Cora had gone into room 17 to get vital signs. Meeting her in the hall, we walked to the nursing lounge together. I told her about Room 16 and his grocery list and she filled me in on Room 17. Room 17's blood pressure had been steadily rising throughout the night but was now over 200 systolically. His heart rate remained in the 70's and was regular. As Cora charted this and contacted the doctor to relay the information, she asked me to go re-check the blood pressure.

Obediently, I grabbed the blood pressure cuff and headed for his room. I knocked and opened the door. He was alone, lying on his bed with his eyes closed. The sun was shining through the window, bathing him in light. He looked incredibly peaceful despite the droop to the left side of his face. Too peaceful. The more I studied, the more I noticed everything that was wrong with the picture.

I approached the bed and placed my hand on his chest. Nothing. I applied the blood pressure cuff and confirmed my suspicions. I was too late. I moved my stethoscope to his chest and listened. Nothing. He had kicked off his blanket at some point, but I laid it gently on him and closed his eyelids. I moved across the room to his window and opened it. Before I left, I quietly said goodbye.

Back in the nursing lounge, I reported my assessment and findings to Cora. None of this surprised her. Part of me wondered if I'd been set up. Had she known he was dead when she asked me to go and get the follow up blood pressure? I shrugged it off. This stuff happened. We worked in a hospice facility.

"Would you like to call his family?" She had mischief written all over her face.

I'd had one other patient die before and I hadn't been the one to call their family. This was foreign territory and I wasn't sure I was ready for this. It hadn't been too long ago that I had been a family member learning of my own loved one's passing and I didn't want to be on either end of that phone call. Cora sensed my hesitation and told me she'd call the family on this one, I could listen to the call, and make the next one. I agreed.

On my way home, I made a pit stop at the grocery store and picked up the supplies for Room 16. As I paid the bill at the register, I chuckled to myself. I couldn't wait to see the look on his face when I delivered the items on his list. It was something so small, but I was sure it was a big deal to him. It was a great honor to fulfill his wish. Potentially, his last wish.

The next morning after report, I made my way to Room 16 and knocked on his door. Recognizing me, I handed him the shopping bags and watched as his eyes lit up. He rifled through the bags for a moment before he leapt from the bed. He collapsed against me in an attempt to give me a hug. I assured him it was a small feat and I was grateful he'd trusted me with his list. I sat him gently on the bed and right before I reached the door, he called for me. Turning around, he thanked me for being kind and showing him love.

"I know my head doesn't always work. It hasn't for a few years now. That's pushed a lot of people away or they just ignore everything I say. Thank you, ma'am, for listening to an old man."

"Anytime." I smiled and walked out into the hallway.

Sitting on the floor under a window, a teenager sat with her head in her hands and crying. Even though I didn't know who she was or who she was with, I sat down next to her and placed my hand on her back and began to rub softly. After a few minutes of silence, she looked up at me, paused, and then fell into my arms in a hug and continued to cry.

"Want to talk?" I asked hesitantly, not sure I really wanted the answer.

"I don't know what to say," she said through sobs.

"That's okay. How about your name? My name is Ellie," I offered.

"Danielle." She pulled out of the hug so she could see me.

"Nice to meet you Danielle. How old are you?"

"Nice to meet you too. I'm fourteen."

"What brings you to Rolling Hills?"

"My sister," she said as a new wave of tears flooded her eyes.

"I'm sorry."

"It's all my fault!" she sobbed.

"What happened?" I asked, wishing I had more experience with this type of thing.

"I wanted her to take me to the party she was going to, but she told me I was too young for parties. I begged and begged, but she kept saying no. So I hid in the backseat of the car when she wasn't looking. As she was driving, she reached into the backseat to find something and instead found me. She freaked out,took her eyes off the road, and we hit a tree. I walked away, but she's.. she's paralyzed." She shuddered as she spoke.

"And you feel guilty?"

"Of course I do! If I hadn't pushed, she would have gone to the party and been back home and been grounded and life would have gone on. Instead, we're here."

"You can't blame yourself for this. You can play the what if game all day long, but no one can see the future and know what will happen."

"My parents are blaming me. They won't look at me. They won't touch me."

What was I supposed to say to that? I felt completely unqualified to be having this conversation, but I'd started it and I had to face it. However, rather than say the wrong thing, I resumed rubbing her back and letting her cry into my lap. I was immensely grateful when Cora arrived and I was replaced with the social worker.

"It's a sad situation, isn't it?" Cora said as we walked down the hallway.

"I didn't know what to say. Is it true that the parents want nothing to do with her anymore?"

"Is that what she said? No, no, no. The parents hate that *she* wants nothing to do with *them* because she's blaming herself. Poor girl."

78

A wave of relief flooded over me as we headed to the med room to get meds ready for another patient. The day had only just begun and I was already riding an emotional roller coaster. One I wanted to get off of, come to think of it. Cora just smiled as I mentioned the roller coaster analogy.

"Buckle up and hold on tight!" she advised.

I had a few days off at the end of the second week. While I didn't plan to work full time, orientation was five days a week. Growing up, there hadn't been a lot of emotions in my house. Seeing the family dynamics my patients were experiencing was really toying with emotions I didn't know I had. I was excited to have time off and celebrate my birthday with a small group of friends. And Asher. It would be the first time my friends were meeting this man that I gushed about all the time, but I had no worries they would like him as much as I did.

Opening my front door, Asher wore a vintage light grey tweed suit, suspenders, and a teal tie. One look at him and I melted. His sex appeal was off the charts and I caught myself imagining what I'd do with him later. It was the suspenders. I loved a man in a suit with a pair of suspenders.

My silver sequin dress hugged my body, the deep v-neck showing off my healthy cleavage and the barely-there back showed off the small curve of my lower spine. I had noticed Asher's eyes examining every inch of my body. Instead of attacking him right there in the doorway, I forcefully jerked myself back to reality, walked to his car, and climbed into the passenger seat.

Arriving at the venue, Asher held the door open for me as I carefully exited the car. He then handed the keys to the valet and escorted me inside and up the elevator to the rooftop nightclub. At our

VIP table, I introduced Asher to my friends, some of whom I hadn't seen in quite awhile.

Most of the friends I'd invited were friends from my elite social circle I had growing up. While we didn't exactly have a lot in common these days, they were a good time and I enjoyed their company in this type of setting. Of course, most of them were married, had kids, and were making their own financial fortunes with start-up money from their parents.

"Who has the kids tonight?" I asked Mary Jane as she introduced her date for the night.

"They're with their dad," she yelled above the music.

"Ah. I'm so glad you're here!" I said.

"I wouldn't miss it! And you look stunning, girl!" she exclaimed as she pulled back and examined me.

"Just embracing another year of life!" I laughed as I twirled around.

I introduced Asher to my friends Natalie, Mary, Veronica, Davina, and their spouses. The waitress magically appeared just then to deliver a bottle of champagne and when everyone had a glass in hand, Asher offered up a toast.

"I want to offer up a toast to an amazing woman. Ellie, thank you for inviting me to your birthday party and introducing me to your friends. You're one hell of a woman and every day that I get to know you more, I find more and more things I love about you. Your adventurous spirit keeps me on my toes, your inner beauty warms my heart, and your smokin' hot body... Well, that's for later." Everyone laughed and he paused. "I know it's been a rough few months, but the future is very, very bright. Happy birthday, Ellie. To Ellie!"

When the toast was finished, everyone headed to the dance floor. Staying back, Asher kissed my cheek as we sat next to each other on the couch. When the song changed to something slower, Asher grabbed my hand and asked me to dance. Unable to refuse, he pulled me close as we swayed to the music. Electricity pulsed through me as our bodies touched. The sexual chemistry was undeniable and I closed my eyes and allowed my senses to soak up all of Asher. The smell of his cologne, the way he touched my body, the sound of his lips moving when he whispered in my ear, the taste of his kiss, and the desire in his eyes had me hot and bothered in all the right ways.

Two drinks and an hour later, I couldn't resist him any longer. I whispered in his ear exactly what I wanted from him and watched as it registered in his brain. Despite the protests of my friends, we said goodbye and practically ran to the elevator. Asher was barely able to hit the button as my hands began to feel all over his body and his mouth met mine. A bell announced the arrival of the elevator to the hotel lobby and we immediately straightened ourselves and headed for the front desk.

Trying to look inconspicuous, Asher fumbled for his wallet as he tried to quickly book the room. It was obvious what was going on, and I was sure the woman checking us in was fully aware of what was about to happen. She'd probably seen it all. When she finally handed a room key to Asher, she told us to have a great stay with a smirk splattered across her face. There was no doubt in my mind we were going to have a great stay, I thought, as we rushed back to the elevator.

When the elevator arrived at the selected floor, Asher picked me up and carried me down the hallway, swiped the card in the door, and carried me into the room. Setting me down, I pulled off my heels and began to unbutton his belt, but his hands stopped me. Locking eyes with mine, he slid off his suit jacket and removed his tie. I was right. He was dead sexy in suspenders and I was finding it hard to be patient.

"Are you sure?" he asked me quietly.

"One hundred percent." I leaned up and kissed him.

"Thank God because I don't think I would be able to pull back at this point," he said into my neck between kisses.

He picked me up again and carried me to the bed. He set me down on the edge of the bed and this time allowed my hands to unbuckle his belt and unzip his pants. As they fell to the ground, I could see he was ready to go. He gently pushed me back on the bed as his boxer briefs dropped to the floor around his ankles. His hands slid up my outer thighs, moving my dress up as they went and I felt his weight lower softly onto me. With his hands on my hips and his mouth on my neck, he pulled me to him as he plunged deep inside me. Losing control, a moan escaped my mouth as pleasure overtook my body.

When we were through, he softly whispered "happy birthday" in my ear and collapsed beside me. I was unable to speak or move.

Fourth Month: June

(Part I)

Heat rolled into town during the first week of June along with stifling humidity. My grandmother had always mixed up a batch of homemade strawberry shortcake when the weather was like that. She always said that there was something about biting into the cold strawberries that soothed the soul when the weather was trying to smother your spirit. I'd always thought of her when I ate strawberry shortcake but I never understood what she meant until I had reached adulthood.

I decided to whip up a batch of Grandma's strawberry shortcake for work the following day as a way to celebrate completing the first part of orientation. I'd stopped at the grocery store for the ingredients and rushed home. As I smashed the strawberries, I smiled thinking of my grandma and then my dad. A strawberry flipped out of the bowl onto the counter and I slid it into my mouth with a satisfying grin. No waste in this kitchen.

Carrying a bowl of crushed strawberries and a bag of homemade biscuits, I opened the door to the nursing lounge the following day. The girls smiled at the sight of me and were happy to share their normal workload with another nurse. The second part of orientation consisted of *having* a shadow rather than *being* a shadow. I'd have my own patients and Cora would be there to answer any questions and to check in with me. Everyone snacked on strawberry shortcake as we received report despite it still being breakfast time. When done, I smiled as I made my way to introduce myself to my patients. My very own patients.

I prepared myself to enter Room 3 as I'd received in report that the patient was actively dying and the family was very upset. Opening the door, I discovered upset was an understatement. There must have been fifteen family members in the room talking loudly and crying. The patient lay on the bed unresponsive with her mouth wide open. The nasal cannula sat positioned in her nose with the tubing extending to the bathroom where the concentrator sat. Unacknowledged, I made my way to the patient's bedside.

"Excuse me. Can I sneak in here for a moment?" I politely asked the woman standing next to the bed.

"No, you may not. You need to back up!" the woman snapped without looking at me.

I took a steady breath before I spoke, "I need to get a quick set of vitals and then I will be gone."

"Oh my gosh. I'm sorry. I thought you were my brother," the woman apologized and stepped aside.

Completing the vitals, the woman looked at me and said, "How much time does she have?"

"Well," I paused as this was my least favorite question to answer. "No one knows for sure. Her vitals are stable currently, but that could change at any time. Our goal is to keep her comfortable."

"So, like a few days maybe?"

"I don't know."

"Well you must have an idea. What does *your* gut tell you?"

"Honestly, I don't know."

"Oh God. Why can't anyone give me a time frame?" The woman let out a burst of anger, threw her hands up in the air, and shot me a nasty look.

"I'm sorry that I don't have the answer. Are you waiting on someone to make it here to see her?" I attempted to probe for the reason behind her insistence as Cora had taught me.

"Hell no. My mother didn't even like half the people in this room." The woman gestured to the people in the room.

"I see. We can ask them to leave if you think she wouldn't want them here," I offered hesitantly.

"Why would I do that? Just because she didn't like them doesn't mean they didn't like her," the woman explained. "I need to know how much time I have to come up with the money for her funeral. I can't handle all of this. I'm overwhelmed and none of these people want to help." The reason for her frustration expressed, she began to sob.

"I can send the social worker in to help you figure out all of that. Right now, you should focus on your mother."

"Get out with that bullshit," she spat at me. "Ain't no one in here going to help us financially figure this out. That's just a line. My mother worked her ass off for years and has nothing to show for it. You can send your social worker in, but we both know she ain't going to help us do nothing."

"Okay," I surrendered, fully aware I wouldn't be able to change this woman's mind.

With that, I was done with the conversation. Clearly, I needed to work on my de-escalation skills a bit more because that had not gone over the way I thought it would. I backed out of the room as the woman returned her focus to her mother and yelled to a child to sit down and be quiet. Closing the door, I took a deep breath and made my way to the social worker's office.

I knocked on the open door of the social worker's office. Connie was a plump, older woman in her sixties. She had dirty blond hair in a bob with gray roots. She sat behind her large desk that was filled with papers and files and had a dim lamp on one edge. She gestured for me to come in and have a seat at the chair opposite of her. After setting down, I relayed the experience in room 3.

"Yeah, I know. The discharge planner at the hospital told me all about the family and their issues. The daughter is very outspoken," Connie informed me.

I nodded. "What funeral home are they going to use? Aren't their programs available to help with the costs?"

"I'm pretty sure it was Hammonds. There are programs, but they all require some effort on the part of the family. We are currently working that part out."

"Okay cool."

Having spent nearly forty-five minutes doing what I thought would take ten, I headed back down the hallway to greet the patient in room 4. Opening the door, I didn't see anyone in the room. I checked the bathroom. No one. With my heart rate rising, I checked my pink paper with my patient information I'd received in report. I had written "escape artist" in small letters next to his name. I was confident another fun day was in store for me on my first day on my own, and off I went in search of Mr. Escape Artist.

As I walked down the hallway towards the front of the building, I checked empty rooms along the way. The conference room, family room, family kitchen, and bathrooms were all empty. The chapel held a few family members, but not Mr. Escape Artist. As I neared the front door, I heard the greeter having an animated conversation with someone. Reaching them, I found her talking to Mr. Escape Artist as he explained he was trying to find his car. A wave of relief came over me like waves crashing on the beach.

Upon seeing me, he immediately began asking if I'd seen his car or his wife. I explained I had seen neither but asked if he wanted to walk with me and we could look. He readily agreed and thanked the greeter for her attempt at trying to find them. As we walked, we talked. First

86

about his car and then about his wife. I tried desperately to steer him away from these topics, but I was finding it difficult.

"Where's your favorite place you've driven your car?"

"Oooo…" He put his hand to his chin in thought and stopped walking. "Alaska," he said at last. "Definitely Alaska. There's bears up there, ya know?"

"I haven't been to Alaska but I've heard there are bears there. My dad had to fly up there once for a business meeting, and told me his plane was delayed for an hour as there was a family of bears on the runway, and they had to wait for the DNR to shoo them along."

"Wow," he said as his eyes got big. "I ain't ever seen anything like that."

"Me either. I try to avoid bears." We both laughed.

"You like to travel?" he asked me.

"I sure do. I've been all over the world, but you got me thinking that I haven't really seen much of our own country."

"I've been all over this country, but never left the States. Well, except for the drive to Alaska. Had to step into Canada for a few, I suppose."

"If you could go anywhere in the world, where would you want to go?" I asked him as I managed to get him to continue walking.

"Oh that's an easy one. I'd want to go to Iceland. I hear it's nice."

"Greenland is ice and Iceland is nice," I chanted.

"Yes! That's it exactly. " He lightly punched my shoulder and laughed hysterically as if he had made a funny joke.

"I've never been to Iceland."

"Me either. I've seen the pictures though. Just somethin' about it that calls to me."

"Do you have kids?" We reached his room, and he sat on a chair next to the bed.

"Oh yeah. I have Bobby and Billy. They are grown though."

"Will they be coming to visit today?"

"Oh no. They don't live here. They gotta to fly in. I think tomorrow." He picked up a notepad and read from it. "Yep, here it is. Be in tomorrow."

"Great. And your wife?"

"Oh she'll be along eventually. She doesn't drive anymore. Speaking of her..." He looked at me with serious eyes. "Do you know where my car is? I'm gonna need it to pick her up."

Unfortunately, my attempt at distraction had brought the conversation full circle. I laughed at myself and reminded him that I didn't know where his car was. I asked if he needed anything else, to which he replied that unless I found the car, he didn't need anything. Before I left the room, I decided to try a last ditch effort to distract him.

"Tell me. If you had a genie who would grant you one wish, what would you wish for?"

He smiled and thought for a long minute before answering, "I'd buy a new car because I can't find my old one."

I gently closed the door as my laughter continued. I headed back for the nurses lounge hoping for another bite of strawberry shortcake. Along the way, my phone beeped, alerting me to an incoming phone call from a patient. Answering it, Ms. Angry Family's daughter informed me that her mother was in pain and I needed to be in there giving her something right then. I assured her I would be in. I changed direction and headed for the med room, telling my stomach that the shortcake would have to wait a little longer.

But there was no shortcake left by the time I managed to get to the nursing lounge. Each time I'd tried to get back there, something would come up that would need my attention. At the end of the day, I was tired and ready to get off my feet. I'd barely used the bathroom let alone eat a meal. Talking to Asher on my way home, he offered to come over and make dinner. The thought of some company sounded wonderful so I hurried home so I'd have time to tidy up before he arrived.

Hauling in a few bags with groceries, Asher kissed my forehead and headed for the kitchen. I pulled up a chair to the table, and he handed me a glass of red wine. I watched as he searched for pots and pans, and began to make what appeared to be fettuccine alfredo. He demanded that I relax and not assist at all. Incredibly handsome as he worked, I did not argue.

"So today, my boss came in and asked me to start assessing a new project and asked if I could make a quick trip to Denver. I didn't know if you might have a few days off that you could join me?" He smiled as he waited for my answer and stirred the pasta.

"I would love that. When?"

"It's flexible, but sometime over the next two weeks. You tell me which dates would work best, and I'll make it happen."

"Let me check my schedule quick." I hopped up and ran for my calendar in my purse.

The thought of spending a few days in Denver with Asher excited me. I'd been to Denver once with my dad, but it had been a brief trip and I hadn't really gotten a chance to explore. We had gone in the winter when the mountains were covered with snow and skiers. It would be nice to explore Denver in the summer.

"Looks like next week I have Tuesday, Wednesday, and Thursday off. Would that work?"

"Yep. I have to be gone for a few more days than that, but we could fly in together. Would you be okay heading home without me?"

"Of course." I sipped my wine.

The following day I was back at work, and I couldn't wipe the permanent smile off my face. After Asher had gone home, I'd spent time browsing Amazon for new clothes, hiking boots, and lingerie. I didn't know if I'd need it, but I was going to be prepared. Entering the nursing lounge, the girls immediately took notice of the pep in my step.

"What's got you so giddy?" Marci said with a sly smile.

Marci had been working at Rolling Hills for about eleven years now. She had shorter, brown curly hair pulled back with a headband. She was known to be "motherly" and had taken me under her wing the moment I set foot in Rolling Hills. Never having had a mother figure, I found myself drawn to her.

"Asher asked me to go to Denver with him next week!" I struggled to contain my excitement.

"Ooooo." Marci said.

"Aren't you lucky," Paige said under her breath in a mocking tone.

As other nurses file into the room, Paige began talking with them and didn't say another word to Marci or me. I hadn't been a fan of Paige, or what I knew of her thus far. She was always making comments under her breath, talking about others, or trying to throw someone under the bus in order to get ahead. I tolerated her, but I drew the line there.

After a few minutes talking about my trip, everyone set about their day. Keeping the same patients from the day before, I braced myself as I entered Ms. Angry Family's room. The daughter sat alone in a chair next to the bed. Compared to the previous day, the room was eerily silent. I quietly knocked on the open door as I stepped inside.

"Good morning," I said softly.

"Ah, good morning."

"Do you mind if I take your mom's vitals?" I asked as I stepped over to the opposite side of the bed.

"No, ma'am."

After taking vitals, I performed oral care on the patient and asked if the daughter needed anything or felt her mother did. For the first time, the daughter smiled at me. It was nice to see her smile and I felt myself relax a bit.

"No, I think she's doing well. Look, I'm sorry about yesterday. I was under a lot of stress, and I took it out on you. I'm really sorry."

"Oh no worries."

"I just want Mom to be at peace."

"Well, you have my number. I'll be here until this evening so if you need anything, or anything changes, please let me know. Would you like me to keep the door open or closed?" I asked as I reached the door.

"Open is fine."

I headed down the hallway to the social worker's office. I found Connie sitting behind her desk working on her computer. The dim lighting of her office was warm and inviting. I leaned against the door frame.

"What changed with room 3? The daughter was *smiling*."

"The funeral home called this morning and informed her that everything had been taken care of and arranged," Connie said.

"What did they mean?"

"Like everything is paid for. The director said that when she passes away, we are to contact them, and they will pick up the patient. The family can then come to the funeral home and arrange the burial and service however they would like. An anonymous donor had paid for the entire thing."

"Wow. That's such a weight off their shoulders."

"You can say that again. It's the best present someone could give to a family."

I smiled as I headed for Mr. Escape Artists' room. Arriving at his door, I again saw an empty room. I laughed to myself as I began to look around the facility for my patient. Finally, I found him sitting in the atrium with two men.

"Good morning! I found you!" I smiled at the trio.

"Ha! I'm gonna make you work for that paycheck." He laughed and introduced his two sons. Both were tall and thin with balding heads. They wore ratty blue jeans and cut off t-shirts and were spitting images of their father.

"Nice to meet you both. Your father told me you don't live around here."

"Nope. I live in Minnesota and Bobby lives in Utah," Billy explained.

"I hope you had good flights."

"Well, they arrived," Bobby stated with a laugh. "The flights were smooth; riding in the car with Billy wasn't. He needs his driver's license revoked!" Both sons laughed at this.

"Oh boy! I'm going to stay out of this one." I smiled.

"Listen dear, can you bring me some of that good medicine. My hips are achin' something awful again." Mr. Escape Artist rubbed his left hip.

"On a scale of 0-10 with 10 being kicked by a cow, how bad is the pain?" All three laughed.

"5," he said still laughing.

"You bet. Comin' right at ya." I headed to the med room to get him pain meds.

Upon my return, the boys were playing a dice game and loudly having a good time. Watching them for a brief moment, I couldn't help but smile. Their smiles were so genuine and even from a distance, I could tell that the three of them had been close. I handed Mr. Escape Artist his med cup with his pill in it and without hesitation, he swallowed it dry.

"You don't want... water?" I quickly asked but didn't manage to ask the entire question before he'd swallowed the pill.

"Nope. Don't need that." He smiled as he rolled the dice.

"Well, alright then."

Back in the nursing lounge for lunch, I made some phone calls and did more online shopping. I listened to the other nurses complain about their husbands, boyfriends, or in the case of one nurse, both. Everything always centered around money and communication. I hadn't told Asher the whole truth when the topic had come up. He'd never asked how I'd come up with money to explore the world at age eighteen and I'd never offered it. He talked about his own family coming from money, but I just hadn't felt like sharing. As far as I could tell, he was completely unaware that I'd inherited millions of dollars.

When my dad died, I vented about the experience in terms of transferring assets, not about the worth of the assets. While I knew Asher had come from a wealthy family, I had managed to leave out the part that my father had been a multi-millionaire and left me every penny along with the company he'd built from the ground up. When he'd invited me to Denver, he had offered to pay for everything. Mostly his company was paying for hotel and car, but he'd offered to foot the bill for the plane tickets. I'd let him. I wasn't ready just yet to let the cat out of the bag.

While I didn't think Asher would view me differently knowing I was worth millions of dollars, I wanted him to get to know me as a regular woman. My co-workers were unaware that I was worth millions of dollars as well. A part of me felt it was my little secret. I was good at keeping secrets.

When I had been working for the lawyer, friends would ask me why I'd needed a job at all. I'd explained that it built character. It seemed impossible for anyone to understand that life wasn't just about money. I'd felt that way too for the longest time, and then I'd gotten a job and understood. Nursing wasn't about the money for me, it was about the ability to help others.

As I sat listening and occasionally offering advice to my co-workers, I couldn't help but feel guilty. Guilty that I wasn't helping the people I worked with every day. Guilty that I kept such a big part of me a secret. And guilty for thinking it even mattered to any of them. Maybe I would casually mention to Asher while we were in Denver. And maybe I'd just keep it to myself awhile longer.

Finishing my lunch, I stepped into the hallway to round on my patients when I heard a loud commotion coming from the direction of my assigned rooms. Rounding the corner, I saw a crowd of grieving family members. My aide rushed to me and whispered in my ear that Ms. Angry Family appeared to have passed away, and we rushed to the bedside. Attempts at taking vitals were futile and I glanced at the clock to pronounced her.

The daughter was sitting on a chair next to the bed with her head laying on her mother's hand, the tears pouring out of her. Across the room, several men wept loudly. By the door, several more family members were crying and in the hallway, family members were beginning to argue. I instructed the aide to usher the family to the conference room. I gave condolences to the daughter, and she hugged me. After a few moments, she let me go, angrily swore at one of the men across the room, and walked toward the conference room. I called the doctor.

Exiting the patient's room, the daughter stopped me outside the door. Her body matched that of a defensive linemen playing football, and she was easily a foot taller than I was. She gestured for me to go back into the patient's room, but I was afraid to be cornered and alone with her based on my previous interactions with her. I stood my ground.

"What can I do for you?" I asked with compassion, hoping to feel out her emotions.

"You." That's all she managed to say before she began to cry again.

"Me?"

"You. Thank you." She pulled me in for a tight hug. "Thank you," she repeated.

My fear subsided as she walked back toward the direction of the conference room. I let out a sigh and made my way to Connie's office. Connie was definitely needed as I knew I couldn't handle this family alone. Instead, I ran into Bobby. He informed me that Mr. Escape Artist had fallen during the excitement of the dice game and hit his head on the edge of a table. Without any hesitation, I followed Bobby.

Asher and I arrived at the airport early on Tuesday morning. I'd packed my carry-on with as much as it could possibly hold, placed everything else into my backpack, and was using the largest purse in my closet. Asher had laughed at me as he loaded everything into the back of his BMW. He'd packed his carry-on and a backpack, but both were obviously lighter and smaller than mine.

Despite dating Asher for the last three months, I was anxious about our first trip together. Would he be annoying to travel with or laid back and just go with the flow? Everything was an unknown, and I was about to find out. As we walked through the airport, he held my free hand. The contact made the butterflies in my stomach flutter. While waiting, he read a sports magazine and I read a romance novel I'd ordered online.

Boarding the plane, he had lifted my carry-on into the overhead compartment, and given me the window seat. He'd leaned over me as the plane took off, peeking through my window, and kissing me on the cheek. When the stewardess arrived for drinks, he casually told her that his girlfriend would like wine. Girlfriend. I instantly blushed.

"Girlfriend?" I asked him as the stewardess continued down the aisle.

"Is that okay? Do you want to be my girlfriend?" he asked quickly, as if he'd made a mistake.

"I don't know. What does that entail?" I joked with a smile.

Rather than answer, he put his hand behind my head, pulled me into him so our lips were barely inches apart, paused for a moment, and then kissed me softly. I kissed him back and my stomach dropped as if I'd been at the top of a roller coaster. Despite the recent losses in my life, I felt like I had won the lottery meeting Asher. In that moment, he was all I wanted and all I needed.

We'd flirted throughout the flight and had been getting stares from other passengers. We didn't care. Landing was smooth, and we exited the plane without any problems. We were in Denver. Just the two of us. Since we didn't have checked bags, we made our way to the baggage claim and would be able to meet our company driver without a wait.

There stood a woman in a black pant suit with long blond hair pulled out of her face with a barrette. She held a sign that read "Mr. A. Grant". She led us to a black SUV parked on the curb and without so much as a word, drove us to our hotel. At the hotel, Asher didn't even give our luggage a second thought as he exited the SUV and held out a hand for me. Holding my hand tightly, he led me up the steps and into the hotel towards the big oak check-in desk.

Fourth Month: June

(Part II)

"Welcome to the Biltmore Hotel. How can I help you?"

"Asher Grant, checking in."

"Thank you, sir. One moment while I locate your reservation," the agent said pleasantly. "Here it is. Looks like everything is all set."

She handed Asher a credit card like key and called for a bellhop to escort us to our room. Once off the elevator, the hallway stretched to the right and left with only a few doors on each side. Our room was at the end of the hall on the right side. The door opened into a living room or seating area with a sofa, loveseat, and two oversized chairs surrounding a glass coffee table. To the left was a small kitchenette. To the right was a bedroom with a king-size bed and a bathroom with double sinks, a whirlpool bathtub, and a shower.

Asher placed his hand in the small of my back and led me toward the wall of windows across from the door that overlooked the city. In the background, beyond the city, were mountains. The view was breathtaking and Asher placed his arms around me and pulled me close, my back to his chest. We stood there pointing out different things we saw for nearly thirty minutes until another bellhop arrived with our luggage, and broke up the moment.

"Does your company always make reservations like this for you?" I smiled as I moved away from the window and looked into the bedroom.

"Never," he laughed. "I asked the office to upgrade my room because I was bringing a guest."

"All this for me?"

"I figured, why not? A beautiful woman deserves a beautiful place to sleep, right?" He winked.

"Is that so?"

"Always." He moved across the room and kissed me.

His kiss was passionate and I felt a desire rise inside me for more. I felt his hands cup my butt as he lifted me off the ground. Carrying me while he continued to kiss me, he walked me into the bedroom and placed me on the bed. He laid himself softly on me and kissed my neck. As much as I wanted this to continue and to progress, I had to stop him. Knowing I'd regret it, I pushed him back lightly.

"I can't right now," I groaned softly.

"As much as I want you at this moment, I respect that," he said as he stood up and pulled me off the bed, into his warm embrace.

"I'm sorry," I said bashfully.

"Don't be. We just arrived. We have plenty of time to make love." He lifted my chin and looked into my eyes and I saw sincerity. He kissed me again and then left for the living room.

I composed myself and followed.

"What's on the agenda for the rest of the day?" I asked, trying to distract myself.

"Food. Food is always at the top of the agenda," he said with a laugh.

"I like food."

"Then, we play it by ear. I have a meeting at 08:00 a.m. tomorrow morning, so we can't stay out too late. I should be done with my meeting tomorrow by 03:00 p.m. and then I'm all yours." He gave me a big smile.

"Sounds wonderful. Thank you for bringing me along. I'm really happy everything worked out and I could come with you."

"Me too!" he said excitedly.

I changed into a pair of blue jeans, a gray off the shoulder top, and white sneakers while he changed into blue jeans, a navy polo, and brown loafers. I ran a brush through my hair and threw it into a fresh ponytail before we took off on foot to find dinner.

Holding hands, we walked back to the hotel after dinner. The street lights provided a beautiful setting and the perfect end to a long day. Standing in the middle of a bridge, Asher stopped me and pulled me into his arms. He smiled at me. His eyes were large and a deep green color, similar to emeralds.

"I stopped here because I don't want this day to end," he whispered into my ear.

"Me either." I nuzzled my head to his chest.

"Ellie, I'm falling in love with you," he spoke as he hugged me close.

He couldn't see my face when he'd said it. I took a deep breath, inhaling his musky cologne. He smelled amazing. Everything over the last few months churned inside me, and hearing him say those words just pushed me over the top emotionally, and I began to cry. He was genuine and real and falling in love with *me*. The truth was, I was falling in love with him as well. Part of me was holding back, not yet ready to allow myself to fall. The other part of me was already in love.

I looked up at him, soft tears still wet on my cheeks, and I kissed him. We then walked back down the street, hand in hand, by the light of the street lamps. I hadn't replied to his confession and that hadn't seemed to bother him. Did my kiss convey that I agreed with his confession? Did my silence suggest that I *wasn't* falling in love with him also? I tried to shut my mind down and just enjoy the moment.

Back in our room, I rummaged through my carry-on looking for the most appropriate pair of pajamas to wear, and went into the bathroom to change. Asher and I had never spent the night together before and this, too, was another step in our relationship. I couldn't wipe the grin off my face when I looked in the mirror. I changed into a linen button up top and pair of shorts, washed my face, and brushed my teeth.

When I stepped out of the bathroom, Asher wasn't in the bedroom. In the living room, Asher had made a bed on the couch, and was laying on it reading. Trying not to read into it, I pushed his legs aside and sat on the couch with him. As I looked him over, I noticed he had changed into a white t-shirt and a pair of boxers. He also wore a pair of glasses. My pulse quickened. The truth was he looked damn sexy. I didn't want him to sleep on the couch. I wanted him to sleep cuddled up next to me.

He set his paper down and smiled at me when I walked into the room. He always smiled at me. The way his cheeks dimpled when he smiled, the flash of his perfectly straight white teeth, and the way his lips curled always gave me butterflies. I couldn't resist his smile. I spoke from the heart before my brain could stop me.

"I'm falling in love with you too."

As the words registered in his own brain, he leaned over and kissed me. Not a gentle kiss, but a hard, passionate kiss that screamed "I want you". He continued kissing me as he laid me back on the couch where his feet had rested moments before. His hands searched my body frantically, touching every inch. With my legs wrapped around his torso, I could feel his excitement as he pressed against me.

His hands found my buttons. He slowly unbuttoned the top two, and then he gingerly kissed my collar bones one by one as his hands continued to unbutton my pajama top. I extended my neck back and closed my eyes, allowing every nerve ending in my body to enjoy the experience. With my top completely unbuttoned, his kisses trailed down my torso. I arched my back, half feeling tickled and half in pleasure.

Before going any further, he stood up, and pulled his t-shirt over his head. This hands then planted on each side of my hips, and he slowly slid my pajama bottoms off my body. His hands tracing along

100

my legs sent electrical pulses through my entire body. I didn't dare open my eyes. Instead, I let him have complete control over me. When I felt his body on me again, he was completely naked. I surrendered all my inhibitions and let him ravage my body.

In the morning, I woke up, alone, in bed. Glancing at the clock, it was already after 09:00 a.m. I sighed heavily and then made my way to the living room. I sat lazily on the couch contemplating what to do with my day when there was a knock at the door. Immediately realizing I wasn't properly clothed to answer the door, I grabbed the robe from the back of the door in the bathroom and answered the door.

With a vase of flowers in one hand, a bellhop stood at the door pulling a cart with his other hand. He smiled. He asked if I was Ms. Arthur, then handed me the flowers, and wheeled the cart into the room. He scurried away before I had a chance to get a tip for him. Alone again, I smelled the flowers and set them on a table by the door. I opened the card and read the message from Asher. "Thank you for last night. You were amazing. With love, Asher."

I glanced at the cart. It held multiple silver cloches and a carafe of orange juice. I lifted one of the silver lids and found a pile of bacon, sausage, and ham. Curious, I opened another and found pancakes. Yet another held scrambled eggs. At the bottom of the cart was a basket of muffins, bagels, and croissants. Laying on top of the cart next to one of the cloches was a note that read "I didn't know what you wanted for breakfast, so I ordered everything on the menu."

After devouring breakfast, I showered and dressed for the day. My flower summer dress was perfect for the weather and I took off to explore a little before Asher came back. While out, I phoned Mary Jane and filled her in on everything that had happened. She was excited for me. After doing a little shopping, I made my way back to the hotel. I grabbed my laptop and decided to check emails while I waited for Asher.

Three o'clock came and went without so much as a phone call from Asher. I assumed he'd been caught up with work and wasn't worried. I didn't call him. Finishing my emails, I decided to read my book for a while. I knew eventually Asher would return.

When my book was half-finished, I looked at my phone. 07:29 p.m.. No phone calls. No text messages. Definitely not a note at the front desk. Irritation was boiling inside me. Where the hell was he? If there was one thing I hated, it was being stood up. To make matters worse, I was being stood up on a trip out of town by my new boyfriend. I shot Asher an angry text message. Polite, but angry.

By 09:00 p.m., I was out of my mind. Where the hell was Asher? I'd now wasted an entire afternoon waiting inside a hotel. Not cool. Deciding it was time for a drink, I grabbed my purse and headed to the hotel bar. I went straight to the bar and ordered a shot of Jack and a Coke. Waiting for the bartender to pour my drinks, I glanced around the room and my eyes settled on him sitting in a corner. Alone. I threw the drinks down my throat.

"What are the chances of seeing you here?" I said as I approached his table.

"Well hello there," Mystery Man said.

"Hello there to you too," I said with irritation.

"I didn't notice you were here. I'm meeting my brother, but he's busy flirting with the bartender and hasn't made it this way yet." He motioned towards the bar where a man was flirting with the bartender.

"Why do you always appear wherever I happen to be? Are you following me?" I asked aggressively.

"I'm not sure. Maybe you're following me?" He played dumb.

"Who are you?" I demanded, the alcohol now in my bloodstream.

"Not who you think I am," he said with irritation.

"What?" I asked, confused.

The bar lights were starting to sway as I tried to steady myself. What had been in that shot? I blinked rapidly a few times trying to clear my vision, but was unsuccessful. Mystery Man just watched me. Had the bartender slipped something in my drink? I had watched him pour the shot, hadn't I? I wanted to make it back to my room before the opportunity to do so under my own control had passed, so I turned and walked away.

Reaching the arch that led to the reception area, I paused and looked back to the bar. The man flirting with the bartender happened to break away and did *not* walk towards Mystery Man, but instead walked out of the bar past me. He had lied. They were not together.

Feeling a bit scared and irritated, I carefully made my way back to our suite. Asher ran to me and hugged me the moment I opened the door. While I'd remembered to grab my purse, I had left my phone on the table. Asher had arrived back, finally, and I had been missing. As he began to ask where I'd been, I interrupted him and told him about running into Mystery Man at the hotel bar, and how I was feeling after taking the shot of Jack.

"Where the hell have *you* been?" I stopped abruptly and asked him.

"My meeting ran late."

"No call. No text. Not even from some secretary? And who works until 09:00 p.m.?" I unleashed all of my pent-up anger, which was now mixed with alcohol.

"Shit. You're right. It's been a long time since I've done this and apparently I'm rusty," he explained.

"That's such bullshit. No one forgets they have a girlfriend waiting for them when they have gone away to a different city. It's not like this was in your routine. I. Call. Bullshit." I said matter-of-factly.

He was silent. When he finally spoke again, he admitted I was right, and he had been incredibly inconsiderate. It was hard to stay mad at him when he was standing before me bearing his soul with an

103

apology. Still dressed in a suit, he was drop dead gorgeous. I accepted the apology but went into the bedroom to change into pajamas without another word. I crawled into bed and grabbed my book. He followed me into the bedroom, stripped down to his boxers, crawled into bed, and began to read papers from his briefcase. This is how I'd imagined growing old, not recovering after a fight.

Returning to work after the trip to Denver, I felt completely unprepared. I had stopped to pick up a large coffee on my way to work and was still sipping on it as I received report. I was pleased to know that Mr. Escape Artist was assigned to me again as well as a new patient. Cora told me she would have the rooms next to mine if I needed anything as my new patient was medically complex. Diagnosed with colorectal cancer, she experienced a lot of pain and had given the night shift nurses plenty to keep them occupied. I wasn't sure if today was the day to have a challenge, but I wouldn't back down from it.

I decided to go to Room 3 first, and attempt to find Mr. Escape Artist after. I took a deep breath and opened the door. A middle-aged woman lay on the bed with an oxygen mask on her face, a nasogastric tube hooked up to suction, and a pain pump next to her bed. It looked incredibly uncomfortable. Her husband sat on the couch across the room, his laptop on his lap, and his phone to his ear. Upon seeing me, he ended his call and set the laptop aside.

"Good morning. My name is Ellie, and I'll be your nurse today. How are you feeling?"

"I'm okay." Mrs. Colorectal cancer spoke barely above a whisper.

"Is there anything I can get for you?"

"Let me think." She tapped her long, pale finger against her chin. "I'd like a hot fudge sundae," she finally said with a smile.

"Oh no! We're all out of fudge! Would you like some vanilla ice cream instead?"

"No, I guess that won't do. How about a new intestines? Do you have a spare one lying around anywhere?" She asked.

"Unfortunately, my last patient used up my last one. I'm striking out here. Not a very good first impression, I suppose." The husband and wife laughed.

"How about pain medicine? Do you need any more pain medicine while she's here?" The husband turned and asked his wife.

"No, I get it from that thing now, remember?" The patient glanced at the pain pump attached to the pole next to her bed.

"Oh, that's right. I'm still getting used to all of these new contraptions."

I emptied the suction canister, verified the liters of oxygen on the concentrator, took her vital signs, and cleared the pain pump. She was weak, but stable at this point.

"Do you need anything else?" I asked as I neared the door.

"A cure for colorectal cancer," she said without any hesitation, "so no one else would have to go through this."

"I'll see what I can do. If you need anything else, just let me know."

"You got it," the husband said as I closed the door behind me.

Peaking my head into room 4, I was surprised to see Mr. Escape Artist in his room *and* lying on his bed. His eyes grew big as he saw me, and he attempted to straighten himself up. His decline was obvious since the last time I'd seen him. He was now wearing a nasal cannula and boasted he'd gotten a pain patch to ensure even coverage of his aching hips. It hadn't even occurred to him that the increasing pain to his hips was the progression of his bone cancer, but I wasn't going to bring down his spirits by pointing it out.

"Where did your sons go? Did they head back home already?" I asked after taking his vitals.

"Oh ya. They had to get back to work and wives and stuff."

"That's too bad. They seemed like a fun bunch."

"You aren't kidding. When they were growin' up, my wife always said they were quite a handful, but I found them delightful. We got into so much trouble. Them boys are my world. I love my wife, but those boys are everything," he said as he thought about them.

"I could tell when you were playing dice."

"Do me a favor?"

"Sure. If I can, I will."

"Take care of them after I'm gone. Remind 'um I love them and that I'm always with them, okay?" My heart proceeded to break.

"Of course I will. I'll send them to Iceland with your ashes while I'm at it," I joked, trying to lighten the mood.

"Now there's an idea! Ashes to Iceland." He thought about this for a moment. "I better call my wife!"

I laughed and headed for the door. He called my name and as I turned around he thanked me and blew me a kiss. Somehow, this crazy old man had stolen my heart. It was patients like this that gave me a purpose. If I could help this man reach his goals in the short time I had with him, then I felt at peace. I didn't go into nursing for the money. I didn't even need the money. I was here for the patients. And for the way they made me feel.

I hadn't been a nurse long, but with each passing shift, my purpose in life became more clear. When I stopped to think about things, I realized just how much I had grown and matured. If I had described my current life with myself at eighteen, I would have been laughed at. At eighteen, my life revolved around trying *not* to work, shopping for the latest fashion trends, and doing whatever worked best for *me*. I had been selfish. The more time I spent thinking about how much I'd changed, the more the plan formulated in my head.

I worked all weekend and Monday arrived like a slap in the face. By the fourth twelve-hour shift in a row, I felt like I had gone through a wrestling match and every muscle in my body ached. By Monday, I didn't bother to shower, feed myself properly, or talk to people. I felt like a zombie as I took report that morning. Even though I worked part-time, I'd picked up extra days here and there to help out co-workers. I was still young enough to work like this, but since I *hadn't* worked this hard in my life, I was still trying to condition myself.

Asher had arrived home from Denver on the weekend. We hadn't had much time to talk since I'd left Denver, but I wasn't upset about what happened anymore. He had invited me to dinner on Saturday night, but I declined. The only thing I wanted to do was sleep between shifts. In fact, the only thing stopping me from sleeping during report was the steaming hot hazelnut coffee in the cup between my hands.

Just as it had been all weekend, I was assigned rooms 3 and 4. I would be off orientation on my next scheduled shift and would have more patients assigned to me, but today I was thankful for only having two. Before I headed off, I chugged the rest of the coffee and grabbed a muffin from the basket on the table.

It was just my luck that both of my patients were actively dying. It wasn't time to be half awake because I needed to be on my toes. Marci and Cora offered to help if shit began to hit the fan, and I was glad to know that I had their support. However, I first had to assess my patients and make my plan of action for the day, even if the plan never seemed to work out the way I'd hoped.

Mrs. Colorectal Cancer had her husband at her bedside along with what I assumed were her children. Her mouth lay open and a gurgling noise came from deep within her throat. Her nasogastric tube continued to draw coffee-ground-like liquid from her stomach. Her brow was furrowed and her forehead had beads of sweat. Her pain pump was still attached and the bag of narcotic medicine was full. The pump was providing the pain medicine continuously with the ability to give an additional bolus every fifteen minutes, if needed. She was no longer able to trigger the pump herself, but her husband stated he was activating it on her behalf when he noticed she was restless or uncomfortable.

Using the glycerin swabs on her bedside table, I carefully cleaned her mouth. I emptied the suction canister into the toilet and cleared the pain pump. I did a quick assessment of her skin and noted mottling to both of her lower extremities. I didn't need a thermometer to note that she had a fever. Her breaths were in a cheyne-stokes pattern and resembled a roller coaster — fast, fast, slow, slow, no breath, no breath, big gasp, fast, fast…

I flashed a small smile at her husband, answered all of his questions about dying, and quietly headed for the door. Before leaving, I squirted hand sanitizer onto my hands and watched Mrs. Colorectal Cancer for a few more moments while I worked it into my hands. I closed the door softly behind me and moved next door.

Mr. Escape Artist was easily located in his room, lying quietly in his bed. For a brief moment, I missed the challenge of trying to find him. His body was soaked with sweat, and he was unable to communicate with me. His wife was at his bedside, crocheting a scarf. She informed me that Bobby and Billy were on their way to the facility, but she wasn't sure if they would make it on time.

For the second time in an hour, I found myself softly talking about what to expect with dying, and she acknowledged that he had been ready for years. However, she wasn't sure if she was ready for him to go yet. I had explained this was common and it was extremely hard. She softly cried and held his hand. His color had grown ashen since I'd last seen him. It was hard to have seen him so lively just a week ago and to see the man he was now.

His heart rate was elevated, his breathing rapid and shallow. His hands and feet were freezing, his torso hot. I answered the rest of the wife's questions as I cleaned his mouth with swabs. I checked his brief, but he was dry. Finished with my assessment, I slipped quietly from the room.

Having a few free minutes, I slipped away to the courtyard to make a few phone calls. The courtyard was private and allowed me to get a few minutes of fresh air. Just as I finished my final call, Marci approached me.

"What are you up to?" She asked with curiosity.

"Nothing," I lied.

"Oh come on," she begged. "I know you're up to something."

"Is that so?"

"Yeah. I'm a good read of people and I sense you're up to something."

I laughed. "No, I'm not up to anything. I've just got lots of loose ends to tie up from my father's death a few months ago. It's been a complicated process and I'm still trying to figure everything out."

"Oh, I'm sorry. I didn't realize you had all that going on."

"It's okay. I didn't really tell people."

"I won't say anything," she assured me.

"Don't worry. It's not a secret."

"Okay. Anyway, I came out here to see if you needed any help."

"I think I'm okay at the moment."

We slipped back into the building and went our separate ways. I checked on both patients and found no changes. I realized I had one more phone call to make, so I returned to the courtyard. I found a bench and made my call. I suppose if I wanted to work on my plan, I wouldn't get the most privacy from the courtyard, but it did allow me to get some fresh air while I did.

The courtyard held a variety of bushes, flowers, and trees with a path from each corner, meeting in the middle with a bird bath. Along each path were garden lights, bird houses, and wind chimes hanging from tree branches. A few benches were placed strategically to allow for a beautiful view and privacy for patients and their families.

Back in the building, all hell broke loose. I had barely set foot down the hallway when I was notified that Mr. Escape Artist had just passed away and Mrs. Colorectal Cancer's nasogastric tube had started to come out when the aides were helping to reposition her. I headed toward Mr. Escape Artist's room, but before I reached the door, I heard yelling coming from the entrance of the building and the fire alarm began to sound.

The heavy fire doors began to close the moment the alarm sounded, and created an obstacle. I pressed the lever in the middle of the door and it opened. Just as I reached the nearest fire extinguisher, the overhead system blared to life and announced that it was a drill. Shoot me now, I thought to myself and proceeded down the hallway to Mr. Escape Artists room.

The sons had not made it in time and the wife sat alone next to his bed. Using my phone, I quietly called for Connie to come sit with her. I did a discreet check of vitals and finding none, I noted the time on my paper. I came around to the wife and gave her a hug as Connie stepped into the room. She quickly took my place and began softly talking to the grieving woman as I stepped out and contacted the physician. As I gave him the information, I noticed a small tear fall from my face and land on my paper.

I quickly wiped it away and moved to the room next door. Mrs. Colorectal Cancer had received an entire bed bath and bed change while I had been in the other room. After discussion with the physician during my phone call regarding Mr. Escape Artist, it was decided that the nasogastric tube would remain out as long as Mrs. Colorectal Cancer was comfortable. If she were to become uncomfortable from the bile in her stomach, the tube would have to be replaced. I updated the husband and he agreed to the plan. I turned off the wall suction, removed the tube the rest of the way, and provided oral care.

Feeling proud of myself for adequately handling both situations at once, I flung the door to the nursing lounge open. The door rebounded and my toe caught the edge of it as it flew back at me. I cried out in pain and began a mixture of laughing and crying. Karma was always right there to remind me not to get too big for my britches, and as I began to sit down to inspect my toe for damage, my phone vibrated in my pocket and alerted me that I was needed in room 3.

Sally, the other nurse in the nursing lounge, had witnessed the entire incident and had been laughing with me. Sensing that I had to take the call, she quickly offered to help me with my toe. We removed the shoe and sock, and found my toe completely intact. Relieved it was just going to be bruised, I replaced my sock and shoe and headed out the door, thanking Sally as I went.

"She's not breathing!" The husband rushed to meet me at the door, loud and frantic.

"Okay, let me check on her." I tried hard to sound reassuring, but I was pretty sure I didn't.

From the door, I could see that Mrs. Colorectal Cancer was extremely pale, if not slightly blue in color. Her chest did not rise and the noises from her throat were gone. I felt for a pulse and found none. I listened for a heartbeat and attempted a blood pressure, but she had definitely passed away. I turned towards the husband and my gut sank when I informed him that she had passed. He collapsed on the floor and sobbed.

Her daughter cried over her body, and her son rushed to the husband and sat on the floor next to him. Still feeling emotional from Mr. Escape Artist's death as well as my overwhelming tiredness, the tears returned to my eyes as I watched the three of them grieve. I felt like a kindergartener had glued my shoes to the floor. I wanted to run from the room, but was unable to lift either foot.

It was almost too much for one day. I'd spent the last four days caring for these patients and their families. I knew that each was dying, but I hadn't expected to witness it, let alone on the same day. Finally, I managed to break away and stepped out of the room to contact the physician, again.

Fifth Month: July

Asher grabbed my hand and squeezed as we walked up the tree lined driveway. The house sat off the road and was well hidden by a row of trees along the road. By all accounts, the house was an old plantation home. It stood two stories high with wrap-around porches on each level. Windows peppered the front wall and were surrounded by black shutters on both sides. Solid white columns ran from the ground level porch to the roof. The porch was lined by a selection of low-lying bushes and flowers. Green grass spread across the lawn and around the house.

As we approached the front door, a well-dressed man opened the door and welcomed us. Looking around, the foyer was two stories tall with a huge crystal chandelier hanging above our heads. Grand staircases leading to the second story lined each side of the room. Straight ahead, an archway led to another room and eventually french doors to the back patio.

Asher took my hand and walked me straight through the house to the backyard. We passed through the open doors and stood on a marble porch. The view of the expansive fields surrounding the house was outstanding. Crowds of people gathered around tables, mingling and drinking champagne, while a live band was set up to one side of the yard playing jazz music softly in the background. In front of us, steps led to a marble fountain with colored lights showcasing the flow of water. A dance floor had been set up near the live band and several couples were swaying to the beat of the music.

"Asher, dear! You made it!" A woman approached Asher, kissing him on each cheek.

"Hello, Mom," he said, annoyed by her kisses and the spit shine she applied to remove the lipstick marks from his cheeks.

"Who is this fine lady you have with you? Is this the one you've been raving about for months?" Asher blushed. Or was it left over smeared lipstick?

"Yes, this is Ellie. Ellie, this is my mother. Marceline Grant." He introduced the two most important women in his life.

Asher's mother, Marceline, was a beautiful woman. Her shoulder-length hair was delicately curled at the ends and held out of her face by small diamond pins. Her make-up was perfectly applied, and a diamond necklace accented her chest. Her dress had a sweetheart neckline and hugged her curves as it fell just below her knee. A diamond belt was buckled loosely across her waist. Uncharacteristically, she was barefoot.

"It's so nice to finally meet you. I've heard so much about you," I said, unsure if I should hug her or shake her hand.

"Likewise. Listen, please, enjoy yourselves. We can talk more tomorrow at breakfast. Asher, did you give your bags to Arnold?" She began walking off towards another group of people as she asked the last question, not waiting for an answer.

Asher looked at me, shrugged, and said, "and now you've met my mother."

The way his mother had spoken to us had an almost stuck-up tone to it, but my gut told me that wasn't her true personality. Asher had always spoken about his family as loving and supportive. His mother had always been there for his school events and field trips, never missing one, unlike my own mother. Marceline's children were her pride and joy. It didn't match the woman I'd just met, but potentially, it was the alcohol speaking instead.

Making our way through the crowd, Asher would stop and introduce me to different people. Most of them were friends of the family or distant family members. The Fourth of July party had taken place annually at the Grant Plantation for nearly one hundred years, minus a few years here and there during wars and the Great Depression. What had started as a backyard gathering had turned into a large shindig over the years that was planned a year in advance.

The plantation, I had learned, had once comprised 399 acres — one acre had been donated to a local church group leaving the Grant's shy of 400. In the 19th century, the Grant family went to auction and bought several slaves, but refused to treat them poorly like their neighbors and friends did. The slaves were paid a low wage for their work, were given their freedom when the work was completed each day, and stayed in well-kept quarters near the main house.

However, the property today was only fifty acres, no other buildings remained besides the main house, and machines did the work that humans used to. Some men running the machines had descended from the slaves who had worked those same fields by hand. At the turn of the century, the Grant family broke up the plantation land, gifting acreage to the families of those who had been enslaved to them as a "thank you" for staying on as paid help when slavery was abolished.

Once we'd made our way through the crowds and I'd been introduced to no less than twenty people, Asher led me to the dance floor. He held me as we twirled around and around. Memories flooded to me of parties similar to this with my dad — either parties we had hosted or parties of his friends and business partners. At first, I'd been put to bed and told I was too young but as time passed and I grew older, I was allowed to join the festivities longer and longer. By the time high school rolled around, I was at the party until the dawn of the new day would arrive and just a few guests remained.

When the sun set, the sky was illuminated by the magical colors of fireworks. They were being fired off from a field a short distance to the left and with each boom, you could feel the vibrations in your chest. They crashed over our heads and looked like they were raining down over the crowd. Cuddling in Asher's arms, I leaned up and kissed him. The entire situation was incredibly romantic. As I pulled away from the kiss and nuzzled into his chest, he looked down at me and whispered into my ear, "I love you". I melted into him, and replied the same.

The fireworks continued for close to an hour before the last explosion of the grand finale was lit in the field. Thunderous applause followed. Then, some in the crowd said their goodbyes and left while others headed to the dance floor. Looking around, I saw a flash of someone I'd recognized. I searched through the crowd with my eyes until I settled on him. Mystery Man. What the hell was he doing here? He had met Asher at the karaoke bar for the first time, so I knew they hadn't known each other for years or some other bullshit explanation. As I tugged at Asher to ask him about Mystery Man, he disappeared through the crowd again.

I frantically searched the crowd but after a few moments, I gave up. Maybe it had been the alcohol and I had just seen someone that looked similar to him. My mind was playing tricks on me. No way would Mystery Man actually be here at the Grant Plantation. When I finally had Asher's attention, I mentioned I was tired, and we headed back towards the house.

Asher took me to his room. It was the room he'd grown up in, and was still decorated as if he had been living there only yesterday. His queen size bed was pushed off to the far left corner and covered with a navy blue comforter that matched the curtains on his three front lawn facing windows. The right wall contained a walk in closet and shelves filled with books, awards, a television, and DVDs. The wall that contained the door leading to the hallway also held a door to a private bathroom complete with shower and bathtub. The dead give away that he *didn't* live in this room any longer was that absolutely nothing was out of place. It was carefully organized, like a museum.

I sat on the bed and removed my heels as Asher fell onto the bed. Literally fell. Arms out wide, he purposely crash-landed himself right onto the super soft bed. He hadn't even removed his shoes. He let out a loud sigh. Thinking that had been a great idea and completely exhausted, and slightly drunk myself, I stood back up and crash-landed right next to him. He simply reached for my hand, held it for a few moments, and then used it to begin exploring my body. Obviously he wasn't as tired as I was.

Finally falling asleep sometime after 3am, I was exhausted when Asher woke me the following morning, and informed me that I had to get up for breakfast. I threw on some shorts and a t-shirt, ran a brush through my hair, and glanced in the mirror to make sure I looked presentable. Yesterday's makeup was still pretty much in place. Asher gave me a once over and told me I looked beautiful. I really felt he might say that no matter what, if my make-up was perfect or if it were running down my face and I looked like I'd joined a circus.

Asher took my hand and led me down the hallway, down a set of stairs, and down another long hallway before we entered a sunroom. The room had windows floor to ceiling along three sides as well as massive amounts of light flowing in from the domed glass ceiling. A long table ran from one end of the room to the other and held about twenty chairs total. The table was set elaborately and had fresh floral arrangements carefully placed along the center. Several people were already seated, but stood when we entered.

"Well hello, Asher. Good to see you this morning. Who is this lovely lady you've brought with you?" A tall, robust gentleman shook Asher's hand.

"This is my girlfriend, Ellie Arthur," Asher introduced me.

"Hmmm… Arthur? That name is familiar," He paused in thought. "Wait, is your father Franklin Arthur?" He asked.

"Yes. But he passed away recently," I sheepishly replied.

"Ah yes, that's right. I'm sorry to hear that. He was a fine man. What a small world. I knew he had a daughter. Asher, if she's anything like her father was, you've got yourself a great catch," he said wagging his finger at Asher.

"Did you know her father well?" Asher asked the man, somewhat confused.

"Oh yes. He was a..."

"I'm starving. Shall we sit?" I interrupted quickly in an attempt to change the conversation.

Everyone sat down, and Asher shot me a dirty glance. Asher wasn't aware of how large my father's company was nor that he owned it. I was sure that the robust man was about to spill the beans if he had been allowed to talk about my father. I don't know why I felt I needed to keep it all a secret, but I didn't want my fortune to change the dynamic of our relationship. Eventually, it would be time to come clean, but breakfast with strangers wasn't the right time. Even though Asher grew up in a similar fashion, Asher had his parent's wealth by association whereas I already had my father's wealth.

Asher's parents entered the sunroom and sat down as a few more couples followed. After a few more introductions, including Asher's sister, Andrea, her husband Benedict, and their two children, Max and Molly, we finally were served. As responsible hosts, their home had been open to anyone wishing to stay who may have traveled far or had a few too many to drink. Like a bed and breakfast, everyone joined in the sunroom for a bite to eat the following morning before heading their separate ways.

I enjoyed watching Asher interact with Max and Molly, and thought about how it might be to have my own children with Asher some day. Watching his family interact, I saw how close they really were. I also confirmed my suspicion that my first impression of

Marceline had been wrong. During breakfast, she was attentive and down-to-earth.

We spent the rest of the morning touring the house and discussing its history. Early afternoon meant good-byes and the long drive home. Later that evening, I was crawling into my own bed and wishing I didn't have to work the next day. Our trip to his parent's home had been far too short, and I had genuinely enjoyed meeting all of them. We assured them we would make another trip soon, and I hoped we would see that through.

As I lay in bed that night, I heard the familiar pitter-patter of rain softly hitting the roof. Spending the day traveling, I hadn't even known it was supposed to rain. We'd had clear skies all the way. I climbed out of bed, careful not to wake Asher, and looked out the window. The clouds were being illuminated by frequent, silent lightning. I crossed the room to my phone and looked at the radar. I was restless, so tired that I couldn't sleep.

I had grown up a storm enthusiast, always wishing my dad would take us tornado chasing. However, he hadn't been a fan of storms and had adamantly refused. Each time I asked, he would mumble something about his childhood, a bad storm experience, and he would signal that the conversation was over. It hadn't stopped my curiosity for storms. The crack of thunder making you jump, the sound of the wind hitting the window, and the lightning illuminating the sky. It all made me excited in that "nature is cool" sort of way.

The radar showed strong storms headed our way and my ability to sleep was zero. I lightly closed the door behind me as I exited the bedroom and headed for the living room. Sitting on the couch, I turned the TV on and looked out the bay window. A severe thunderstorm warning was flashing across the bottom of the screen for our county and I could hear the rain picking up outside. A few quiet rumbles of thunder and the living room would momentarily light up.

I grabbed the blanket from the chair and cuddled up on the couch, watching out the window and keeping an eye on the TV for updates. I could hear tree branches being blown against the house as the wind picked up and whipped them back and forth. The rumbling thunder became louder and the lightning more intense. Sometimes just the clouds would light up and other times I could see a bolt touch the ground in the distance. I heard a loud crack followed by a big thump and my reflexes caused me to jump. I heard the power go out and five seconds later, the generator turn on. Crossing the room to the window, I could see a very large branch from my oak tree laying in my yard when the lightning lit the sky.

As quickly as the storm rolled in, it died down. The soft rain continued, but the patches of orange and red were gone from the radar. I quietly crawled back into bed and curled up next to Asher, and fell back asleep. My dreams of tornado chasing visited me in my sleep that night, and I woke five minutes before my alarm just as the fictitious tornado was about to hit my house.

It was a busy morning at work due to the storm. While Rolling Hills hadn't sustained any damage, many home hospice patients had. Most were simply without power, but a few had damage to their houses. I was to receive a patient around 10:00 a.m. for temporary respite admission due to her home being uninhabitable after the storm.

When she arrived, still wearing her pajamas, she collapsed into the bed and closed her eyes with a sigh of relief. Her son explained that she had been awake all night with fear. The large walnut tree in their side yard had crashed down on their room, collapsing it into their living room. It had landed mere inches from where he had been sleeping on the couch. After the shock from the fallen tree had settled, the rain had continued to fall, flooding their living room.

"Mom, it's going to be okay," the son assured her as I worked on my admission paperwork.

"Terrance, you're so optimistic that you aren't seeing reality," she snapped back at him.

"Are you having any pain?" I interjected.

"No," she answered sharply before continuing with her son. "You cancelled the homeowners insurance six months ago to pay for my treatments. Who's going to fix the damn roof? Who's going to pay for the repairs? Who's going to replace the damaged stuff? I'm going to die in this hell-hole rather than in my bed thanks to that damn tree. I told you to chop it down years ago, but you didn't listen," she barked at him angrily.

"Would you like anything for anxiety?" I asked her, sensing her anxiety level rising rapidly.

"No, thank you."

"Mom, just listen to me. I'll get this figured out. I don't want you to stress you out with this," he pleaded with her.

"Too late. How can I *not* stress about this. Do you see where we are?" She shot at him.

"I do. I know it's my fault. I'm going to do whatever I can to make this right," he assured her again.

"Bullshit. You won't even get a job."

"I'm going to step out. Is there anything else you need at the moment?" I asked trying to stay out of the conflict.

"Could you get me something to eat?" She asked sweetly and politely.

"Of course."

"And maybe a new roof if you have one," she joked.

"Well, I'll see what I can do, but no promises."

After my admission paperwork was completed, I snuck into the courtyard for another round of phone calls. Sitting on the bench, I saw

Marci eye me from the window and head in my direction. With the same sly look she'd had before, she asked what I had up my sleeve again. I finally decided to confess to her about my father leaving me with a company. I explained that during these calls, I was answering questions, making decisions, and finalizing deals. It wasn't anyone's business what I was up to, but I felt that the only way to get Marci off my back, was to provide her with some information. Whether the information was completely true or not was my own secret.

When she accepted my explanation, I asked if she wanted to get the girls together and go for drinks after work. Considering the fact that a few of the nurses were also without power, she gladly accepted. She bounced off excitedly to invite the other girls. I returned to my phone calls. I had just one more to make before I needed to return inside and check on Mrs. Homewrecked again.

At the restaurant that evening, I ordered a round of drinks for everyone. There were six of us who had been able to make it. The restaurant was a small hole-in-the-wall type place. As our drinks arrived and we chit-chatted, Paige leaned forward and asked if anyone had noticed some odd things happening around the facility lately. After receiving questionable looks from the rest of us, she explained.

"Come on guys! You know what I'm talking about. We have residents come and go and everything, but lately when the residents go, shit happens!" More curious looks were shot at Paige's direction.

"What in the world are you talking about?" Grace asked.

"Well, do you remember that one lady who had the big family and the daughter was always super ticked off about everything? You know, the one who hated all the family being there but refused to kick them out of the room?" We all nodded. How could you forget that family?

"Well, Connie said that she had been pissed off because she couldn't afford the funeral and stuff. But then the funeral home called and said an anonymous donor called and offered to pay for the entire thing! Whatever they wanted, paid free and clear!" She said looking for affirmation from us.

"What's weird about that?" Jan asked.

"Who the hell pays for a stranger's funeral?" Paige tilted her head as she asked.

"Maybe it wasn't a stranger," offered Jan.

"Fine. Maybe it wasn't a stranger. What about the crazy old guy who kept trying to escape? Ya'll remember him?" We again nodded.

"Is he back to haunt us?" Grace joked as she finished off her first drink.

"No!" Paige said shooting her a death stare. "I heard that his children opened an envelope at the funeral containing two plane tickets to Iceland to spread his ashes. Who the hell does that?"

"Uh, he could have had some old buddy who had gone to Iceland with him or something and had the money? You don't know that it was a conspiracy," Marci suggested.

"I don't buy that for an instant." Feeling deflated, Paige sighed heavily. "Connie went to another patient's funeral as she was friends with the family. The family was asking for donations for the Colorectal Cancer Association and someone left a $10,000 check in her memory! Explain that." She finished off her first drink.

"Let me order another round," I said as I left the table for the bar.

"I think you're being dramatic," Jan stated as she accepted her drink when I returned.

"I'm not being dramatic. Sure this kind of cool stuff has happened before, but not with this frequency! *Something* is going on and I'm going to find it out and prove you all wrong!" Paige said finally throwing in the towel.

I wasn't a huge fan of Paige. From the very beginning, she had watched my every move, made comments under her breath, and had been quick to criticize things that I'd done. Most of all, I didn't like that she had easily picked up on the things happening around Rolling Hills.

After we had finished the second round of drinks, three of the girls headed home while the rest of us ordered a third round. Jan talked about her grandkids getting to spend more time with her in the summer and Grace talked about the summer class she was taking. As the last gulp of my drink went down, I said my goodbyes and headed to the parking lot to meet Asher. I called him to drive me home after I'd drank half of my second drink and had felt a little intoxicated, and he hadn't hesitated to drop everything to rescue me.

By the following week, my temporary resident was no longer on our patient census. I wasn't exactly surprised, but I was curious. Of course, some patients decline quickly, but something told me that wasn't the case for this woman. When I'd asked Paige where she had gone following morning report, Paige hysterically laughed in my face.

"The day after the storm, a contractor showed up at their house with his crew and repaired the roof. Guess how much they charged?"

"No clue."

"Nothing. Ab-so-lutely. Freaking. Nothing." She grinned.

"Maybe it was a church group or some felon needing to do community service?" I offered as I laughed.

"Wrong. I just know it. You're dead wrong," she said matter-of-factly. No one was going to convince her it was all coincidence no matter how hard anyone tried.

"I'm not sure what to tell you, Paige. I have no clue what's going on, or that anything even *is* going on."

Paige stared at me and said nothing. Her eyes had plenty more to say, but her lips didn't move. I felt as if she were trying to glare into my soul or to read my thoughts. It was intense. With that, I left the nursing lounge not wanting to discuss conspiracy theories with Paige all day.

Instead, I went back to my patients. Mrs. G-tube was complaining of extreme nausea, so I headed to her room first.

She was a quiet, petite woman who'd suffered a stroke about five years ago that had caused major paralysis to the right side of her body. She had a positive spirit and re-learned to walk and talk and write, despite the limitations she was faced with. The one thing she hadn't been able to re-learn was to swallow. Despite how much she *wanted* to swallow, she had remained unable and a permanent gastrostomy tube had been placed above and to the left of her belly button.

In getting to know her throughout the week, I'd learned that her husband had died around the time of her stroke from an industrial accident. The tractor's cab wasn't enough to protect him from the steel beam that fell from a crane and crashed through the cab. He'd died on impact, the doctor had told her. No pain. It was she that was left with all the pain.

Their three children had rallied around their mother despite their own grief. They took turns living with her while she recovered that first year. Eventually, their own families grew tired of the constant change and when she'd learned enough to survive on her own, she'd been left to her own devices. After one year of living on her own, she knew she needed more help and didn't dare reach out to her children again, so without telling them, she hired a moving company, sold her house, and moved into an assisted living facility across town.

She'd flourished. She made new friends, got stronger, and even began dating a fellow resident. She had truly cherished their time together and enjoyed the companionship, but his dementia progressed faster than either had anticipated. Six months into their relationship, his children moved him into a nursing home, and she sunk into a depression that she couldn't kick. Having no desire to get out and do things, she began to spend the entire day, minus meals, sitting in her recliner.

One day, during her weekly bath, her aide noticed her stomach had swollen, and she looked pregnant. With further questioning, she had been experiencing nausea, heartburn, and stomach pain for over a week. After alerting the nurse, she was taken to the hospital for further evaluation and diagnosed with gastric cancer. Deconditioned, she was no longer able to return to the assisted living facility and was admitted to Rolling Hills to spend her last days.

She admitted she hadn't talked to her children in over a week, and they were unaware she had been admitted to the hospital, diagnosed with cancer, and was now a patient at a hospice facility. Feeling guilty, calling her oldest daughter was one of her top priorities. Upon receiving the phone call, angry and confused, all three children rushed to be with her. She'd had one of them at her bedside twenty-four hours a day since.

Slipping into the room, Mrs. G-tube looked up at me and half smiled. I explained that I had brought her some meds for her nausea. I uncapped the med port on her gastrostomy tube and administered the medicine with a syringe. After I flushed it with water, I asked her if she had any pain.

"No, dear. Thank you for always asking," she said politely.

"You don't have to thank me. It's my pleasure to make sure that all your needs are taken care of," I said softly as I patted her hand.

"That's sweet of you."

"Do you mind if I sneak down to the kitchen and get a snack?" The son interrupted and asked his mother.

"No, dear. You don't need to starve on my account."

He slipped from the room and left the two of us alone. My other patient had stated he'd wanted to take a nap, so I had time to sit with Mrs. G-tube while her son was gone. I pulled up a chair next to her bed and sat down, happy to take some pressure off my feet.

"You've had so much change over the last few years. Have you thought at all about what your goals are now that you're here?" I asked.

"My only goal is to die. Please understand me," she pleaded. "It's not that I *want* to die, I just understand it's the outcome of all this, of life that is. If it's going to happen one way or another, I'd rather it be sooner rather than later."

"That makes sense," I acknowledged my understanding. "Can I ask you something off the wall?"

"Sure."

"Is there anything you wish for? Anything you wish you'd done or had?"

"I would say world peace, but that's too generic." She said, laughing at her own joke.

"You're silly," I teased.

"What do I wish for? Hmmm. I've never been asked before." She seemed taken aback by the sincerity in the question.

"I always love to hear the different answers. Take your time. Something you wish for," I repeated the question.

"Other than world peace, right?" She let out a giggle.

"Other than world peace." I grinned.

"I suppose I want to know my family will stay together when I'm gone. I see them interact when they perform their little changing of the guard here each day. I saw it when they lived with me. They love each other. They just don't spend enough time together. They never stop their crazy, busy lives to just be together. You know?"

"I wish I had a family like that."

"Some of my favorite memories growing up were with my cousins. I adored the hours we spent swimming in the lake, making up games, and telling ghost stories in the dark. I want that for my grandchildren. I want to leave this Earth knowing my children will stop their busy lives and make time for making memories. Before it's too late."

"That is beautiful," I said as I felt an urge to cry.

"Oh no. Now I've got you tearing up. Don't cry, dear," she demanded.

"I didn't have siblings growing up and my cousins were far too old or too young. I didn't even know my mother's side of my family," I confided in her. "But that's a little secret between us, I suppose."

She squeezed her thumb and pointer finger together near her mouth and twisted her hand making the international signal for "I'll keep my mouth shut" just as her son stepped back into the room. Her eyes twinkled as she watched him cross the room to her and plant a kiss on her forehead. I gave her hand another squeeze, thanked her for the talk, and left the door open as I went down the hall.

I found myself busy the rest of my shift and feeling as if I might never get caught up. Between charting, calling the doctor, and receiving new orders, I was flustered. I'd made time to sneak into the courtyard to catch up on some phone calls, but none of them had gone the way I'd hoped. I was searching for an answer, racking my brain, but nothing was coming to me. I had zero answers to solve my problem. Until I had the perfect answer, I knew I wouldn't be able to shake the flustered feeling.

Before I left for the day, I stopped in to say goodbye to Mrs. G-tube. I had the next few days off and needed her to know that I would be thinking of her. In this line of work, if you don't say goodbye, it was very possible you'd never see the patient again. She had grabbed my hand before I pulled away, thanked me for taking the time to listen to her, and assured me that everything would be alright. I wasn't one hundred percent sure, but I felt pretty confident that she was going to be one of the patients that I'd remember for my entire life. One of the patients who shapes who I am as a nurse.

Sixth Month: August

(Part I)

Sweat dripping down my body, I threw off the sheet covering my naked body and sat on the edge of the bed. August had arrived. The previous night had been cool and I'd turned off the air conditioner and opened the windows. Clearly, this was a mistake because the room was sweltering hot and humid. I looked over at Asher as he lay sleeping and saw the beads of sweat glimmering on his chiseled back in the sunlight.

Feeling my eyes on him, he rolled over with nothing more than the other half of the sheet covering his lower body, smiled, and said "good morning". I looked at him, trying to be seductive, and motioned for him to follow me as I made my way into the bathroom and turned on the shower. Within seconds, he was behind me kissing my neck. We took turns washing each other's body in the shower and when we knew they were good and clean, we made passionate love right there on the ceramic tiles of the bathroom floor.

I enjoyed the nights that Asher spent the night. We rarely slept at his apartment. Instead, we usually found ourselves in my bed. It was comfortable and I liked having someone next to me while I slept. I found he was spending more nights in my bed than in his own and made a mental note to brooch the subject at some point in the near future.

Refreshed, I headed for the kitchen and opened the pantry, rummaging through looking for anything that could be combined to create breakfast for two. Nothing. Absolutely nothing. I always seemed to fail when it came to having groceries in the house. The pantry held an empty box of saltines, a box of elbow macaroni, a spare bottle of ketchup, a can of tomato soup, flour, sugar, salt, and a small opened box of baking soda. No combination of these items would make a breakfast I'd eat.

Asher entered the kitchen, drying his hair with a towel. He wore only a pair of tight, black boxer briefs. Droplets of water remained on his chest making his body glistened as the sunlight poured in through the window. I felt my pulse quicken as my mind flashed back to fifteen minutes ago.

"What's for breakfast? I'm starving," he said with a boyish grin.

"Apparently, cardboard because all that I have is empty boxes and carbohydrates. Not exactly appetizing."

"Get dressed. We'll make a stop at the grocery quick, and we can make breakfast together."

The grocery store was a short drive, and we struggled to find a parking spot at this time on a Saturday morning. We'd decided on omelets and made a shortlist on our way there of the items we'd need. Basically everything. Something as simple as a trip to the grocery store felt so natural. Everything with Asher felt amazing.

"How does this pepper look?" He held up the green pepper and fondled it like he had my breast that morning.

"Ripe," I said with my best impression of a sexy voice.

"Nice." He laughed.

"Hey, I was wondering if I could take you out for coffee sometime?" I playfully joked with him as I realized this was practically the same spot we'd met.

"Only if I can take you home afterwards…" His sentence drifted off as he drew me into him and planted a kiss on my lips.

"Okay, okay. We're in public!" I blushed as I smiled and leaned against him.

We'd rounded up everything on our list and paid, while doing our best to avoid further PDA. In the parking lot, I heard someone call my name. Turning around, I was face-to-face with Delilah and Jonah. A brief feeling of panic swept through me as my professional and personal lives collided. Was I supposed to introduce Asher to them? It reminded me of running into my grade school teacher on a Saturday and realizing she had a life outside our classroom.

"Oh my gosh! How are you guys? I never got the chance to tell you I'm so sorry for your loss." I gave Delilah a compassionate hug.

"Thank you. We can't say thank you enough for the wonderful care we received from you and the other nurses."

"Oh, it was my pleasure." Why hadn't nursing school taught us how to handle situations like this? Maybe they could have called the class "Meeting Families Outside Work 101".

"Dad was an amazing man, and he's been missed, but I just know he's watching over all of us. He even found a way to pull through for Jonah."

"Oh yeah. How was the graduation party, Jonah? Congrats on your 4.0, by the way. That's quite an accomplishment. Are you off to college next month?"

Jonah smiled, "Thank you. I will be off to McKinley State to study pre-med. Grad party was great."

"Speaking of the graduation party, can I ask you a question in private quick?" Delilah asked me as she pulled me aside and lowered her voice. "Do you remember what I told you about the car?"

"Yeah. It was sold at auction, right?"

"Yeah…" She drug that word out. "But a box with the keys to it appeared at Jonah's graduation party with a note that said 'from grandpa' and nothing else. I've asked everyone I know if they know what happened. Thought I might ask you too."

"A box with the car keys in it?"

"Yeah. And the next morning, the car was sitting in our driveway. I called the auction house to ask what the hell was going on, but they told me they couldn't disclose the name of an anonymous buyer. When I explained that the car was in our driveway, the guy told me that the car had sold at auction and had been removed from their lot at the end of the auction and from there, they have no idea what happened to it. A week after the party, the title arrived in the mail."

"Wow. Do you think Randall did all that?"

"I just don't know how he could have. It's been a big mystery to all of us."

"I bet. I'm sorry I can't help you with answers." She nodded understanding.

She called for Jonah to follow her as they waved goodbye. Asher and I had a breakfast date waiting for us. On the way back to my house, we talked about the auto auction and the mystery Delilah had asked me about. Asher just smiled and told me that miracles happen when you believe in miracles.

"Do you really believe that?" I asked.

"Of course I do. Some people believe in karma, I believe in miracles."

Mr. ALS greeted me mid-morning on Monday as my new admission. He had instantly recognized me, although he couldn't recall my name. I had re-introduced myself and shown him to his new room. His kids quickly climbed onto the couch and began playing with their handheld video games while I began my admission assessment with Mr. ALS and his wife. Since we'd last seen each other, he had continued to decline and was now wearing a ventilator via mask during sleep, using a machine to help himself cough, and had a feeding tube.

The wife had finally cracked and admitted to him that she could not care for him *and* the children anymore without sacrificing her own health. A decision was made for him to enter Rolling Hills. He sat slouched on the side of the bed and removed his shoes with the help of his wife, then leaned back.

Once settled in, his wife and kids kissed him goodbye, and then found their way to the door. He cried quietly as I undressed him to assess his skin. Rolling to his side, a shallow pressure sore was visible on his coccyx and deep purple bruises lined the sides of his back. I saw bruising to both of his knees, and he flinched as I evaluated shallow cuts on his left inner forearm. His wrists had another set of deep purple bruises.

Quietly, I asked, "What happened?"

Silence.

"How did you get these bruises? And these cuts?"

Silence. Quiet crying turned into loud sobbing as his walls crumbled down before me. His chest heaved as he pulled in air desperately and shook as he exhaled. His pain was more emotional than physical. And it was deep. Deep to his core.

"What happened?" I asked again after a few moments.

"She did," he covered his eyes.

"She did what?"

He hesitated before saying, "She has destroyed me."

My phone rang. Shit. I couldn't ignore it. I didn't want to interrupt the conversation with Mr. ALS right as his wall was crumbled around him and his pain was spilling out. I quickly answered the call. I then turned back to Mr. ALS to see he had composed himself. The door to sharing had seemingly closed.

"I'm so sorry for the interruption."

"It's okay. I am feeling better now."

"I'd like you to tell me what happened and how you got the bruises and cuts."

"I can't."

"Did she give them to you?"

Silence.

"Are you afraid of her?"

Silence.

"Okay."

Armed with this discovery, I got up to leave when he called out to me.

"She threatened me."

Now I was the silent one.

"If I needed something, she would become angry. She would punish me. She would tie me down to the bed if she had to go somewhere and didn't want me to cause problems."

Speechless. I was absolutely speechless. I could not imagine this life.

"She's had a boyfriend for the last month and has paraded him around in front of me. If I said anything, she would slap me. She lied when she said I made the decision to come here. I've been begging to come here, or anywhere honestly, for a while now. I'm tired. I'm losing control of my body. I'm only still alive because I can't leave my kids like this. I can't give up on them." He swallowed. "If I commit suicide, she doesn't get my life insurance and my kids suffer. I'm a ticking time bomb waiting to self implode. Waiting for the right time to just let go. I've had so many hours staring at the ceiling, thinking about the end. I have lived through war. She won't break me. But," he paused, "what about my kids? They cannot live through this. I have to find my voice before it's gone forever."

I reached for his hand, but he grabbed mine hard before I reached it and held on tight. Then, he whispered as if his life depended on me, "I've trusted you with my darkest secret. I trust you to help me. To help my kids. I've seen it in your eyes. I know you can help me."

"I will help you." He let go but I remained close to him. I took a moment to collect my racing thoughts, and then repeated, "I *will* help you."

I felt lost when I left the room. I needed to vent in a safe environment. I needed to know *how* to help him. I had never imagined when I'd asked about his skin that his answer would be his wife was abusing him. I had never experienced something like this let alone had someone ask me to help them out of the situation.

My view of nursing had been badly misguided. In my mind, everything was so simple. Even nursing school hadn't been realistic. The patients we cared for in nursing school were extremely uncomplicated compared to this. The instructors would have removed a student nurse from the room the moment this type of information was revealed and a student nurse certainly wouldn't be responsible for helping find a solution.

Even my own "hard times" weren't hard compared to this. I'd grown up with rose colored glasses on. Now, I found myself in a situation I felt completely unprepared for. I felt sick. Most of all, I felt alone. I knew I couldn't keep this a secret if I genuinely wanted to help him, but I didn't know who to trust with the information.

Knowing I *couldn't* shoulder everything alone, I went straight to the social worker's office. By the time I had finished telling her what had happened, my eyes were red and puffy from crying. She had reassured me that we would help him and had encouraged me to pull myself together for the sake of Mr. ALS as well as my other patients.

I splashed cold water on my face in the bathroom and gave myself a pep talk. I visited my other patient and by the time I headed back to the nursing lounge, a police officer was waiting to interview me. I took a long, deep breath and introduced myself as I was led back to the social worker's office.

By the following week, Mr. ALS and I had begun to grow close. He often cried when I came in to care for him. Some days I felt as if I was more of his friend than his nurse, but that was part of my job, wasn't it? He not only needed someone to help him with everyday tasks like bathing, brushing teeth, and eating, he needed friends. He needed protection. He needed emotional support.

When the police had finished my interview, they had interviewed Mr. ALS. The police called Child Protective Services and his children were removed to the care of Mr. ALS's parents. At that point, everything had been chaos. Staff contacted police when they saw her arriving at the facility. She was filled with rage when she charged into his room. Luckily, the patient next door had a buff family member visiting who was able to intervene when the wife began throwing things in the room. She had been arrested quickly thereafter.

All of this had been a big relief for him and he had declined significantly in a short amount of time. It was as if he had allowed himself to stop the self torture and to just relax. His parents brought his kids to see him every day and they were handling everything as well as could be expected. His parents had enrolled them in counseling, which had been the smartest thing to do.

When they would leave, he would cry for hours. His biggest fear was that his wife would get out of jail, even if waiting for trial, and get them back. That she might hurt them to spite him. Most of all, he feared she would come after him. And at this point, his fears were valid and no amount of assurance was enough to quell his fears

And then one day a lawyer appeared at his bedside, introduced himself, and stated that he would be representing Mr. ALS and his children. Explaining that his job was to keep the wife behind bars, and to secure the adoption of the children to his parents, Mr. ALS wept. He wept tears of joy. Having a sense of security and the promise of success, Mr. ALS died that night. I found a letter in my mailbox in the nursing lounge from him at the start of my next shift.

In the letter, he expressed gratitude for all of my help and friendship. He thanked me for listening to him vent, to caring for his every need, and for ensuring he could pass away under his own terms. He didn't have all the answers though, he admitted. He didn't know what would actually happen in the court system, but he placed great trust in the lawyer. He didn't know who had paid for the lawyer, but when the lawyer appeared, he'd explained that his fees were paid in full and there would never be charges sent to his trust or his parents. This had allowed him to finally step off the metaphorical ledge and finally feel peace.

I cried reading his letter. I had felt his pain. I had held his hand as he tore open old emotional wounds and attempted to glue them back together again. I had never known trust like the trust he'd placed in me. It was truly an indescribable feeling and the greatest honor. I would frame this letter and hang it on the wall in my office because this letter was exactly why I became a nurse. Maybe I was better prepared for nursing that I had originally thought.

By Friday though, I was mentally and physically drained. Asher had recognized this and surprised me with a home cooked dinner. Pulling into the driveway, I noticed his car parked in his unofficial spot. I saw multiple lights on inside and assumed he'd used his key to let himself in while waiting for me to get home. I wasn't exactly sure why, but I honestly didn't care. I was happy to see I wouldn't be alone. He would be heading to Spain next week and I would be alone and practically unable to reach him even when I wanted to.

Opening the door, I instantly smelled a delicious aroma permeating the air. I followed my nose towards the kitchen and stood in the door watching him work without saying a word. The way he bent over to place a plan in the oven, the way he brushed his hands on the hand towel, how he viciously mixed ingredients in the bowl, and how he hummed to himself as he worked made him incredibly sexy. He had earbuds in and was dancing, his back to me. I hated to break up his party for one.

He started a mini twirl when he stopped dead in his tracks, finally noticing me standing in the doorway. Pulling an earbud from his ear, he grinned like a young boy who'd been caught doing something he'd been told not to do. He looked around the hopelessly messy kitchen, flashed his pearly whites, and told me dinner would be ready in about thirty more minutes. I playfully rolled my eyes and backed out of the kitchen.

With thirty or so minutes to kill, I went to my office and logged onto my laptop. I sat up straight, took a few deep, calming breaths, and tried my hardest to think and focus as I checked my emails.

Just as I was starting to feel relaxed, Asher appeared in the door to the study. He walked up behind me and began to rub my shoulders as he informed me that dinner was served. Seeing I was working on something, he stood behind me glancing at my screen. Part of me wanted to slam the screen down and yell at him for invading my privacy while the other part of me wanted to tell him my problems and seek advice. In the end, I closed the screen down, twirled around in my chair, and exclaimed I was starving.

The next morning, Asher and I loaded his suitcase into my car and headed for the airport. His trip to Spain had arrived. We'd talked about it on our first date and I hadn't imagined then that his travel across the globe would impact me, but here we were and now it was. The airport was about an hour from my house, and we drove in silence. We were at a point in our relationship where we didn't need words. We felt complete just being near each other. Just having him by my side was enough and I didn't want that to change.

I'd been thinking for the past week or so about this exact thing. How when Asher left at night to go home, I felt the most alone I had in my entire life. I never wanted him to leave. I was sure he felt the same way based on how he lingered on the doorstep before finally pulling away. To broach the subject though was another story. I wanted so much to be brave and just say what was on my mind, but the fear of rejection was strong.

When we arrived at the airport, I stood by the trunk as he unloaded his bag and held back my urge to cry. I didn't know why I was feeling so incredibly sentimental and emotional. He was only going to be gone a little over a week, but I was falling apart inside. I told myself that everything would be fine, that I was a strong and independent woman, which I knew to be true, but I was struggling with agreeing to those feelings. Finally, the inner turmoil burst to the surface as he kissed me.

"Will you move in with me?" I said quickly.

"What?" He looked at me in surprise.

"Will you move in with me?" I said more slowly this time, feeling slightly more confident.

"I was wondering when you'd ask. Of course I will." He pulled me close and kissed me again.

"Please be safe. I love you." I waved as he headed towards the entrance, and I returned to my car.

I'd signed up to work most of the week since Asher would be away. I figured, why not? We'd been having a steady stream of new admissions and all twenty beds were usually occupied now. Knowing I'd be missing Asher, I'd decided that keeping myself busy was the absolute best thing to do with the week.

Besides working, now that Asher was moving in, I had things to do around the house. On top of the priority list was redecorating my — *our* — bedroom and the office. I wanted to buy a bigger bed and maybe change the paint color. I thought adding another desk to the office would be nice so that Asher would have his own workspace.

While I had plenty of money to pay people to come in and do all the work I could imagine, I just didn't feel that is what home ownership was about. I wanted to take pride in my home, not just because of how it looked, but because of what I had done to it. Growing up, I lived in a mansion with a staff of people and my father's wish was their command. It felt more like we were living in someone else's house and not necessarily a place of our own.

I didn't want a mansion, or a staff for that matter. I did have a cleaning lady that came in every other week to spiffy things up and I paid a neighbor teen to mow the lawn. That was more about convenience than necessity. But maybe my dad felt the same way about his staff. Maybe they were more of a convenience than a necessity? I wanted to try to live a more "normal" existence. I felt I had grown up living a fairytale and now that I have worked with many different people, I realized that having people at your beck and call just wasn't what I wanted. I realized that the struggle of life gives you strength and personality.

I was still mentally making my to-do list the following day when I met a ninety-one-year-old woman who had been newly admitted to our facility. She had been admitted to the hospital originally and diagnosed with adult failure-to-thrive. The hospital had offered a feeding tube but the family had declined all lifesaving measures and requested hospice. Once that decision was made, the discharge planners didn't waste any time getting her to Rolling Hills.

Extremely slender, her bones were visible through her frail skin. The little hair she did still have was as white as a ghost, and she couldn't see any longer. Her hearing, on the other hand, was as sharp as a tack. She laid on the bed wearing a thin nightgown with her arms neatly folded across her abdomen. At first glance, she appeared as if she were already laying in her casket and a cold wave of shivers ran through my body.

I crept into the room, and softly called her name. She didn't bother to lift her eyelids knowing she wouldn't be able to see me anyway, but she had heard me and welcomed me in. After my usual round of questions, she asked me if I could do her a favor. Unsure what she could want from me, I'd told her I wouldn't make any promises, but I could always try. What could she want from me anyway? Maybe something simple like a glass of water or a steak?

"Are we alone?" She asked cautiously.

I looked around the room and told her, "yes."

"Good. Can you help me find someone?" She said barely above a whisper.

"Help you find someone?" I questioned.

"Yeah, can you help me find someone."

"I can try. Who are you trying to find?"

"Well, a long, long time ago, I gave birth to a daughter and my mother forced me to give her up for adoption," she said as my mouth dropped open in surprise. "I was very young and unmarried. My mother scolded me like a schoolgirl when I'd told her I was pregnant."

"I see."

"She hid me for a few months and told everyone I was real sick. That I'd come down with something contagious and didn't let anyone come in the house. Of course Daddy knew and so did my sisters, but no one else," she explained and then paused.

I was speechless. Instead of responding, I sat patiently waiting for her to continue. It had been such a different time period, and there was no way to guess what else she could say, so I just waited.

"I've always wondered about her. It's the one thing I've regretted most in my life. I should have kept my baby and ran away like many women did. I would have sacrificed marriage and lived poor if it meant keeping my baby, but it didn't happen that way. Instead, my mother told me I didn't have a choice and after the baby was born, before I'd even delivered the after birth, she swaddled her up in a blanket and handed her off to Daddy. He took her to another family. I never even got to see her." Quiet tears started to stream down her face, and I leaned over to hold her hand.

"Once I was cleaned up, my mother told me to stop crying. We never discussed it again. I finished school and went to college. I met a nice sailor. Got married. We had children and I never spoke of my first daughter to anyone. It's like she'd never existed. But she existed to me. She was always on my mind."

"Wow. How old would she be now?" I asked.

"She would be older than my oldest son and he is 71. So maybe 75? If she's not still alive, maybe she has children or grandchildren who are? I just need to find her," she said with a sense of urgency.

"Do you know her name?"

"No. I don't even know where she went."

"Well, that is going to make this more challenging then," I said, beginning to jot down some notes.

"I can tell you she was born on December 20th in Springfield, Illinois. Maybe that will help?" She offered.

"It's a good start. I'll see what I can find, but again, I don't offer any promises."

"I just don't want to die knowing I never looked for her. All of these years I've wanted to look, but never had the courage. I'm sure she would hate me for giving her away like that." She shook her head.

"You didn't have a choice. Maybe she doesn't even know that she was adopted?" I offered.

"Maybe. Listen, don't tell my children about this. If we find her, then we can tell them. If we never find her, I don't want them to know she even existed."

"Fair enough. If I find this woman, what about your life would you want to make sure that she knows? What would you want to tell her most about you? What would you say to her?"

I was genuinely curious what I was supposed to offer this woman if I did, in fact, find her. What was her expected outcome? It wasn't the type of abandonment my own mother had put me through. I couldn't begin to imagine the pain that this woman had gone through being forced to give her child up for adoption. It's the greatest sacrifice and gift of love. My mother hadn't done it out of love or sacrifice. She'd been a part of my life and then selfishly chosen to leave it. She had chosen the booze and drugs over her daughter.

"I would tell her that I have loved her since the moment I first felt her kick within my belly." It was poetic and beautiful. "I would tell her that despite giving her up, I always loved her."

"Let me see what I can find and let's see if we can't let her know that you have always loved her," I said

Sixth Month: August

(Part II)

As quietly as I'd arrived, I slipped back out of the room. I felt a surge of ambition within me to find this woman. Unsure exactly how, but thankful that I'd have the help of the world wide web. As I walked down the hall to the next room, I thought about how I'd even start the process of trying to find her. No name. Just a birthday. They didn't play by rules in that generation and there weren't agencies keeping records. It was a shameful thing and everything was kept hush hush. This was going to be a challenge.

I'd never been one to give up on a challenge. This was going to be difficult, but not a reason to never even try. With Asher gone all week, I'd have plenty of time to plan my attack and start searching for the missing daughter. Was she really even considered missing? Was she even alive? My remodeling would have to wait because the clock was ticking on my search. If I wanted to give this dying patient peace of mind, I was going to have to find this daughter and find her fast.

Eating my lunch, I began to think of different ideas. Since I didn't have a name, I tried searching through obituaries, looking at birthdays and people in the Springfield area. Unfortunately, the daughter may have never even stayed in the Springfield area so this probably wasn't the best way to start my search. With a deep sigh, I realized that the most efficient way to make this search happen was to start a viral Facebook post. The problem with that was HIPAA. How was I going to get around breaking her privacy rights?

Back in her room later, I explained to her the best plan of attack for finding her daughter. It would have been easier if Mrs. Birth Momma's own family knew there was a daughter out there in the world, but they didn't. To my surprise, Mrs. Birth Momma told me that she had a Facebook page and that if finding her daughter meant telling her family, she would tell them.

As if we'd summoned them, her daughter appeared in the doorway at that exact moment and asked what we'd been talking about since she'd heard just the last part of our conversation. It was time for Mrs. Birth Momma to come clean. I excused myself and left the room. This was a private conversation that I didn't want to be a part of. I'd go visit my other patients and come back.

By the time I returned to the room, the mother and daughter had finished their serious talk and were laughing and joking. The daughter looked up at me as I entered and thanked me for taking the time to listen to her mother and offering to help her. The daughter stated that a Facebook post would be wonderful if I thought it might help find her sister. She'd accepted this long given up baby already as her sister. This made me happy.

Together, the three of us worked on what our post would say and look like. Around ten minutes later, I hit the post button, and we waited. It was like watching a pot of water waiting to boil. Would we even see something right away, or would it take some time? Would anyone even share the post? Did the post have enough information to make identification possible? There were so many unknowns, but it was worth a try.

As I finished up my day, I checked my phone and saw that the post had already been shared over one hundred times! Many of my friends thought that philanthropy is something heroic and something as simple as sharing a post would change the world. The problem is that their visions were so shallow considering their vast wealth that could be used for greater change and good, but instead they felt they were *above* that type of thing. However, they were sharing my post so there was that.

I'd set up an email to be used if anyone had any information, and so far there hadn't been any emails received yet. Many people had commented on the post, which would help it's popularity, but no one had posted about finding the missing daughter. Before I left for the day, I updated Mrs. Birth Momma and her daughter.

Rather than driving straight home, I drove myself to a furniture store and marched right up to the salesman in the bedroom department. I needed to buy a new bedroom suite. Something with a mix of masculinity rather than the delicate and girly set I currently owned. After browsing through the many different styles and types of wood, I settled on a beautiful Amish oak sleigh bed and matching set. Then, I laid on probably fifty different mattresses, and decided on the perfect one, in king-size of course. The queen had been big enough for me by myself, but now that I'd have someone to lay next to me each night, I needed a bigger bed. I needed my space and my beauty sleep! I headed for the register.

As I waited in line, it was hard not to eavesdrop on the woman in front of me arguing with the cashier. The cashier looked to be just a teenager with his first after school job, but he was insisting to the woman that there was nothing he could do for her. She, a woman in her thirties, was pleading her case. Apparently, in an attempt to gain sympathy from the cashier, she'd explained that she'd left an abusive marriage and was trying to keep everything together as she supported her three children. She'd bought furniture using a credit card and was behind on the payments and had received a letter than they were going to repossess the furniture.

I'd never heard of this type of thing before, but I'd never actually opened a credit card. She had paid over half of the original balance, but they did not care and were going to take all of her furniture. She had bought a bunk bed, a twin bed, a queen size mattress, and a couch. Realizing she was not getting anywhere with the young cashier, she asked if she could step away to make a phone call, and he looked relieved.

When he offered me assistance, he reset his smile and took the ticket I handed him with my items on it. He and I arranged a delivery date and as he began to give me my total, I stopped him and told him to add the woman's remaining credit card balance to my own balance. His jaw nearly hit the floor, and he began to stutter as he asked me to repeat myself for clarification. I hadn't been kidding. I had decided that I wanted to do something greater with my wealth than just put it in the bank and watch it grow. I was never good at that type of thing. There was a woman with a genuine need and here was another woman with the ability to help her out.

As he read off my new total, including my bedroom set, mattress, delivery fees, and the woman's credit card debt, he looked at me with a look of shock, and waited for me to give an excuse about why I couldn't pay my bill either. Instead, I whipped out my gold Visa, and handed it to him. Cha-ching. Card accepted. I smiled at him mockingly, thanked him, and said I'd look forward to my new furniture the following day as I walked away from the desk.

On my way out of the store, I casually walked up to the woman and told her that the cashier had made a mistake and needed to speak with her. Confused, she quickly finished her phone call, thanked me, and went back to the cashier. I knew that I should've just left and felt good knowing I'd made a difference, but selfishly, I wanted to see her reaction. I didn't need *her* to know I'd done it, but I wanted to watch her reaction. I hung out by the front door, just out of earshot, and pretended to be looking at table lamps. I watched as she received the news that the bill had been paid in full, and she finally owned everything, free and clear. She cupped her hands to her mouth in complete shock and then began to cry, falling to the floor.

I spent the rest of the evening getting my bedroom ready for my new furniture, and packing up things that I didn't need in there any longer. When I finished, I was completely exhausted. I checked my phone and saw that there were still no new emails. I checked the post and saw it had been shared over one thousand times and continued to have many more comments, but none finding the daughter. I turned on the bedside table lamp, pulled back the covers, climbed in and began reading my book. Before I knew it, I was fast asleep with the book open on my face.

I spent the next morning shopping for a new bedding set and clearing out the office to make room for Asher's stuff. My phone was alive with shares and comments from the Facebook post, but no messages or emails yet. I assumed stuff like this took time so worry hadn't set in yet. My hope was that her daughter could be found quickly, but I realized that wasn't necessarily realistic. I was taking it very personal too. Putting my own feelings of my mother abandoning me into the situation wasn't the best thing to do, but it was too late. I wished my own mother had done something like this. I wish she'd have tried anything at all to come back to me.

After I'd made a list of things I needed from the store, I ventured out, hoping to make the most of my day off. Arriving at the local Walmart, I grabbed a cart and started on the right side of the store and began browsing isles. Even though I'd made a list, I was really just browsing. Growing up, shopping with my friends had always been something I enjoyed. I'd loved going to the stores and see all the things I could buy. My father would try to limit my spending, but one little twist of a smile, and he'd falter. Things had slowed as I'd gotten older and when I entered nursing school, I'd practically stopped. Now, it took an actual need, or Mary Jane, to get me to go shopping. I appreciated money more than I had before. I saw the work that went into making a dollar. I was growing up, I thought to myself as I selected a new bedding set and placed it in my cart.

When I reached the register, my cart was loaded with quite the assortment and I laughed at myself. Looking at the woman ahead of me in line, I felt a little ashamed of myself. She was lugging around a screaming toddler who was touching everything he could get his hands on while she tried to corral him. Her cart contained the basic grocery assortment — milk, eggs, cheese. She was dressed in yoga pants and her stretched out t-shirt had stains around the chest from spilled food, or maybe even thrown food based on the toddler at her hip. Her hair was placed in a messy bun, her glasses were crooked, and she wore shoes that appeared to be long overdue for the trash can. I couldn't help but feel for this woman.

I began to talk and play with the toddler and a look of relief crossed her face. I could tell that she was used to people giving her mean stares or making comments under their breaths about her unruly tot. All I could see was a woman trying to make it and support her family. I grabbed a gift card from the end cap and handed it to the cashier right before he rang up the last item from the conveyor belt. She looked at me startled, but I placed my hand on her forearm and assured her everything was going to be okay.

"How much do you want on the card?" The young cashier asked.

"$1,000 please," I stated without hesitation as the cashier and the lady whipped their heads in my direction with expressions of shock. "What?" I said, shrugging my shoulders.

"Are you nuts? I can't afford that," the woman gasped.

"You don't have to!" I exclaimed as I handed my debit card to the cashier. "I've got you."

The woman, upon realizing that her entire bill was paid, sprang at me and wrapped her arms around me. Big, fat tears rolled down her face, and her toddler danced around us singing a Disney toon. When I assured her that "we've all been there," the lie stung coming out of my mouth. She continued to thank me over and over as she headed for the door, toddler in tow.

The cashier wouldn't stop staring at me as he rang up my own items. When he gave me my total, he picked up the card from his keyboard and swiped it again. When he handed it back to me, he paused.

"Why did you do that?" He asked.

"Why not?" I replied.

He blushed. "I guess I don't know," he stammered.

"Well, alright then. Sometimes we all just need a little help," I said, taking my receipt from his hand and pushing my cart toward the exit. I wasn't about to have a conversation with some cashier about my own deeply personal reasons for my financial giving. I didn't want, nor did I need, a therapy session in the middle of Walmart.

After I loaded my haul in the car, I headed to Home Depot. I spent the next ninety minutes searching for just the right shade of blue paint, buying a new light fixture, and being drawn into the fascinating world of home appliances. I could have spent all day dreaming in the store, but I didn't have the slightest idea how to install or fix anything so that would require additional work of hiring someone. In the end, I bought a can of paint and a new light for the bedroom. No appliances.

The moment I carried the last load of bags inside the house, the furniture delivery truck pulled into the driveway. Perfect timing. Three men jumped from the truck, flung open the back door, and began to find my items. An hour later, they were back in the truck and headed down the road to their next stop, and I was left with a room full of new furniture and a living room with its own set of bedroom furniture.

I called the local women's shelter to see if they wanted the bedroom set I no longer needed. As I hung up, an alert appeared on the screen notifying me of a new email waiting to be read. My pulse quickened and I prayed it would be something positive about the missing daughter. Instead, it was a survey regarding my experience with my recent furniture delivery. I sighed, irritated, and closed the phone.

Once details for the pick up of the old bedroom furniture had been arranged, I felt my stomach rumble and realized that in my excitement for the day, I hadn't eaten anything. Rather than even look in the cupboards and attempting to pull together a meal, I said screw it and ordered pizza. Thirty minutes later, as I crammed a slice of cheese pizza into my mouth, my doorbell rang. From my phone, I saw that it was the people from the women's shelter to pick up the bedroom furniture. I set the pizza aside and answered the door.

When 08:00 p.m. rolled around, I was exhausted. With work scheduled for the next morning, I crawled into bed. My new mattress was covered with brand new, freshly washed sheets and a new comforter. The pale blue color was calming and I already felt myself drifting off to sleep when my phone rang a familiar tone. Asher!

"Hello?" I answered with excitement.

"Hello sexy," the dark, gravely voice replied.

"Asher? What time is it there?"

"Two o'clock in the morning."

"What are you doing awake?"

"Thinking about you."

I laughed. "You woke up at two o'clock in the morning to think about me?"

"Well, I didn't have to wake up to think about you."

"Okay. Go on," I said waiting for him to continue.

"My dinner with my client ran much later than it was supposed to and after several bottles of wine, I came back to my room thinking of you."

"I see," I said, realizing he was drunk and wondering about the type of clients he was meeting with.

"Thinking of your breast in my hand and kissing your neck. How you smell of flowers and taste like salt…" He trailed off.

"Asher…" I said trying to redirect him.

"Ellie…" he mocked before trailing off. "Your hand trailing down my stomach as my mouth moves from your neck to your breast."

"Asher. What are you doing?"

"What are *you* doing?"

"I'm getting ready for bed."

"Perfect."

Phone sex wasn't exactly something I was into, but I missed him and didn't want to turn him down, so I played along. At some point, I'm not exactly sure what point though, his words began to slur enough that I couldn't understand him, and he fell asleep. With a little giggle, I ended the call. It would be fun to tell him all about this tomorrow.

Before I set my phone down, I took one more glance at it and saw another new email! Opening the app, my heart jumped as it was from someone I didn't recognize and was titled "Long lost daughter info." I read the email three times before it finally processed in my brain. How was I going to sleep after reading this? Adrenaline was pulsing through my veins like I'd drank two cups of espresso. I would need to get some sleep eventually, so I replied to the email and took a Benadryl in hopes of forcing sleep on myself.

I rushed into work early, excited like a kid at Christmas, so I could share the email with Mrs. Birth Momma. She was already awake and listening to the early morning news when I barged into her room. After explaining that I had received an email about her missing daughter, she demanded that I read it aloud to her. I could see hope written on her face.

The letter read:

To whom it may concern:

I saw your post on Facebook looking for a woman. I may know who you are looking for, but I am not 100% sure. My mother adopted a baby girl on December 20th in Springfield, Illinois. I wasn't born yet and I never knew she was adopted until a few years ago when my mother told me what had happened. Supposedly, a woman at church had received a child from a young mother and knew my mother wanted a little girl, so she was given to her. My mother died last year, but my sister is still alive. If you'd like to talk, give me a call.

Sincerely, Martha

Mrs. Birth Momma began to cry big, wet tears. I told her I'd sent a reply email and that later, I would help her contact the woman if she wanted. I encouraged her not to get her hopes up because, after all, it was still a long shot that this *was* her daughter, but it was too late. After being thanked profusely, I headed to the nursing lounge to receive report and start my shift.

I picked Asher up from the airport around noon on Sunday. I couldn't wait to see him, and ran straight into his arms when I finally saw him coming towards me. I hadn't realized how much I was missing the little things, like the way he smells, or the side smile he throws my way, until he hadn't been there for so many days in a row. The sight of him wearing a pair of grey sweatpants and a white t-shirt immediately brought the middle of the night call to my mind. I whispered into his ear how much I'd missed him, and tried my best to add a hint of seduction. It must have worked because he gave me a little smirk and told me he'd been thinking about me all week.

"I spent some time thinking about the best way to approach moving everything to your place this week," he said.

153

"Is that so?"

"Yeah. I hope it all works out. I hired a moving company to come on Tuesday and pack up my apartment. They will then deliver everything to your house Wednesday. I'll have to spend Thursday unpacking. I thought maybe we could have a date on Friday to celebrate the long week."

"It sounds exhausting," I mentioned.

"It sounds *exciting*! I can't wait to have you in my arms each morning when I wake up, and each night when I go to bed." That sounded wonderful.

"I agree. I work on Monday, Tuesday, and Wednesday. Sounds like Wednesday might be a little chaotic, but we will make it work. We also do, right?"

At home, I quickly showed him the new bedroom suite and the space I'd made for him in the office. He didn't say anything. He just leaned in, kissed me, then he playfully threw me over his shoulder and carried me to the bedroom to carry out what he'd started during his middle of the night phone call. Conversation wasn't necessary to show his gratitude when he could show it in other ways.

In the morning, I was off to work while Asher was off to his apartment to begin packing up smaller stuff the moving company wouldn't pack, or he didn't want them to pack. It was a beautiful day, and I was feeling so incredibly positive that I didn't think anything could break my spirit. I had been wrong. We had three nurses call in for diarrhea, leaving the rest of us extremely busy and overwhelmed. When my shift was done, I couldn't make it home fast enough before my own stomach was churning and I had to run for the bathroom.

Asher arrived home while I was still in the bathroom, and I was immediately mortified. While I knew it was perfectly normal that people poop, it just hadn't been something I'd done around him yet. I don't even know why I was embarrassed, but I was. The second time he called my name looking for me, I didn't have a choice but to answer. He was moving in and this was a fact of life. I needed to get over it. In my haste to make it to the bathroom before I would have shit my pants, I hadn't even closed the bathroom door.

"I'm in the bathroom," I yelled from my position on the toilet.

"Oh." I heard his footsteps moving closer to the open door. "Whoa!" He laughed as he appeared in the doorway.

There I was, scrub pants around my ankles, sitting on the toilet with a foul odor permeating the air and wafting down the hallway. I looked at him standing in the door, sweaty from working all day, and gave him a sheepish grin.

"Hi," I said meekly. "Can you close the door?"

He laughed, "nope."

"What? Are you kidding?"

"Babe, it's just you and me. People shit. Time to face the facts. You stink, by the way. But not to worry, so do I!" He said still laughing. "You don't have to be embarrassed. I still love you, no matter what comes out of you."

"Thanks. I love you too. Now close the door," I said more firmly.

"Okay, okay. Be sure to spray when you're finished," he said, closing the door, and walking off down the hallway.

When I finished and emerged from the bathroom, I could hear the shower running. Mortified didn't even begin to cover how I felt. Did I have time to make a run for it? I wouldn't have made it far because as I entered the living room, there were boxes everywhere. He had worked hard, and we had lots more work to do to prepare for the moving company. Where would we even put all the stuff? Where had it all come from? I peeked inside the box closest to me and saw dishes. The next box held comic books. As I looked inside a few more, I felt like I was peaking into his life, and it felt intrusive. But there was a saying about karma...

"Comic books, eh?" I said as I entered the steamy bathroom.

"Going through my boxes, are ya?" He asked with a smile as he stepped from the shower.

"Maybe."

"Yep, comic books. Did you find my naughty box?" He asked.

"Oh man, I seemed to have missed that one. I'll go look really quick!" I said jokingly.

Stark naked, he hugged me, still wet from his shower. "I've got nothing to hide from you." He said as he planted a kiss on my forehead.

By the end of the hectic week, we had mostly everything arranged, rearranged, and rearranged again. This had been more work that I'd anticipated. In my head, he would just appear at my house every day and live there. I hadn't exactly pictured all of his stuff joining mine, but here it was. At the end of the day, I was happy. I felt settled. I'd become so domesticated and it was scary.

Seventh Month: September

(Part I)

The September sun was warm as I drove to work on my day off. It had been two weeks since I'd learned about the daughter my patient had given up when she was just a teenager. Facebook had led us to a woman who felt her sister just might be that daughter and everyone had agreed to try DNA testing. Thankful for expedited results, a match had been identified. Joy filled my soul as I'd picked Alice and Martha up from the airport, and we chatted as I drove them to Rolling Hills.

The courtyard was the perfect setting for a first time meeting, but Mrs. Birth Momma was too weak to sit in a wheelchair today. As we stood at the door to my patient's room, I asked Alice if she was ready to meet her birth mother. Admittedly nervous, she said she had waited her whole life for this moment. I knocked on the door, and we stepped inside.

Without a word being spoken, everyone in the room teared up as Alice rushed to Mrs. Birth Momma's bed and gave her a gentle but firm hug. They stayed locked together for what seemed like an eternity while Martha slowly walked over to Mrs. Birth Momma's other daughter and gave her a hug.

"I have loved you from the moment I felt you first kick in my stomach. I have thought about you every day since. I have always loved you and I always will," Mrs. Birth Momma said with a quivering voice as tears rolled down her cheeks.

"I have thought of how this moment might be my entire life. I'd given up thinking it would happen. Thank you for never giving up on *me*!" Alice cried and squeezed Mrs. Birth Momma's hand.

Satisfied I'd done my good deed, I silently slipped from the room and headed home. I'd send a car for Alice and Martha when they were ready to head to the hotel later. Once home, I made lunch and sat down at my computer to log into my corporate email and catch up. I knew it would be boring and there would be hundreds, but it was necessary and I had the time before Asher was home from work.

I got to work late the following Monday, but immediately noticed that Mrs. Birth Momma's name was no longer on the dry erase board. Grace filled me in that after finally meeting Alice, Mrs. Birth Momma had gone unconscious that night and passed quietly the following morning with all of her children at her bedside, including Alice. I couldn't stop the smile from forming, knowing that she had passed away having her final wish granted.

I felt rushed the rest of the morning as I struggled to stay on top of everything. As I was eating lunch in the nursing lounge, the admissions nurse came in and began writing information for a new admission on the dry erase board. As I watched her write out the information in her perfect penmanship, my mind began to race. Had she made a mistake in writing the new patient's name? Could it be the same person? As I continued to read to the diagnosis, I knew. Without a doubt, one hundred perfect. It was *my* mother.

I almost choked on the bite of sandwich in my mouth. I hadn't seen my mother since I was five — nearly thirty years ago — and here she was, dying in my facility. Questions without answers began to form and reform in my mind. Would I go see her? How had she been? Obviously, not well judging by where she was. What had she been doing all these years and why had she never even attempted to come back to me?

Emotions began to flood me. Anger. Irritation. Abandonment. Everything was flooding back to me like pulsating waves in the ocean. How could she come and invade my space after all this time? Who did she think she was? Did she know how much she had hurt me? Or how empty she had made me feel? Did she know about the years I spent wishing she would show back up and pretend it had never happened?

Unable to finish my lunch and armed with years of anger, I made the decision that I would go see my mother. If I didn't, I would forever regret it. This was my one chance to say goodbye once and for all to the woman who kissed me goodbye and left my life forever. My chance to finally have a voice.

Stepping into her room, my mother sat on her bed eating a sandwich. Her hair was long, thin and light brown with gray showing at her roots. Her body was too thin and I could see her collar bone under her pajama top. There was a man sitting beside her on a recliner chair and two younger girls sitting on the couch across the room. I could tell the man was tall. He was balding and had a gray mustache. The girls appeared to be teenagers and each had long blond hair pulled back in a ponytail. I wasn't sure if they were twins or if there was an age difference. Neither looked up, too engrossed in their technology to care that someone had entered the room.

I suddenly felt foolish standing there. My mother and the man looked up when they heard me enter. My mother dropped her fork and immediately froze with her hand halfway to her mouth. The man watched me for a moment more, looked at my mother, and then stood in alarm.

"Can I help you?" he offered.

I was fighting back tears as resentment and the few old memories I had overtook me. I wanted her to speak first. To acknowledge me. To know she recognized that it was me standing in front of her. I wanted her to introduce me to this family that comforted her as she was dying. To introduce me to the family that she chose to keep and not abandon. Again, questions kept coming to the tip of my tongue, but I was unable to speak. I had dreamed of the moment I would see my mother again. It had been so real. To now be looking directly at her, the moment having arrived, it was nothing as I'd imagined, and I was speechless.

Softly, she spoke just one word and the tears began to stream down my cheeks, "Ellie."

She recognized me. I became a five-year-old little girl all over again as my mother held out her arms asking to embrace me. Instead of running into her arms and burying my face in her chest, I asked her one short question.

"Why?"

"Oh, honey."

It felt so insincere. How could she think she had a right to call me honey? She hadn't been the one fixing up scraped knees or listening to drama with friends. She hadn't even sent birthday cards or bothered to call me. And now, she's holding out her arms and calling me honey?

Seeing this exchange, the man became confused and looked toward my mother, silently asking for an explanation. Still, the girls continued on with their ear buds in and iPads on, completely ignoring everything around them. Then, my mother sat up straight and introduced me to Ben, her husband. Ben's mouth moved between shock and disbelief before he poked the two girls and ushered them from the room, leaving my mother and me alone.

The girls eyed me with irritation as they passed me and headed out the door. Ben stopped for a brief moment, locked eyes with me, and nodded his head in a silent hello.

"How did you know where to find me?" she asked coolly.

"I work here," I replied with a steady tone.

"You're a nurse?"

"Yes."

"I'm so proud of you."

With this, my resolve broke and the flood gates crumbled, unleashing a rath I'd only dreamed of. "You don't have the right to be proud of me. You gave that right up when I was five. You gave that right up when you kissed me goodbye and walked out the door knowing you weren't coming back," I said viciously.

"I didn't know what else to do, Ellie," she pleaded.

"Counseling? Rehab? A goodbye?" I suggested.

"I was scared. I was drunk and high. And I knew I was no good for you."

"You're not drunk now," I said as a pain started in my stomach. "You have an entirely new family."

"I deserve for you to be angry at me. After a few years of drinking myself silly, I got sober and I met Ben. Before I knew it, along came Ramona and then Lily. And when they were only a few years old, the stress overwhelmed me and I began drinking again," she explained.

I let out a loud sigh. I honestly didn't want to hear excuses because nothing she said could make this better, but she continued anyway.

"Ben wouldn't let me leave. I wanted to so many times. I wanted to close the door and be alone in my miserable existence. But Ben wouldn't let me leave. Frank... Franklin... Your father... told me to go. He paid me to leave. He didn't want me to be around you."

Shock replaced my anger. My father had *paid* her to leave? It didn't seem possible. Could I even believe her? It did sound like something my father would do. I just wasn't sure how he could have done that, and still tolerated himself while I cried, knowing he'd sent her away.

"And you listened? I was your daughter. Your flesh and blood. How could you abandon me like that?"

"I'm sorry. I didn't know what else to do. And I was desperate. At that moment, I was lost and looking for direction. Your dad gave me a direction. It just happened to be away from you."

"Do they know about me?" I asked sharply.

"Ben does. He's known about you since we met. I used to write you letters, and one night he found them. I had tried a million times to explain what had happened, but nothing was ever fair enough to send to you. I didn't know what I could say to express my sincere apology for what I had done, so I just never sent any of them." She looked down and shook her head.

She continued, "and now it's too late for an apology. Days turned into weeks turned into months turned into years. How could I expect anyone to forgive me for abandoning them when I still haven't forgiven myself?"

"I see," I said quietly.

"And now the drinking has caught up with me, and I'm dying from cirrhosis."

"Is that why you're here?"

"I'm here because Ben has to go to work. Someone has to pay the bills and take care of Ramona and Lily. He can't just stay home and take care of me all the time."

Fighting another round of tears, I said, "I have to get back to work now."

I headed for the door but she called after me.

"Will you come back?" she asked, scared.

"Did you?" I shot back and walked out the door.

It was harsh, but the words felt so good as they left my lips. I felt so many things, but most of all I felt manipulated. My mother was trying to manipulate me into feeling sorry for *her*. Her entire story revolved around her. She hadn't changed from the monster that left me. Had she ever been the perfect mother from my dreams?

Out in the hall, I ran into Ben and the girls. Ben smiled at me, encouraged the girls to continue on without me, and quickly approached me. Before I had a chance to turn and run, he hugged me.

162

"I know you don't know me, but I have dreamed of meeting you for so long. I heard what your mother did to you and she asked me not to try to find you, but my conscience told me I should anyway. I was going to wait until after all this was over, but here you are." He spoke quickly and with a nervous tone in his voice. "I don't know if it will ever be possible, but I'd love for you to have dinner with us and get to know the girls. Your sisters."

He paused before continuing, "I know I could have looked up your dad and all, but every time I tried, your mother caught me."

"My father passed away a few months ago," I said.

"Oh my gosh. I'm so sorry!" he began to backpedal. "I didn't know. I didn't know."

"It's okay. I didn't even know you existed until a few moments ago. Not to mention, that I had sisters." I choked back tears. I'm sure my eyes were completely red at this point.

"Do they know about me?" I asked timidly.

"No. I didn't want to get their hopes up if I couldn't find you, or if you didn't want to meet them," he said. "Do you want to meet them?"

"Yes. Not today, but I would love to meet them when this all registers in my brain," I said.

I said goodbye and quickly walked to the nursing lounge, and cried my eyes out. I didn't care who saw or who knew. Eventually, someone would have to know something personal about my family, I supposed. To add to my dismay, Paige entered the nursing lounge just then. She always had horrible timing.

"What's wrong with you?" Paige asked, giving me a side glance as she walked to the refrigerator.

"Not today, Paige."

"What's your problem?" she quipped.

I didn't satisfy her with a response. Instead, Cora suggested I take the rest of the day off since our census remained low and I didn't argue.

How could I? I knew I wasn't able to focus on my patients, and that was dangerous.

I sat in my car for nearly thirty minutes, lost in thought. Then, I drove to the cemetery and cussed out my father for his part in my mother's story. I didn't know whether to believe my mother's story, but in case she had been telling the truth, I had to speak my peace. In all honesty, I really didn't know this woman I called my mother. She was nothing more than a figment of my imagination as my memories had been replaced by dozens of repetitive dreams over the years. I would meet my sisters, but not because Ben or my mother wanted me to. I would meet them because they deserved to meet me.

I didn't know how to stop the storm of emotions swirling inside me. However, one emotion I was certain of was exhaustion. Before bed, I took a Benadryl and a hot shower. I didn't know what exactly I wanted other than a good night sleep. I crawled into bed, covered myself up to my chin with blankets, and closed my eyes. I was haunted by memories and dreams throughout the night, waking drenched in sweat. When the sun began to peak through my bedroom window, I abandon the idea of sleep.

Giving myself a pep talk, I opened the door to the nursing lounge to get report that morning. Her name was still on the board. I prayed she wouldn't be assigned to me, and felt a wave of relief when she was assigned to Jan. Instead, I had the two rooms on the opposite side of the building from her. I said a silent "thank you" to the assignment Gods and took report.

Approaching my first patient of the morning, I was still a bit on edge and was overwhelmed by the number of people in the room. The patient sat in a recliner by the television while five or six kids ran around the room. At least ten adults stood in groups chatting throughout the room. No one even noticed me enter the room. I walked over to the patient, crouched down to her level, and introduced myself.

"Good morning. I'm Ellie. How are you doing today?" I asked as everyone else continued to ignore me.

"I'm tired," she said with a sigh.

"Alright," I said to her. Then, I stood and spoke loudly for everyone else to hear. "Excuse me! I need everyone to head to the conference room while I do my assessments, if you don't mind."

Everyone stopped talking, looked at me, and then began to leave. It had worked. Assertive wasn't exactly on a list of adjectives that describe me, but today it did. After a few moments, everyone had gone and just a single woman remained. She introduced herself as the daughter and asked if she could stay, which I allowed.

"Is that better?" I asked her as I crouched next to her again.

"Oh yes," she said looking relieved.

"Alright then. Are you having any pain?"

"A little in my back," she said motioning to her lower back.

"On a scale of 0-10, how bad would you say your pain is currently?"

"A five. It's okay for right now though. It always seems to act up if a storm is coming. Maybe there is a storm coming" she offered in explanation.

"Well, I'd like to get you some pain medicine before it gets out of control, if that's alright?"

"Sure."

"How about any other discomforts? I read that you had an upset stomach last night and took some medicine to keep you from being nauseous."

"Yeah, that wouldn't hurt. I do feel a little sick to my stomach. I figured it was from the eggs I had for breakfast," she said with a smile.

"Probably not, but you can never be sure," her daughter interjected with a giggle.

"Let me empty your foley quick and then I can get your meds," I said as I stood and headed to the bathroom for the triangle collection container.

Wearing gloves, I unhooked the drain from the bag and emptied her urine into the collection container. I set it on the floor and realized that the alcohol prep pad that I needed to clean off the drain was in my pocket. Not a good start to the day. I took off my gloves, grabbed the alcohol prep pad and quick grabbed a new set of gloves. As I crouched back down to clean off the drain and hook it back into the bag, I kicked over the collection container and spilled the urine across the floor.

Inside, I screamed "fuck" but on the outside I remained composed. The daughter jumped back quickly. I grabbed towels from the bathroom and quickly cleaned up the spill without saying a word. The patient had closed her eyes and hadn't even known there was a problem. With the towels in the laundry hamper and everything hooked back up, I explained I would be back shortly with her medicine and left the room.

With all of her morning medicine in a cup, I returned to her room. I asked for her name and date of birth and handed her the cup along with a glass of cranberry juice. She tossed the pills in her mouth and with a large gulp of juice, swallowed them. I rolled her wheelchair closer to her bed and locked the brakes. Giving her a hug, on the count of three, we stood together. I pivoted her into bed and lowered her down. As I moved to swing her legs into bed, her foot jerked and kicked me in the face. Shocked at the sudden movement and hurting from the pain in my nose, I let out a yell.

"Ouch!"

"Mom!" the daughter chastised her mother.

Then, I felt it. The warm blood began to stream from my nose. I quickly covered my nose and headed for the bathroom. Using paper towel and applying pressure to the bridge of my nose, I stood looking in the mirror for a long moment before I emerged from the bathroom, apologized for my hasty departure, and headed for the nursing lounge to stop the bleeding.

"What the hell happened to you?" Jan asked as she peeked into the room.

"Ha! I got kicked in the face by a patient."

"Shit," she said as she laughed.

"You need me?" I asked, still holding the paper towel to my nose.

"Well... Uh... Kinda of."

"Oh boy. This sounds dangerous."

"Your mom is asking to see you," she said quietly.

"What?" I said irritated.

"Your mom. She's been asking for you since I came in," Jan hesitantly said.

"Tell her no. Plain and simple. I'll come see her when, and if, I chose to," I said defiantly.

"Okay. I told her I'd ask, and now I have." She stood and walked to the door before pausing, "I don't blame you for not wanting to see her."

"Thanks," I said, checking to see if my nose was still bleeding.

Finally able to see my other patient, I prayed for a better experience. Inside the room, a man lay motionless on the bed with cheyne-stokes breathing and a deep gurgling noise from his throat. The pauses in breathing were nearing thirty seconds at times. His color was pale, and he was clammy. His feet were marbled with various shades of red and purple. His lips were chapped and his tongue dry. A washcloth lay across his forehead. An old woman lay beside him on the bed, her head resting in the crook of his armpit.

"How many years have you been married?" I asked.

"Sixty-two," she said without lifting her head.

I couldn't imagine what it would be like watching my partner of sixty-two years dying. To know that very soon I wouldn't have him anymore. I told her not to move, and I would work around her. I swabbed his mouth and gave him a new washcloth. I placed a syringe into the corner of his mouth and gave him Roxanol and then some atropine. He groaned and swallowed. Once his room was picked up, I asked if his wife needed anything or felt that he needed anything.

She smiled and quietly replied, "time."

Seventh Month: September

(Part II)

I gave her hand a squeeze and told her to call me if she needed anything before I slipped out the door. On my way back to Ms. Kung Fu, my phone rang. Ms. Kung Fu's daughter was calling to let me know her mother was in excruciating pain, despite the medication only two hours ago. I made a u-turn and headed to get her medication. When I finally made it back to her room, she was in the fetal position on her bed and crying.

Slowly, she sat up and tried to take the cup from my hand but her own hands shook, and she dropped the cup and the pill onto the floor. Shaking my head in disbelief from the luck I was having, I ran to get another pill and to waste the fallen one with another nurse. When I finally returned for round two, I poured the pill into her mouth and handed her a new cup of water with a lid and straw. She slowly sipped the water, swallowed, paused, and then projectile vomited all over my shoes.

Wanting to cry, I assured her I would call the physician to get her orders adjusted, get her medicine for nausea, and return yet again. My day had been shit. Nothing had gone right. Despite wiping my shoes off, I smelled like vomit. Not just any vomit. Bile. I smelled like bile. All I could do was laugh at this point. I couldn't stop the laughter from exploding out of me. Before I knew it, the daughter came into the hallway to investigate the noise. Upon seeing me leaning against the wall laughing, she too began to laugh. She walked over to me, gave me a hug, and went back to her mother.

Finally able to compose myself, I called the physician to get new orders. On my third attempt to get Ms. Kung Fu relief from her pain, I was successful. Her order had been changed to liquid. I had drawn it up, she had taken it down, and most importantly, she'd been able to keep it down with the help of a dissolving Zofran tablet. Feeling victorious, I ran from the room and went straight to the bathroom to finally relieve my aching bladder.

As I sat down to lunch minutes later, my phone rang again. Ms. Kung Fu was continuing to have ten out of ten pain to her lower back. I assured the daughter that she just needed time for the medicine to work and I would check back in with them in thirty minutes. The microwave chimed that my soup was ready and just as I dipped my spoon into the bowl, my phone rang again. It was the elderly wife of my other patient calling to say she didn't think he was breathing any longer. Setting my spoon down and covering my soup, I gave up on the idea of lunch and went to assess my patient.

"I don't know what to do. He.. He.. Isn't breathing, is he?" she stammered as big fat tears rolled down her face.

"Let me take a look," I said as I began to feel for a pulse.

She watched over me as I checked for signs of life. Having found none, I gave her the grave news. To my surprise, she sat bolt upright.

She looked me straight in my face and said, "It's about time."

"What do you mean?" I said in shock.

"He's threatened to die on me for years. He finally followed through," she said smiling.

I was speechless, confused, and unsure how to respond. The wife picked up on this.

"Look sweetie, when you've been married as long as we have, you start to have conversations about death. We have spent nearly our entire lives together, and we knew it wouldn't be possible to stay that way forever. At some point, one of us would be called home and neither of us would have control over it. You start to accept it," she explained.

"Ah," I said faking my understanding.

"We made a pact years ago that when one of us was gone, the other one would keep on living. We never held each other back in life, and we don't want to hold each other back in death." She looked at him with love in her eyes and planted a kiss on his cheek. She continued, "Now, I'm going to make our dreams come true. I'm going to follow his wishes and live my life."

"What will you do?" I asked curiously.

"Oh, that's easy. See, we never had children. It's always been the two of us. By the time he retired, he was too sick to go traveling across the good 'ol U.S. of A. together, so we didn't. But now, that's exactly what I'm going to do! I'm going to sell the house, buy an RV, and see all 48 contingent states. That's what I'm going to do!" she said with excitement.

"That sounds like fun. What is he going to do?" I asked motioning to the patient.

"Oh, he's going to come with me," she said matter-of-factly.

"Well, be sure to send me postcards of your travels if you have time," I said.

"Oh I will. You're sure he's dead, right?" she asked me.

"Uh… Yes," I replied hesitantly.

"Okay good. I'm going to go to the funeral home to make some quick arrangements and then home to meet with my realtor. I've had her on stand-by for a few days now."

I watched in surprise and horror as she practically skipped from the room, humming to herself. Sixty-two years. Was she in shock? I didn't have time to dwell on it as my phone rang again and Ms. Kung Fu's daughter screamed that her mother was *still* in pain. As I hung up, I called the doctor again to get new orders for stronger pain meds. I headed my tired feet towards the med room and glanced at my watch, hoping it was closer to end of shift. My stomach growled.

As I searched through the narcotic box looking for the higher strength morphine, I froze.

"Shit," I said to myself. "Son of a bitch."

Being in a hurry to get her pain medicine after she'd puked on my shoes, I'd pulled the wrong strength morphine. My first med error. She was suffering in pain because I'd pulled the wrong dose of pain medicine and under dosed her. My stomach dropped as I called my supervisor. Everything about this day had been wrong and this was the cherry on top. There was a leach somewhere on my body, sucking everything from me. I felt lower than the dirt under a casket.

After we'd filed the report, given the correct dose, and finished my day, I couldn't wait to get home. As I sat in the nursing lounge waiting for my relief to arrive, Paige walked in. She took one look at me and walked to the dry erase board.

"Looks like you screwed up today, eh?" Her tone was full of ridicule.

"Yep. We all make mistakes."

"Is that what you tell yourself? Mistakes in nursing can lead to someone dying." She finished scribbling on the board and then without another word, left the nursing lounge.

My phone rang. Answering it, I learned that my relief would be an hour late. I laid my head in my hands. Was I being punished? I was aware that every day in nursing wouldn't be perfect, but why was it always the bad days that went on and on like the Energizer bunny?

Leilani, our evening shift charge nurse, came in an announced a new admission would be arriving in about thirty minutes. Of course, the new admit was being placed in one of my rooms. I softly thanked her and put my things back in my locker. I read the board and then headed to the room to get it ready for the new admission.

I smoothed the comforter on the bed to make it look more presentable when my phone rang. It was the hospital calling report on the new admission, a man with dementia. I pulled out a piece of scrap paper and began to write the information.

"He has dementia and had gotten up in the middle of the night to use the bathroom, but ended up falling down a few stairs into the garage instead. The wife didn't know what he was trying to do. Anyway, he broke his femur."

"What is he taking for pain?"

"Tramadol scheduled and Roxanol as needed. Well, while he was here we found a UTI and pneumonia. His wife is his power of attorney and does not want to treat these infections. However, she can't care for him in his current state so he is coming to you."

"How does he take his pills?"

"Whole with applesauce. And he's been bed bound since he's been here."

"When is he leaving the hospital?"

"He left about twenty minutes ago. I was a little late at calling report to you."

"Thank you." I rolled my eyes.

I'd barely hung up when the ambulance arrived with him on a stretcher, screaming and yelling. When was my relief coming again? I wanted to scream and yell myself, but instead I calmly welcomed him to Rolling Hills and assisted the medics with transferring him into his new bed.

When my relief, finally arrived, I was overjoyed! I barely took a breath as I gave her report. I had started the admission, but hadn't finished it. I explained what I had and hadn't done, handed her the phone, and practically ran for the nursing lounge to gather my stuff.

Just as I reached the door, to my horror, was Ben. I'd had the toughest day of my career and now I'd be expected to deal with the bullshit of my mother. There was nowhere to run and hide. I had to face him if I wanted to get home.

"Good evening," I said as I approached the door.

"I've been hoping to see you all day. Please hear me out. I know Mags asked her nurse to see you. And I know you said no. But I want to set something set up for you to meet the girls. I know you're mad at Mags, but I hope you can keep forgive us for what she has done to you. Whether you forgive Mags or not, that is between you and her." He said with desperation in his voice. "I want the girls to know their sister. When Mags is gone, they will need a female role model and a part of me hopes you'll be in their lives and be their role model."

I paused and tried my best to take in everything he was saying and have it register in my brain. I wasn't sure if I was ready for a new family, or if I'd ever be ready for *this* family. I know that these girls, Ramona and Lily, may potentially want to meet me, but I had to ask myself if I really wanted to meet them. Of course, deep down I knew that there was no way I would pass up the opportunity to meet my sisters. Just when I thought I had no family, I found out I had sisters. They didn't abandoned me. They hadn't even known about me. I had to meet them.

"I will meet them."

"Thank you. What day would work best for your schedule?" He asked with excitement.

"Wednesday. Say 05:30 p.m.?" I suggested.

"Yes. Yes, that will work." He pulled out his phone and gave me his phone number.

Promising to call him later, I rushed out the door and practically ran to my car. I jumped in, closed the door, and quickly locked all the doors. I wanted nothing more than to be left alone. I wanted to leave this terrible day behind me.

Once I'd composed myself, I drove straight home. I did not pass go and I did not collect two hundred dollars. I couldn't stop thinking about what I would say to these girls. These sisters I'd just learned I had. I know none of this was my fault, but how do you introduce yourself to someone like this? I went straight to the cupboard and grabbed a wine glass. Once it was filled, I drank. When the cup was half empty, I refilled it and drank some more. Sure, it wouldn't help anything, but mentally I would feel better. It was a momentary patch to blur my feelings.

When the bottle was empty, I laughed at the ridiculousness of drinking an entire bottle of wine by myself in one sitting. I couldn't stop the laughter from erupting out of me. I could feel the stress melting away the longer I laughed but eventually, my stomach began to hurt. I stopped laughing when the sudden urge to vomit hit me and I ran for the bathroom.

Kneeling before the toilet, I heard the doorbell. I froze in sheer terror. Who was here? My brain was foggy and I thought if I didn't move, whoever it was would just go away. Then, I heard a key in the lock and the door open. There were only two people who had keys to my house - Mary Jane and Asher. One I wouldn't mind being here at this moment and the other I would be mortified. I was silent listening. And then I heard it. I heard his voice calling for me as he searched the house.

Wiping my mouth, I went to the bathroom door, opened it and peered out. I surrendered myself and Asher looked relieved to see me. I felt like a teenager having been caught doing something I wasn't supposed to. I stood there with vomit breathe and still drunk from an entire bottle of wine.

"Are you okay?" He asked as he rushed up to me and hugged me.

"What are you doing here?" I asked.

"You told me to come save you!"

"I did?" I blushed.

"Yes…" He paused and looked at me funny. "Have you been drinking?"

"There is a possibility." I said with a smile. I could feel the laughter begin to bubble up in my stomach again, but rather than laughter, vomit erupted from my mouth.

"Oh Ellie!" he said as he quickly launched me towards the toilet..

When I was sure I was done, he grabbed my hand and led me to my bedroom. He delicately replaced my scrubs with pajamas, pulled back the covers on my bed, and tucked me in. He left the room and returned with Motrin and a glass of water five minutes later. After forcing me to take them, he laid on top of the covers next to me. After watching me take the medicine and drink the water, he finally spoke.

"Want to tell me about it?"

"Not really." I confessed.

"Okay," he swept the stray piece of hair from my face and smiled at me. "You make a cute drunk, you know that?"

"Thank you, I think." A giggle erupted from me.

"I've got you now. Everything is going to be okay," he said as he stroked my cheek.

"Thank you." I said and a few tears fell from my eyes suddenly.

"You're welcome," he leaned in to kiss me but stopped short of my lips. "Why don't you brush your teeth first and then I'll kiss you?" he said jokingly.

"Deal."

My brain continued to be fuzzy as the events from the day swirled inside. Between the reaction of my dead patient's wife, the events in Ms. Kung Fu's room, and the whole mother stuff, I was emotionally drained and the wine was only making me feel more unsure of my feelings. I wasn't ready to tell Asher about my med error or anything else that had happened.

I fell asleep to Asher rubbing my back but awoke in the morning, alone, an hour before my alarm would be going off. My head was slightly foggy, but no headache considering I'd drank an entire bottle of wine. After laying there for a few minutes, I climbed out of bed and went to the bathroom for a shower. There was a yellow sticky note taped to the glass door from Asher.

"You were amazing last night. Love, Asher"

I laughed. I was completely head over heels in love with this man. And I could see that he, too, was madly in love with me also. I'd been in love with men before, but never like this. None of those men loved me for who I was, instead they loved the idea of me. They loved my bank account. Asher loved *me*, but did I really allow him to see the whole me? My thoughts were too deep for the morning.

Asher held my hand as I knocked on the red door of the white duplex situated at the middle of a quiet street. Their house was so different from the one I had grown up in.

From inside, we could hear the girls talking animatedly as they fought over who would be the one to answer the door. Asher squeezed my hand. I was anxious. My entire life I'd been an only child and in just a few minutes, I would be introduced to the sisters I never knew I'd had.

When the door flew open, two teenage girls greeted me and invited us in. Ramona was tall and slender while Lily was shorter and had a more muscular frame. Ben made formal introductions before letting us know that dinner was ready and leading us to their small dining room that set off the living room and looked directly into their kitchen.

Little cards with our names written on them were perfectly arranged at each place setting. Taking my seat, Asher sat to my left and

Ramona to my right. Ben began to bring the food to the table and the girls began passing the dishes around to the right. Chicken, mashed potatoes, carrots, and garlic bread.

"What do you do for work?" I asked Ben as everyone began eating.

"Oh, well. Mostly odd jobs, but right now I'm working for a local construction company. Helping them finish up a new subdivision across town."

"What will you do when the work is done?" I asked, wondering if I was being too personal.

"Not sure. I will find something. Always do," he said hopefully.

"What do you do, Asher?" Ramona asked.

"I build roads and bridges. Well, I help design them and watch their progress as they are built to make sure they are safe."

"Wow!" Lily exclaimed.

"Do you like being a nurse?" Ramona asked.

"Yeah. It's not exactly what I had imagined. There are good days and bad days. Overall, I am enjoying it."

"Are you girls enjoying school?" Asher asked.

"No!" Lily said immediately and everyone laughed.

We continued having small talk until everyone was done eating. I was relieved that my father and the way I'd grown up hadn't been discussed. Asher still didn't know that my father had owned his own company or that I had inherited everything.

Dinner was delicious and when it was over, conversation continued to flowed easily and I learned all about the girls, their lives, and their past. Finally realizing it had gotten quite late, Asher and I promised to visit again soon and to keep in touch as we said our goodbyes. Despite my feelings for my mother, I really liked Ben and the girls. They were kind, welcoming, and gracious. They expected nothing from me beyond a relationship and I knew that I needed that more than I wanted to admit. These girls were my family. They had welcomed me with open arms.

I still had so many questions for my mother, but I wasn't sure I wanted to hear her answers. In a way, she had emotionally abandoned Ramona and Lily but remained physically present in their lives. I wasn't sure which was more damaging to a young girl. The similarities caused the three of us daughters to genuinely bond and I knew that it would be an unbreakable connection.

By Saturday, I was eager for a dinner with the girls from work. As the first round of drinks were delivered, everyone chatted about the start of school for their kids, their plans for Halloween, or just the everyday things that came up at work. Generally, we tried to avoid talking about work when we got the chance to get out, but we always found ourselves sharing experiences.

It didn't take long for Paige to bring up her suspicions that weird things were happening at work. She was obsessed with figuring it all out. She had to know everything that was happening at work or things weren't right in her world. It was extremely annoying because I didn't want her knowing my business.

From the moment I met Paige, she'd watched me closely and pointed out my mistakes with a harsh sarcasm that I didn't appreciate. Something in the way she interacted with me gave off the "mean girls" vibe. Apparently, she was one of the nurses who "eat their young" that you hear everyone talk about. In general, I tried to steer clear of her, but anytime we were having an outing, she found out about it and showed up.

"I don't know what to believe anymore. It's all good, of course. Awesome things just keep happening and I can't quite figure out why or where they are coming from. I talked to Connie at lunch the other day, and she told me about even more fabulous gifts received by families

179

after their loved one passed away. It's like someone is reading their minds and making their wishes come true. It's our own personal fairy godmother or something," she exclaimed.

"Paige, that stuff doesn't happen. Rolling Hills isn't a Disney movie," Marci said with a laugh.

"Yeah, no one has a fairy godmother granting secret wishes," Jan piped in.

"You all have no sense of imagination!" Paige quipped in reply.

"Oh, I have a very active imagination, thank you very much!" I said defensively.

"You do, do you?" Paige said, raising one eyebrow.

"Sure do," I said with confidence.

"Explain what you think is happening then," she said with attitude.

"What I think?" I questioned.

"Yep, what do you think is happening?"

"Well..." I said trying to think of a plausible explanation. "I think that somehow, someone is figuring out what people wish they could do for their families and then making it happen," I said, directing my attitude back at her.

"Well that's obvious! But *how* and *why* are my real questions!" Paige continued.

"How? How about someone is just asking them? Why? Maybe because someone is just super awesome," I suggested.

"That's lame. No imagination in that answer," she said with a laugh.

The conversation took a turn and another round of drinks was ordered. As our food was delivered, Paige sat down next to me and struck up a friendly conversation.

"You really think you're cut out for nursing?" she asked quietly.

"Yes I do."

"We will see."

Then, like a record, she returned to the wish granting as if I held the key to all the answers.

"So what do you think is really happening?" she asked, leaning in closer. "You can tell me what you really think is happening."

"I don't know. I haven't thought about it. I don't notice it," I said nervously, feeling as if she were demanding answers from me.

"Have you noticed that none of this started until you arrived?" she asked with a hint of attack in her voice.

"Huh?"

"You started at Rolling Hills and then all of these families start receiving expensive, elaborate gifts when their loved ones die." She watched me carefully, looking for any type of reaction.

"I guess I hadn't noticed."

"Interesting."

"What's interesting?" I asked with irritation.

"That you haven't noticed. Of course, you wouldn't."

"What are you talking about?"

"I think you're the missing link," she said quickly, finally getting to her point.

"How do you figure?" I said trying to keep my calm.

"I haven't figured it out yet," she said suspiciously.

"Well, I'm not sure what you want from me."

"Me either," she said as she stood up and returned to her seat across the table.

Eighth Month: October

(Part I)

As the first chilly day arrived, so did October. My newest admission was a sweet, younger woman. Pictures hung on her bulletin board by her husband after they arrived showed a healthy, attractive woman with a thick head of jet black hair. Now, her hair had begun to slowly grow back after extensive back-to-back rounds of chemotherapy and was sticking out of her head in small, thin white curls. Her voice was thin, her skin was pale. She no longer weighed much and her skin drooped off her bony frame. Cancer had not only shortened her lifespan, it had changed her definition of beauty. Per her husband, her smile never faded or changed.

Her husband was attentive as I completed her admission assessment and he provided her history as I asked questions. Occasionally, he would kiss her on the forehead or squeeze her hand. Her daughter arrived shortly after I'd finished. She was in her twenties, short and spunky. She kissed her father on the cheek in greeting him and then immediately turned her attention to her mother.

After initial greetings and small talk, the husband and daughter sat quietly on either side of her bed. Settling in, they read or worked on their computers, ensuring she wasn't alone. If she needed anything, one of them would help the best they could or alert me if they were unable to do whatever was needed. The three of them were patient, kind, and a pleasure to work with. Their dynamic was full of love, and I wished that my own family had been like theirs. I was jealous.

Towards the end of my shift, the husband and daughter kissed her goodbye, and stepped out to go get dinner. She appeared tired, and I sat in the empty chair next to her bed to spend the few free moments I had with her. Outside of wishing my own mother had been like her, I was drawn to this woman.

"How's your pain?" I asked.

"It's okay right now. It comes and goes, but right now it's okay."

"Okay. Is there anything else I can get you?"

"No, I think I'm alright."

"You have a beautiful family. Will they be back tonight?"

"No. My husband had to go home to our pups and my daughter has to work tomorrow so she went home to get some sleep," she said as her eyes welled up.

"What's wrong?" I asked as I touched her hand.

"It's just lonely when they leave."

"I have a few minutes. I can stay with you if you'd like."

"No, that's okay. I know you have work to do."

"I have the time. What does your husband do for work?"

"He sells real estate. Luckily, he's been able to work his appointments around mine for the last few months. I know that this hospice thing is very new for him, and he feels very helpless. He's trying so hard and he's doing such a great job. He doesn't get much sleep between being here, appointments, and getting a walk in with the pups."

"That definitely happens. Being a caregiver is a lot of work sometimes. Giving it up is very hard for husbands or wives because it feels like defeat or like they have given up on their spouse."

"Yeah, he has said that. My daughter has been great with helping him, but he and I know she has to work and has her own husband to spend time with."

"What does she do for work?"

"She's a nurse. She's definitely handling this differently than he is. She knows the ins and outs and is very realistic. She tries to help him the best she can, but sometimes it's just tough. There are just some things he wants to do all on his own."

"Yeah. That's tough. What did you do for work?"

She smiled then and said, "I actually was trying to go back to school when all this cancer stuff happened. Before that I was a nurse too, but I wanted to try something else. I had started my pre-reqs when I was diagnosed."

"Wow. Did you know what you wanted to do?"

"Not exactly. I was burnt out. I'd been screwed over by the company I was working for and it was kinda my last string, ya know?"

"I've heard a lot about burn out lately. Nursing isn't for the faint of heart, that's for sure."

"No it isn't. But I'm glad that there are still nurses out there. Where would I be without them?" It was a rhetorical question.

"So true. This is my first year as a nurse. My father had cancer and it was while I was taking care of him that I realized I wanted to take care of others. So I went back to school."

"I love that. Is it hard to take care of people with cancer after having gone through it with your dad?" she asked sympathetically.

"I've never really thought about it, to be honest." I answered truthfully.

"Hmm. We need people like you. People who have a connection to their patients."

"Thank you. How long has your daughter been a nurse?"

"Just a few years. She does a great job taking care of me though, so I know she'll have a successful career. She's just smart and intuitive."

"Do you have any grandchildren?"

"Of course not! I'm not old enough for grandchildren, am I?" she said with a laugh. "My daughter and her husband have been married for five years and have been unable to get pregnant. I always thought 'maybe someday' I'd be a grandma, but I'm realizing that it's just not in the cards for me. My daughter saw a specialist a few years ago who recommended IVF, but she didn't have the money to go through with it."

"I had a friend who did IVF and it was very expensive. It's such a difficult path. So many ups and downs. Who did she see?"

"It's such a rollercoaster from what I've seen. I think my daughter saw a doctor at CCRM, but I can't quite remember. Do you have children?" she asked me.

"No. No children and no husband. A boyfriend though. Maybe someday." We both laughed.

"My friends have all told me that grandchildren are the absolute best. They say that the moment you hold your first grandchild in your arms, everything changes. My husband and I have talked many times about ways we could help them, but it's just never been something we could afford either."

"It's so hard to want something, and be unable to do anything to achieve it."

"Yeah. My heart breaks for them. Maybe someday though, ya know?"

"I'm sorry." I squeezed her hand.

"Don't be. I have everything I need in life. I have love. It's the most important thing. Nothing else really matters besides feeling loved." I thought about that for a moment when she said it.

"Well, you get some rest. I've got a few things to finish up before the end of my shift. Just call if you need anything, okay?"

"Thank you for the talk. I appreciate it, and I'm feeling much better."

I closed the door softly as I left. My phone rang, and I was informed of a new admission coming. In the five months I'd worked for

185

Rolling Hills, I hadn't felt stressed by the number of patient's I had, but today I found myself feeling overwhelmed. Maybe I was just being emotional. Was it the talk with Mrs. Cancer? Was I due to start my period anytime soon? Maybe I was premenstrual.

Report for my new admission stated that the woman was coming from home, being brought by stretcher. She was a morbidly obsese woman and had been bedridden for quite some time. She hadn't left her house in a few years, but the admissions nurse felt she would get better care at Rolling Hills than if she remained at home since her husband was unable to do just about anything for her anymore. When she arrived a few moments later, I guided the EMS workers to room 10.

Moving her from the stretcher to the bed required the assistance of six people. As the aide and I rolled her around to begin her skin assessment and remove the extra sheets under her, an odor permeated the surrounding air. The stench of dead skin and feces was overwhelming. The family that arrived soon after did not seem to notice, nor had they been able to bathe her in what appeared to have been a very long time. Making a list of priorities, bathing was at the absolute top of the list. I asked the aid to gather the supplies, and we could do it together, and she left the room.

"Good afternoon. Wait. Is it afternoon yet?" I said as I looked at my watch. "Yep, it's 12:05 p.m."

"Good afternoon," she said, her voice gruff and scratchy.

"I'm Ellie and I'll be your nurse for this afternoon. I'm glad you're here. Just to give you a quick idea of how the afternoon will go, we're going to get a set of vital signs, give you a bath, I'll ask you a bunch of other questions for my admission assessment, and then, we can talk about our goals for your care while you're here. How does all that sound?"

"It's okay. Just tell me what you need me to do. I'm pretty flexible," she said kindly.

"Great. Who did you bring with you today?" I asked motioning to the trio of people sitting on the couch watching my every move.

"That's Alden, Augustus, and Ada. My kids," she said proudly.

"Nice to meet you. Please, make yourselves comfortable and don't hesitate to let me know if you need anything. I may not always be able to make it happen, but I can certainly try," I said with a smile.

The aide returned and began to get set up while I kicked her sons out of the room. Her daughter chose to go with them, and the aide and I were left alone in the room to give the patient a bath. Beginning the bath, the woman told me that she frequently has itchy skin under her breasts and to not be surprised if there are scratch marks. Lifting her right breast, the chunky, white paste coated her red, excoriated skin. It was the same under her left breast. More of the same sat under her lap fold and both sides of her groin. Once her front was washed and dried, we rolled her onto her side to begin her backside.

The smell made my stomach roll and looking to the aide, I saw her face had gone green as well. A flash of movement caught my eye and I peeled back her brief with fear. Sure enough, there it was. Her complaint of pain to her bottom was identified and it took all of my might to not look away. Clearly, she had spent hours upon hours sitting on her coccyx because before me sat a gnarly wound complete with maggots. Red, raw skin surrounded a deep crater centered on her tailbone. Maggots wiggled and climbed, feasting on dead tissue like a Thanksgiving feast.

I admitted defeat, and excused myself to step out of the room. I immediately called for Marci to come and assist me. She'd been reluctant, but I didn't blame her. Together, we finished her bath, dressed the wound, and made her as comfortable as possible.

"You owe me. Big time," she said as we finally left the room.

"Oh I know. Thank you for helping me."

"You ready for lunch?" she asked with a sly smile.

187

"Hell no. I may not eat for the next week." I made a puking motion and we laughed.

"A true sign of a nurse is to eat lunch after dealing with something that most people couldn't handle, ya know?" she joked.

"I'm sure I'll get there. Maybe. Someday. But not today," I replied.

Instead, I headed to check on my patients in room 11 and 12. Both were resting with their eyes closed, so I headed to the nursing lounge to finally get some charting done and to get off my feet. I hadn't been sitting long when my phone buzzed and room 10 was asking for pain medicine. Today was going to be one of those days, and I just accepted that.

By the next day, I felt better prepared for Ms. Stage 4, but she wasn't assigned to me. I was relieved to see I'd been given a completely new assignment because I wasn't really sure my stomach could handle changing the dressing today. Better prepared, yes. Ready, maybe not. When we reached my name on the assignment board though, I realized that it included my worst nightmare. My mother. I'd have to spend the entire day with the woman I had been purposely avoiding. I'd been able to avoid taking care of her for an entire month, and I was at least thankful for that. I wasn't sure which was worse, maggots or my mother.

It's ironic how I spent so many years wishing for my mother to come back to me, and now that she was, I wished she would go away. In all the years of thoughts and dreams, I was never angry with her when she returned. Every part of me was conflicted when it came to her. My heart wanted to love her, but it was still so damaged from when she tore it apart and my brain didn't want to let the healing happen. Even meeting the family I didn't know I had, I still remained conflicted.

Irritated, I decided to get it over with and just get her morning care out of the way first. I sucked it up, pulled her medicine, and made my way as slowly as possible to her room. I stood outside her door for a moment, bracing myself, and then I knocked. I heard nothing. I opened the door and peaked in but the room was empty. I was disappointed because I had readied myself and now I had to delay the inevitable. Rather than looking for her, I moved on to the next room.

The door was open and inside I saw a young woman bargaining with an elderly man who was threatening to throw a remote control at her. Cautiously, I walked in and introduced myself. He was distracted long enough for the young woman to take the remote from his hand. He looked at her with evil in his eyes and threatened to kill her.

"Don't touch me!" he said to me.

"I won't. I just want to talk," I said in a quiet, calm tone.

"That's what they all say before they attack" he yelled as he steadied his eyes at me.

"I'm sorry you've experienced that. I can sit over here and we can talk. We don't have to be close." I motioned for a chair across the room from him.

He didn't say anything, but took his time weighing his options and then backed up and sat on the edge of his recliner. I slowly moved toward the chair I'd pointed to without turning my back on him. The woman hadn't moved an inch. Finally, when the patient and I were seated, she backed herself into a chair closer to me.

"What do you want?" he said.

"Again, my name is Ellie. I'm your nurse today. How are you doing?" I remained calm and spoke in a steady tone.

"How am I doing? How am I doing? Can't you see? I'm under attack from these people!" he shouted.

"Where are the people? What are they attacking you with?" I asked, anxious since I clearly hadn't seen any people attacking anyone.

"Behind you! They have swords! You're with them, aren't you?" he sneered.

"I'm not with them," I said trying my best to imitate being offended by such a question.

"Good. Watch out, they see you! They'll get you too!" he said.

"Can you protect me?" I asked, hopeful.

"Yes, get over here! Do you have any weapons we can use to defend ourselves?"

It was as if he didn't even see the young woman in the room any longer because he did not acknowledge her as I slid off my chair, crouched low, and hurried to his side as if I were also being attacked. I'd never dealt with a patient like this before, but I was thankful that the lecture on patients with dementia was coming back to me. The main point I remembered was to try to live in their world rather than trying to orient them to ours. I had to admit, it was kind of fun playing along.

"Are you having any pain?" I whispered, keeping my eyes trained on the fictitious army across the room.

"No, that last sword just grazed my shoulder, but it'll heal. How do we get out of here?" he asked without taking his eyes off the fictitious army.

"I'm thinking if we can quietly make it to the door, we can escape. Think it'll work?"

"Yeah, it's our only hope."

He took my hand, and we worked our way slowly across the room, taking careful and quiet steps until we reached the door. He grabbed the handle of the door as we passed it and swung the door shut loudly and then gave me a tight hug around my neck.

"Thank you, thank you, thank you! You saved me!" he said happily.

"Let's not waste time celebrating now. Let's get to the safety zone first." I said as I escorted him towards the library.

I encouraged him to sit on the leather couch and told him to wait for me while I went looking for supplies to bandage his shoulder. He had been extremely receptive to me once I'd begun living in his world. When I returned ten minutes later, he had completely forgotten about the fictitious army and his pretend wound. Instead, he asked if I could help him to his room for a nap, to which I obliged him.

Feeling victorious after our battle with the fictitious army, it was time to go and assess my mother. I steeled myself as I opened her door. This time, I found her napping in her bed. Her skin had taken on quite the yellow tone, and she looked like she had a glow around her. There was a woman sitting on the couch reading that I didn't recognize, but she introduced herself as a friend. My mother didn't bother to open her eyes as I did a quick assessment and checked her equipment.

My heart skipped a beat when she opened her eyes and spoke my name. Instantly, I reverted to the kindergartner she'd left. I wanted to be angry with her still, but seeing her like this softened me. I'd turned off my emotions when I'd first entered the room and I'd assessed her as just a normal patient. But now, speaking my name, she was my mother again. I needed her love. I was ready to accept her apology.

"Ellie," she croaked with a hoarse voice.

"Mom," I said softly, grasping her hand.

The woman on the couch looked at me, horrified, as I said it. Clearly, she didn't know about me. She probably thought I was some nurse overstepping and playing a role to satisfy a dying patient. I didn't care what she thought. Right now, it was just me and my mom.

"I'm sorry," she whispered, unable to make her voice work.

"I know. I accept your apology," I said quietly and gave her hand a squeeze.

"I have always loved you."

"Everything is going to be okay. Do you need anything?"

"Not anymore. I have everything I've ever wanted."

I kissed her forehead and ran from the room as salty, wet tears began to stream from my eyes. Locking myself in the staff bathroom, I

191

sat on the floor and let them fall. Years of hurt and pain were released from within as I cried quietly. I felt lighter. I felt calmer. I hadn't meant for this to happen, but I felt at peace that it had. I didn't have control over the exchange but I knew that it was long overdue. I should have done this when she first admitted, or maybe the following week. I shouldn't have waited so long, but at least it hadn't been too late.

Laying in bed with Asher a few nights later, I finally opened up to him about the interaction I had with my mother. While I was never exactly guarded with my past, I hadn't offered many details about some of the more painful things. Working with dying patients really forced me to evaluate my own relationships and to see things in a different light.

"I know this is something we've kinda talked about a little bit," I started cautiously. "But, I love you, Ash. I think that you're my person. The one I'm meant to be with forever."

"I love you too, El." He kissed me. "And I *know* that you're my person and the one I'm meant to be with forever."

"I know. It just seems so crazy that we've only known each other like eight months. But I have loved every minute with you, especially since you moved in. I wouldn't want to do life without you." I paused.

"Yeah. Where are you going with all this? Are you going to propose to me?" he teased.

"Ha! You wish. Wouldn't that just take the pressure off you?"

"Uh, yeah. Of course it would," he laughed.

"In all seriousness, if we both feel this way, I really think it's important that you meet my mom before she dies." Silence. "You didn't get a chance to meet my dad. Despite the fact that I barely know her, she's still my mom," I trailed off.

"I agree. I didn't want to push or to ask, but I've been hoping you'd invite me since we had dinner with Ben and the girls last month."

"Okay then."

And the following day, Asher met my dying mother. She didn't speak much and kept her eyes closed most of the visit. Ben and the girls had been present since it was a weekend. I had to admit that it was nice feeling like a family. We promised to have dinner again soon as we said our goodbyes at the end of our visit.

Eighth Month: October

(Part II)

The sun was shining, the air was chilly, and there was dew still on the grass as we pulled into the parking lot and prepared for a day of tailgating. Asher and I had flown into town the night before and reached the hotel late. Asher's alma mater sat nestled in the Midwest and was surrounded by trees turning beautiful shades of orange, red, and yellow. My father had played football in high school and college, but had raised me primarily loving "da Bears" and nothing else. Asher had grown up loving mostly just college football. When he'd gone on to graduate school, he had fallen head over heels in love with their football team and had never turned his back.

Homecoming week meant an annual pilgrimage back to college, tailgating with friends, and watching a football game. Eager to meet some of the friends Asher had spent so much time talking about, I felt prepared but had been grossly mistaken. When we arrived at the parking lot at eight o'clock in the morning, the boys had already set up a tent next to an RV, were grilling hot dogs, and were already two or three beers deep. I had underestimated them. While I had envisioned a mature gathering, I was instead transformed back to the partying ways of college students.

Eyeing us, a group of guys high-fived, chest bumped, and fist pounded Asher. As I was introduced, I was roughly hugged and handed a beer. A group of women sat on bag chairs, wrapped in blankets, and sipping steaming hot coffee from colorful mugs. Clearly, the wives didn't revert ten years when their husbands did. Watching Asher with his friends, I wanted to be a part of the wives club.

"Hey, Ash! You want a shot?" Dexter shouted as he headed back into the RV.

"Naw. Not yet," Asher hollered after him. He grabbed my hand and walked me over to the wives club.

"Ladies, I want to introduce you to my love, Ellie. Ellie, this is Holly, Jillian, Kelsey, and Bette."

"You want coffee?" Holly asked without hesitation.

"These guys are gonna get pretty lit before long and the coffee seems to help us tolerate their shenanigans much better," Kelsey added.

"That would be fantastic!" I said enthusiastically.

Before long, I was sitting in my own bag chair, cuddled under a blanket, and sipping gourmet coffee from a bright blue insulated mug. The women were friendly and inviting, explaining that they had all met through their husbands, and they had been attending these annual weekends for years. Asher was the last remaining bachelor of the group and the thought crossed my mind that I might just be the last puzzle piece to their perfect group.

Originally meeting in graduate school, the five guys all studied engineering together and had rented a house off campus. Despite moving to different parts of the country after graduation, every year the guys returned "home" as they called it, for one football game each season. At first, it was just five guys drinking beer from the back of a truck, but as they grew in their careers, their accommodations got swankier.

When Dexter married Holly two years after graduation, the annual weekend included a beat up RV rather than the back of a truck. The following year, Mark married Kelsey and a canopy was added next to the RV to house food and a portable television. Brad married Bette two years after that and brought along a grill that year. Two years after *that*,

195

Jake married Jillian and they brought along an upgraded RV complete with an outdoor television wired into the side and wet bar.

None of the couples brought their children along - this was an adults only weekend. I learned that Mark and Kelsey had three, Brad and Bette had one, and Jake and Jillian had one. All of them had dropped their kids off with their parents.

"Isn't it nice to just sit in your chair alone, Bette?" Jillian asked.

"And use the bathroom alone!" Kelsey added.

"Oh yes. I actually had the chance to sit for five minutes playing on my phone before Jake interrupted me," Jillian said. The group laughed.

"Look how stupid they look right now," Bette pointed to the guys, who were apparently having a hot dog eating contest.

"Ugh. It's going to be so hard to get that stain out of his shorts!" Jillian laughed as one of the guys dropped ketchup in his lap.

"Good luck with that," Holly laughed.

"I'm just glad this only happens one weekend a year," Kelsey added.

"What do they do the rest of the year during football season?" I asked with curiosity.

"Act like this in the privacy of our home!" Holly joked and we all laughed.

"It's finally noon. Time to switch to coffee with Kahlua," Jillian noted.

"Gotta keep up with the guys, right?"

"Something like that." Jillian jumped up and ran into the RV for the bottle of Kaluha.

The guys spent the next few hours tossing around a football, trying to outshine each other in whatever stupid talent contest they could think of, harassing fans of the opposing team, and continuing to drink a variety of alcoholic drinks. The wives club chatted and laughed as they were entertained by the guys. By the time we all closed up the tailgate and headed to the stadium, everyone was feeling warm from the inside out.

As we headed towards the stadium from our makeshift camp, I thought I saw someone I recognized. By the time my brain registered the sight, I had to scan my eyes left and right to find him again. Finally, leaning against a gate near the entrance, I spotted him again. He was watching us. Well, he was more than likely watching *me*! Realizing I spied him, he gave a quick flick of his wrist to wave hello and then lost himself in the crowd headed into the stadium. What the hell was Mystery Man doing here? Why did he appear everywhere that I went? If he hadn't waved at me, I'd have thought the alcohol was playing tricks on me. I was more certain than ever he was following me, but completely uncertain how to make him stop.

As we took our seats, I was amazed at the sheer size of the stadium and the amount of people. I cozied up to Asher, and he put his arm around me. The entire atmosphere was electric — the team, the band, the fans, the tradition. A party erupted with every touchdown.

Since no alcohol is permitted in the stadium, by the time the game was over, everyone was sober again and I had completely forgotten about Mystery Man. The celebration continued as we drove back to Dexter and Holly's house, a short drive from the tailgate.

All five couples usually continued the party into the night, crashed at their house, and then enjoyed a brunch the following morning before everyone would head their separate ways again. Seeing Asher with his friends showed me a new, more playful side of him, and I liked it. It felt good having him show me off to the world like I was his most prized possession. Once in a while, I'd catch his eye from across the room and his face would light up. Being here, with him, was comfortable.

In the backyard, a bonfire was lit and everyone pulled chairs around the pit. Pizza was delivered for dinner/snack and everyone was gleefully drinking again. Back at the house, it felt more like a grown up version of the college party from the morning. The wives club sipped wine instead of coffee and the guys traded beer for rum and coke or something equally hard. Their shenanigans continued, but their tricks seemed slightly more sophisticated than they had earlier.

"Excuse me! Can I get everyone's attention?" Asher said as he stood on top of a log, trying to keep his balance and prevent himself from falling.

"I want to raise a toast to Dex and Hol for having us again this year, and to everyone for being able to make it to what I hope is my last homecoming weekend as a bachelor!" Asher toasted, smiling down at me.

"About time," one of the guys hollered.

Everyone clinked glasses, laughed at Asher's last comment, and high-fived me. Asher carefully climbed off the log, reached for my hand and pulled me to my feet. He stole my glass of wine, took a swig of it before handing it to the nearest person, and then he proceeded to shock the hell out of me.

"Ellie. From the moment I saw you in the grocery store, I knew there was something special about you," he said as he lowered himself onto his right knee and fumbled for something in his pocket. "I am the luckiest guy alive getting to fall asleep with you in my arms and wake up next to you in the morning. You truly make me happy, and I cannot imagine living my life without you." He flipped open the top of the burgundy velvet box in his hand and revealed a diamond engagement ring sparkling in the dim lighting. "Will you marry me?" he asked.

My heart pounded and my hands covered my mouth. Tears of joy formed in my eyes. I couldn't believe this was actually happening. I wanted it to, of course, but I still couldn't believe it. I stared at the ring. Time felt like it was standing still, and while I was sure I hadn't hesitated, it felt like everything around us stopped.

Finally, I pulled Asher to me as I repeated the word "yes" over and over again until his mouth met mine. The wives club dabbed at their own eyes and clapped. The guys hooted and hollered. Once the ring was securely on my finger, the wives club swooped in to get a look and the guys began to joke with Asher.

"Welcome to the club," Bette said.

I spent the rest of the evening cuddling with Asher and enjoying the fire. It all felt like a dream, to be honest. Not only did I love Asher, I loved his friends and family. I knew I'd have to come clean to Asher about my actual bank account at some point, but tonight wasn't the time.

"So, what will you be adding to our tailgate next year? Seems like each new marriage has ended with an upgrade to our setup." Mark commented.

"We have a year to think about it!" Asher said. "Don't rush us!"

The day had been stressful long before I made it to Mrs. Leukemia's room. I had picked up the afternoon shift to help out and everything that could go wrong, had. Every patient had uncontrolled pain. Everyone was in a foul mood, and that included me. Maybe it was the weather or some rotation of the planets.

Ghostly pale, her skin was nearly translucent. Her green eyes were almond shaped and accented her round face. The dark circles under her eyes were what spoke to me the most and drew me in with the stories they had yet to share. She was tired.

She was too young for dark circles under her eyes. Barely of age to drink, she had been fighting leukemia for three years, and was finally too tired to continue fighting this losing battle. Her young husband sat on the couch as she relaxed in the recliner, blankets pulled up to her chin.

"It's cold in here," she said quietly, and he placed another blanket across her lap.

"Are you having any pain?" he asked her as I checked the liter flow on her oxygen.

"No, I'm just tired," she replied barely above a whisper, adjusting the nasal cannula in her nose as if by reflex.

"I will need to change your dressing on your bottom soon. Would you like to do it now or in an hour?"

"Let's do it now, and then I will rest."

Without being asked, the husband lifted his wife from the chair and placed her gently on the bed. Her total weight, blankets included, couldn't have been more than ninety pounds. She was small framed, but now smaller and more fragile. He was muscular in his arms and shoulders but carried a little extra weight around his middle. As I set the supplies out on a table, he undressed her bottom half and rolled her away from me on the bed, exposing her butt in my direction.

I worked quietly as I pulled off the old dressing, cleaned the wound, and applied a clean dressing. She flinched when I cleaned it, but she never made a sound. I pulled her nightgown down and placed a pillow under her before rolling her onto her back once again. Her eyes were moist, but she still did not speak.

I placed my hand on hers and asked, "Are you doing okay?"

"Yeah, I'm fine," she replied, as conditioned.

"Honestly, how are you doing? I understand if you don't want to talk to me, but I can see that you're not fine," I admitted as I looked into her eyes.

"I am afraid that if I admit it, it will control me," she confided.

"Sometimes, admitting it has the opposite effect, and sets you free."

"I hurt. Not physically. Emotionally. Mentally. I don't feel *anything* physically. Everything is now emotional pain and discomfort.

200

I hurt seeing my husband and family. I feel their pain and it hurts me. I hurt seeing you girls attend to my every need and not being able to do anything for myself. I hurt thinking of the things I have left on my bucket list that I'll never be able to do. I am tired. And I hurt," she said with a sigh.

"I wish I could say that I understand, but I have never been in your shoes. However, I can empathize with what you've said. This is never easy."

"I just wish things were different." She glanced over at her husband and noticed he was asleep sitting up.

"Understandable."

"I wish I could have given him a child. I wish I could have grown old with him. We are childhood sweethearts and I can't remember a time before there was an 'us', ya know?"

"Yeah." I nodded understanding.

"I'll be leaving him soon. I ask myself often what am I leaving him with and I hate the answers. Debt, a mortgage, heartbreak, medical bills…" she trailed off.

"Memories," I added.

"Is that enough?" she asked philosophically.

"I don't know," I admitted. "I don't have the answer to that."

"Me either. I wish I could leave him with more positive than negative. He has done everything for me and at any cost, but at the end of the day, it isn't enough, and he'll be left with all the cost and yet no me. Does that make any sense?"

"It makes perfect sense." I looked down at the floor and tried to think of something insightful or helpful to say but nothing came to me, so I said nothing.

We sat in silence for a few minutes listening to the soft snore from her husband, the quiet hiss of oxygen being delivered to her nose, and the birds chirping happily outside her window. My stomach growled loudly, and her head jerked my way, and she giggled the way a child might after accidentally farting.

"What can I do?" I finally spoke, my voice cracking.

"Pay off my house?" She laughed.

"Ha! I wish!" I said with a nervous laugh. "I'm a nurse, not a millionaire."

It was nice to see her finally laughing. If it were ten years ago, and I was having the same conversations with patients, I knew that I wouldn't feel the same emotions. I was selfish and immature even though I thought I was beyond my years. The situations my patients were facing, the death in front of them, was a tough pill to swallow. I am glad I waited to go to nursing school so that I would be mentally and emotionally equipped to have real conversations with patients with real empathy.

Leaving her room, I made my way to the nursing lounge for lunch. Just as I'd warmed my frozen dinner, Paige and Jan entered. The thought of eating when Paige was anywhere near me always made me lose my appetite. She was downright mean to me.

"I hear you're working over tonight," Paige said to me.

"What are you talking about?"

"Sally called in sick. You're the low man on the totem pole. Looks like you're working over tonight."

She was trying to make me angry and I knew it. It was working. Just hearing her voice lately was making me angry. The way she rolled her eyes, the way she lifted just one eyebrow before she spoke, and the tone interlaced with attitude she used when speaking to me were enough to make anyone's blood boil.

"Oh Paige, stop," Jan chided.

"What? I'm being serious!" Paige shrugged her shoulders. "Fine. Wait and see if you prefer." She smiled with satisfaction, having achieved her goal of ruffling my feathers.

"I am *not* working over tonight," I said calmly.

"Whatever you say," she mocked.

She won. She always won. I felt anger boiling inside me. Why did she always have a way of getting under my skin like this? If I hadn't just started my lunch, I'd have walked right out of the room. Instead, I sat at the table stewing.

When I finally took the last bite of my microwave dinner, I tossed the trash in the garbage can and left the nursing lounge. I took a few deep breaths in the hallway and then headed straight for the supervisor in charge, Sarah.

Sarah was a dainty woman, in her fifties, with long auburn hair. She had worked at Rolling Hills from the time it opened. I liked her as a supervisor, she was understanding and fair. I found her sitting at the charge nurse desk, concentrating on the screen of the computer. She looked up when she noticed me at the door.

"Ah, just who I needed to see," she said in a chipper voice. "Sally called in tonight and I need you to work over to cover her shift."

"I can't do that."

"Well, I'm not sure what to tell you. Rarely do we mandate, but I can't reach anyone to cover tonight and you're the newest nurse."

Working over meant that rather than getting off at eleven tonight, I would be working until seven tomorrow morning. An overnight shift. Flashbacks of my last night shift played in my head and my arm instinctively ached to remind me of that horrible night. I was filled with dread.

I stood in the door debating if I should explain to her *why* I couldn't work overnight or if I should suck up one of my biggest fears and give the night shift a second chance. Sarah had gone back to her computer screen. Finally, deciding I needed to act like the adult I claimed to be, I left her office.

I went straight to the bathroom, and locked myself inside. I knew I could overcome my fears, but it was easier said than done. I reached out to the only person I knew that could put everything into perspective for me — Asher.

Ninth Month: November

(Part I)

Small dazzling white flakes drifted down from the cloudy sky as November arrived. Coat, scarf, and mittens were required anytime I left the house. Heading to work was no exception. I shivered as I waited for the car to thaw. Had I been smarter, I'd have started the car while I was still getting ready for work and it would have been warm and ready to go when I finally climbed in. But I wasn't and my car was still freezing cold.

By the time I arrived at work, I was toasty warm and hated having to get out of my car. It wasn't even necessarily so cold outside, but the wind made it feel colder and the snowflakes tricked my brain into thinking it was sub-zero outside. I had procrastinated so long at home that I was now late for work. Being late was something I fiercely hated, but at this point I had to own it.

Before I could enter the nursing lounge, I was pulled aside by Penny, the director of nursing. My stomach did somersaults as I followed her back to her office, feeling anxious and fearing I was in trouble for something. Was I getting in trouble for being a few minutes late? Did I do something wrong and not realize it? Had a patient complained about me? My mind envisioned various made-up horror scenes.

Penny's office was across from the nursing lounge. Her large desk sat in the middle of the room with two plush chairs directly across from it. A few indoor plants sat in one corner. A window looking into the courtyard was behind her.

I sat in one of the chairs, but instead of sitting in her own chair, she moved a few things around on her desk and then sat on the corner of it, facing me. I wasn't sure if this was a good or bad sign.

"I wanted to grab you quick, before report, to talk with you."

"Okay," I hesitated.

"Your mom," she started, and I exhaled with relief. "Your mom is unconscious and actively dying. Her husband asked for us to let you know before you saw the board."

"Hm. Wonder why he didn't bother to just call me."

"He's been here all night. He knew we'd be able to catch you first."

I didn't buy that answer. I didn't blame Penny, but my irritation with the whole situation had returned in the snap of a finger. Ben not calling me with this crucial update was not only irritating, it was hurtful. Over the last month, I thought I had made progress on my relationships, both the one with my mother and the one with Ben and the girls. Yet, I was still the red-headed step daughter in Ben's eyes.

"Got it."

I stood and walked out of her office and straight to the nursing lounge as she half attempted to follow me, but abandoned her attempt just before she reached the nursing lounge. I was going to go to work. If nothing else, the lack of a phone call with the status change showed where I stood, and if that was how Ben felt, then I would just accept it. I had been let down by her before and my scars hadn't actually healed yet anyway.

The only empty seat in the nursing lounge when I got there was next to Paige. I hadn't spoken to her since our last exchange over a month ago. I noticed as I glanced at the board that we'd had a few patients pass away over the last few days and that my mother was most likely going to be next. The patients I had been assigned were all fairly new to Rolling Hills and all pretty stable from the looks of it.

I hadn't exactly been open with my coworkers about my childhood, my mother, or my current life. Clearly they thought I was closer to my mother than I actually was. Maybe I should have shared with them how she had abandoned me at the young age of five or that Ben hadn't even bothered to give me an update with her change in condition. I'd had sisters for years that I hadn't even known about. I hadn't told anyone because I didn't want to influence the care they gave her.

All the anger and hurt that had melted away last month was returning with hurricane force and the realization that I wasn't over it after all was at the front of my mind. Rather than dwell on it, I made up my mind on how I wanted to handle the situation and no one was going to change my mind. I wasn't going to be vindictive because that isn't who I am, but I wasn't going to pretend everything was fine.

"I see that I've got your mother today. Anything special I should know about her?" Paige asked me just as I was about to leave the nursing lounge.

"I'm the last person you should be asking." I struggled to hide my anger.

"I see. Being your mother and all, I thought you'd know what she needed most." Paige was reaching for information.

"You thought wrong."

"Is there something wrong? I'm not sure why you're being so hostile."

"My mother and I aren't close. Until she was admitted, I didn't even know if she was still alive. I never met her husband or her other daughters until she arrived here. I'm the last one to give you help when it comes to that woman," I snapped.

"Ah. Well, I guess she won't be on your gift list then." She watched me for a reaction.

"My what?"

"Look, I did some research on you," she whispered so that only I could hear. "I read about your father passing away and leaving you the CEO of his company and every last dime he had. You're not just a nurse like us. You don't even need to be here. You're loaded. Why don't you just go run your Fortune 500 company? What are you doing *here*?"

"Just because I'm loaded doesn't mean I don't have a desire to follow my passions like everyone else."

"Well, I kinda think it does."

I didn't entertain her with a reply. Who researches their coworkers? Why did she *care* so much about what I did and didn't do? And why would having a padded bank account make me a different kind of nurse than anyone else? Somehow, Paige knew just how to word something to get under my skin. I wouldn't satisfy her with a reply or a reaction. I knew *her* type. She was fed by drama. I wouldn't play that game or stoop to her level.

I marched myself out of the nursing lounge and straight to my mother's room. I didn't knock and I wasn't quiet as I walked in. Upon seeing me, Ben rose from the couch and headed in my direction but before he could put his arms around me, I placed my hand firmly on his chest and didn't allow him to complete the hug. I began to soften seeing my mother in that condition, but I didn't allow myself to deviate from my plan.

I went to my mother and bent down. Whispering in her ear, I told her I forgave her and that I would always wonder what it would have been like if she had stayed. I promised to right her wrongs and always stay and fight for what was right. I then kissed her forehead and without a word to Ben, left the room. Practically running, I made it to one of the private bathrooms before I collapsed against the closed door and let my emotions and feelings flow.

Honestly, I was sick of crying in bathrooms. I hadn't cried this much in my entire life. Even as a hormonal teenager, I hadn't been this confused or distraught over my own emotions. I had become someone I didn't even recognize.

I had so many reasons to cry. Legitimate reasons. I wasn't a hateful person or at least that's not who I wanted to be. The truth was my wounds were too deep. Were they too deep to ever heal? Would they heal when she was finally gone? I had been naive to think that they could be repaired with just a few words and a hug. I had spent many years wishing, hoping, dreaming, hating, and fighting. I was pretty sure that the only thing I felt now was confusion.

Finally, I pulled myself together and looked in the mirror. My eyes were red and puffy, but felt better after I splashed some cold water on my face. I straightened my scrub top and exited the bathroom just as Paige turned the corner and spotted me. Pretending I hadn't seen her, I began to walk in the opposite direction, but it was futile.

"Ellie! Wait!"

"Hey," I said as I spun around to face her.

"I've been looking everywhere for you. Wanted to let you know that your mother passed away just now. Wasn't sure if you had gotten a chance to see her or not."

Paige was completely aware that I had just gone to see my mother as she had followed me down the hall after report. Paige wanted the pleasure of breaking the news to me and potentially watching me crumble. Instead, I stood there feeling completely blank. I didn't move a muscle as I tried frantically to think.

"Perfect. Thank you," I muttered when my brain finally made the decision to speak.

"So, now what?"

"Now what? Now I go see my patients and get my day started."

"Really?" Her words dripped with attitude mixed with shock.

"Really."

"Wow, you're cold," she said hatefully.

"Really?" Now it was my turn to deliver attitude.

"I don't get you," she said after a long pause and studying me with her eyes.

"What's there to get?"

"You are this super generous, caring person who gives thousands of dollars to patients, but you don't even give a shit when your own mother dies?"

"I never said I was a super generous, caring person who gives thousands of dollars to patients. *You* have made that assumption. You also assumed to know the relationship between my mother and I. The moral of this story is simple. You don't know me."

"So, you deny that you're the one granting the wishes?"

"Is that really what you're taking away from this conversation?" I sighed heavily and walked away, completely done having any conversation with Paige.

With perfect timing, my phone rang and Penny let me know that she was sending me home and had transferred my patients to one of the home care nurses who was coming in to cover my shift.

"Standard protocol," she'd said when I asked why.

Frustrated, angry, and feeling impulsive, I reverted to a very old trick of burying my emotions: shopping. It wasn't the type of therapy recommended by most people, but it worked for me. It worked at pushing my emotions back to where they belonged and away from the forefront of my brain. When I was a teenager, I had done major damage to one of the credit cards my dad had given me, and he had hit the roof when the monthly bill arrived. As a young adult, I turned to travel when I became too wrapped up in myself and escaped my current reality for whatever I imagined might make me happier.

Mary Jane had been shocked when I took her on my first "therapy" session and thanked me for not turning to alcohol and drugs. Instead, I turned my focus on Neiman Marcus, Saks, Coach, and Louis Vitton. After a boyfriend had broken my heart once, I'd gone out and bought a brand-new car and paid cash. I'm sure an actual therapist would tell me that my coping mechanism wasn't healthy, but I didn't think I had big enough problems to justify seeing an actual therapist.

I was aware that money couldn't buy my happiness — I'd learned that many years ago. However, it made me happy long enough to organize my thoughts. Long enough to figure out why I was feeling the way I was at least.

Leaving work, I called Asher with the news, and he offered his condolences. He asked what I planned to do. He thought I was going to go to the funeral home and help make arrangements. He was wrong. I doubted Ben would even call me with the arrangements once they had been made. As I talked with Asher, I felt myself finding inner peace. He was doing something to me through the phone that was equally amazing and relaxing.

Instead of heading towards the luxury stores, I headed to the spa. It had been a brilliant idea because when I left two hours later, I felt lighter. I felt clarity. I felt *joy*. Asher had pretty much saved me from my own self-pity. Being angry with my past wouldn't fix it. I had spent the last two hours being rubbed and soaked and mentally making peace with the past, and I felt I was a better person because of it.

I was downtown and tall skyscrapers were all around me. A small park, if it could be called that, was directly in front of me and contained a fountain that had no water. The grass wasn't visible beneath the snow and tracks went in all directions. I smelled coffee and fresh snow. I closed my eyes and felt a cold chill down my spine before I snapped them open and back to reality.

I was only a few blocks from Asher's office and made the decision to walk there. I needed a hug. I needed to feel his warmth. The good vibes from the spa had begun to wear off, and I felt myself spinning again. I was a hot mess.

When I finally made it to Asher's building, I took the elevator to the third floor where the office was located. A man in a business suit watched me as we rode the elevator, but didn't say anything. I thought he might follow me when I got off, but he continued on with the elevator.

"Asher Grant, please," I said to the receptionist.

"May I ask who you are?" she said politely.

"Jennifer Aniston," I said, trying to keep a straight face.

She eyed me up and down, then picked up her phone and called to Asher's office. I could tell he asked who was here to see him because she glanced at me sideways as she repeated "Jennifer Aniston."

"He'll see you, Ms. Aniston." She motioned to a door to her left.

Asher pulled me into his arms the moment I closed the door behind me. Without warning, I lost control. Feeling his arms wrap around me, I turned into a child and began to sob. Big, ugly tears rolled down my face and began to pool on his shirt. Was it just the death of my mother I was crying about? Or was I finally allowing myself to grieve my father? Asher just held me tight and let me cry.

I spent the next two weeks trying to find myself again. This time, rather than running, I'd had Asher by my side. The way he cared for me made me feel safe. He had become my family, and most importantly, my best friend.

By the time Thanksgiving rolled around, I was back to my normal self and trying to get back into a routine. Asher and I were scheduled to head back to his parents' house on Wednesday and had decided to make it a long weekend. It would be the first time visiting since we'd gotten engaged, and I was looking forward to being around his family again.

On Tuesday evening, Asher and I were in our room packing our bags when I noticed he wasn't saying much and I felt a distance between us. Ignoring it, I finished packing and rolled my suitcase out to the front door. When I returned to the bedroom, Asher was sitting on the bed fiddling with a sweater in his hands anxiously.

"Can I ask you something?" he said with hesitation.

"Of course."

"Do you want to go with me to my parents for Thanksgiving?"

"Of course," I repeated. "Why would you ask that?"

"Well..." he hesitated. "I was in the office the other day looking for the water bill when I found a receipt. I wasn't snooping! I just knew I needed to pay the water bill. Well, I ended up finding a few receipts. If you have something to tell me, I'd rather you just say it now." He looked up at me, fear written on his face.

"Huh? What are you talking about?" I was completely confused.

"You know what I'm talking about. I'm not judging your spending habits, but some of the things you've bought have been... suspicious for someone who is engaged to be married," he said. "Not to mention, I'm not sure where you got the money for such.. large.. purchases."

"Oh my God!"

It hadn't occurred to me that Asher might find the receipts for the gifts I'd bought anonymously. I was horrified at how this must look to Asher. I hadn't tried to hide the receipts. I had laid them freely on my desk, planning to return to them at some point.

Asher and I still hadn't discussed the financial aspect of merging our lives. He had offered to help with expenses and asked for a few bills to pay on his own. I wasn't upset or angry with him for searching the papers on the top of my desk. Instead, I was upset with myself for not coming clean much sooner.

"That's all you have to say?" he asked angrily, his voice steadily rising.

"You have it all wrong," I said with assurance.

"Really? I have it all wrong? I found receipts for an entire house, a motor home, a family practice lawyer, a contractor, a fertility center, and a trip to Iceland. Not to mention you spent a ridiculous amount on the furniture! How do you explain all that?" he accused.

I sat down next to him on the edge of the bed, trying to think of the right words to explain it. Could I? What would he think when I spilled my secrets this far into our relationship. I had messed up and I wasn't sure if I could fix it.

"Asher, listen," I began before he cut me off.

"If you have someone else, just tell me," he said abruptly.

"I don't have someone else," I responded quickly. "I can't exactly explain it right now, but I promise you that it's nothing bad. You're the only man I want to be with for the rest of my life. I do not have someone else."

"Okay," he said quietly, looking down at the floor.

"When the time is right, you'll know everything. I promise. Please trust me on that."

"I do trust you," he replied.

"In terms of the large amounts and where I got the money... I haven't been completely upfront with you about that."

"What?"

"My dad was wealthy. When he passed away, he left *everything* to me." I paused to let that absorb.

"Of course. Wow. How didn't I see that before?"

"What do you mean?"

"Well, you're an only child. Why wouldn't he leave everything to you? Who else would he leave stuff to?" Asher rationalized.

"Good point."

"This explains a lot. Whew. Wait — who were those purchases for then?"

"That's the part I can't explain to you just yet. I need you to trust me and trust that everything is okay."

He watched me before responding, "Okay, I trust you."

I wasn't sure if he was truly okay with me not explaining it all, but he would have to be for now. I wasn't ready yet to spill *all* beans. To be honest, I enjoyed keeping the secret to myself.

Ninth Month: November

(Part II)

"Ellie! I'm so glad you and Asher could join us! Let me see that ring!" Marceline said with excitement. "I cried when I heard the news."

"Thank you for having us. I'm glad we were able to come down for Thanksgiving. I've never done the big family meal thing, but I am looking forward to it."

"Well now, we have so much to be thankful for, and so much to discuss, don't we? By the way, I'm sorry to hear about your mother."

Marceline hugged me and then sent us to the living room where the rest of the family was waiting. Our bags were carried upstairs by Albert. Everyone had a look at the sparkler on my finger, and then returned to their conversations. I was exhausted as we'd spent the morning and afternoon traveling, and I excused myself to go take a quick nap. Asher followed me to our room, and snuck in just as I closed the door.

"Everything okay, hon?" Asher asked.

"Yes, just very tired."

"Okay. Mind if I nap with you? I'm feeling a bit run down myself."

"Not at all." I said as I fell onto the bed and closed my eyes.

It didn't take long for me to fall asleep. I was a bit surprised because I wasn't one to nap during the day, but today, I was exhausted. When I did finally wake, it was dark in the room and Asher wasn't next to me. I looked at my phone and saw it was 7:00 p.m.! As my eyes adjusted to the darkness, I noticed my stomach growling with hunger. I sat up on the edge of the bed, and without warning had the sudden urge to vomit.

When I returned to the bedroom, I sent Asher a text message and hoped he would see it. I didn't want to walk downstairs and see his family at the moment. Besides not wanting to see anyone, I didn't want to share a viral illness! I just wanted to crawl into our bed and sleep the night away. I changed into my pajamas and crawled back under the covers when there was a soft knock at the door and Asher peeked his head in.

"What happened?" he asked as he sat on the edge of the bed.

"I don't know. I woke up and my stomach was upset. When I tried to sit up, I got sick to my stomach. I'm guessing I'm viral."

"That's not any good."

"I know. It's the last thing I want to have happen when we're visiting your parents, but obviously I didn't pick the timing."

He smiled. "No one wants to be sick. Just stay in bed and get feeling better for tomorrow! I love you."

"I love you too. I'm sorry."

"Don't be sorry. Just get some rest."

He swept the stray hair off my face and kissed my forehead before he tucked me in. Things between us had changed ever so slightly since our talk in our bedroom before we made the trip to his parents. I knew he was still suspicious of my purchases, but he trusted me and didn't say another word about it. I noticed he slept a little closer to me, hugged me a little tighter, and held my hand more often. I was okay with these changes.

I felt better by morning, and Asher and I made our way to the breakfast nook where everyone had gathered. A table had been set up with different kinds of breakfast foods laid out in beautiful arrangements. Three different styles of eggs, bacon, sausages, potatoes, biscuits and gravy, bagels, cheese, and fresh fruit. The smell was delicious. I sat down and poured a glass of orange juice and began to sip from it when Asher's mother noticed I didn't have a plate of food in front of me.

"Darling, aren't you going to eat anything?" she spoke with her uppity southern drawl.

"No, my stomach is not completely settled from yesterday just yet." I replied, rubbing my stomach.

"Oh dear. Let me have Albert fetch you the Mylanta," she said to me as she turned and called Albert into the room and told him what she wanted.

When Albert returned, he carried a small cup with a viscous green liquid in it and served it to me as if it were an exquisite elixir. I slung the cup up and poured it down my throat like a shot of whiskey. It tasted horrible and I struggled to keep it down, but just barely managed. Everyone laughed seeing my face contort, but Asher laid his hand across my upper back and rubbed it.

"So, when is this wedding?" Andrea asked as she bit into her bagel.

"The fall would make for a beautiful wedding, wouldn't it?" Marceline chimed in.

"Maybe in the spring by the lake?" Andrea suggested.

"Whoa, everyone needs to slow down. Ellie and I were waiting for things to settle down a little, and then we'd discuss it. We will let everyone know when we think of some dates!" Asher retorted.

"I have a gala at the end of August that I'll be working hard to plan for. Please keep this in mind." Marceline said.

"Noted." Asher said with a nod. "Where is Max and Molly?"

"Nice distraction technique, Ash. The kids are outside playing." Andrea replied.

"I learned from the best," Asher said with a smile.

"Stop the fighting you two," Marceline interjected, swatting at their hands. "Ellie, are you feeling any better?"

"Yes, thank you."

"Asher, lets go get settled before kick off," Benedict said as he stood and headed in the direction of the theater.

Asher followed and everyone else continued to chit chat as Albert cleared our plates, but I was lost in my own thoughts. I loved sitting in the middle of their kitchen, watching the siblings fight, their mother pleading for peace, and every one happy to be together. I hadn't had a family like this and I loved that I would get to spend the rest of my life as part of this one. I sat quietly just listening to them until another sudden urge to vomit sent me running for the kitchen sink.

Marceline fixed my pony tail as my head hung over the sink, Albert handed me a cool washcloth, and Andrea headed outside to find the children. Marceline continued to dote on me as she settled me on the couch in the living room and sat in the chair next to the couch and grabbed her magazine. Andrea had offered to get Asher before she'd left to find the kids, but Marceline had refused and insisted on caring for me herself. It had been so many years since I'd had a mother and I loved the way Marceline seemed to know just what to say and do.

I vaguely remembered a time when I was young that I had gotten sick and my mother had stopped dead in her tracks when she saw me sitting on the floor and vomit surrounding me. She began to pace in the hallway and yelled at me, saying I was naughty for making a mess. She swore my dad would beat me if I didn't clean it up right away. Scared, I'd found a rag and cleaned it up the best I could, which hadn't been well. When my dad got home, she was passed out in their bed and I had met him at the door, crying. When he saw and heard what had happened, he had given me a bath, cleaned up the floor better than I had, and tucked me into bed with a story. I heard a lot of yelling from their room afterwards. It wasn't long after that that my mother left us.

"Ellie, honey, wake up," Asher called to me quietly as he brushed the hair from my face. His voice was smooth and I just wanted him to keep talking.

I startled and looked around the room, finally settling my eyes on him, and smiled. He assisted me into the dinning room where Thanksgiving dinner was ready. The table had been elegantly decorated with a fall theme and set with gold trimmed dishes. A giant turkey sat on a platter in the middle of the table with a variety of steaming dishes scattered along the tabletop between the decorations. Wine glasses were filled with a sparkling white wine and everyone held a glass, toasting to new family and another prosperous year.

Everyone at the table was dressed nicely, except me. I had on faded blue jeans, a t-shirt, and my hair desperately needed a brush. It didn't matter to anyone what I was wearing as I was ushered to a seat after the toast and everyone began asking how I was feeling. Max and Molly argued about who would get the biggest serving of pie after dinner, Asher and Benedict talked about the football game, and Marceline looked around for Asher's father.

"Where's Dad?" Andrea asked as she noticed her mother looking for him.

"I'm not sure. He ran into the office to grab something and said he'd be right back."

"On Thanksgiving?" Andrea asked.

"You know your father. He never stops working."

"Should we wait for him?" Asher asked.

"No. Let's all get something to eat. I'll set aside a plate for him for later," she said with a look of anxiety. "Andrea, why don't you start the thankful list."

"This year, I'm thankful for my kids, having a wonderful job, and another year of health," Andrea said proudly.

Benedict, taking his cue, "I'm thankful to have a roof over our heads and this fabulous meal before us."

"I'm thankful that I have a nice teacher this year," Max said with a big smile and looked at his sister.

"I'm thankful for Mommy and Daddy," Molly said.

"I'm thankful that all of you can be here with us today. I'm thankful that we have Ellie joining our family. And I'm thankful that we are all healthy," Marceline said as she winked at me.

Asher squeezed my hand as I spoke up. "I'm thankful for my new career, finding Asher, and joining this family."

Asher planted a kiss on my cheek as he held his glass of wine in the air for another toast. "I'm thankful to have met someone so absolutely amazing, loving, and caring. And thankful she agreed to become my wife! She is the last piece of my puzzle."

Everyone raised their glasses in thanks and began to fill their plates. Roasted turkey, cranberry sauce, mashed potatoes, fresh bread, green beans… It all looked baked to perfection and I felt some appetite returning despite my fear that I might become sick again.

After everyone was stuffed, Asher and Benedict headed back to the theater for more football, leaving the girls and children in the dining room. Marceline picked up her plate and took it to the kitchen. I had to admit I was a bit shocked since every time I'd been to Asher's parents, Albert had done everything for her. Andrea followed suit and I assumed that Albert was given the evening off on account of the holiday. How generous, I thought sarcastically. I stood and began to take my own plate to the kitchen when I was stopped by Marceline and told that she and Andrea would take care of everything. I was to go rest on the couch.

Without argument, I returned to my post in the living room. From there, I heard when Asher's dad returned home and argued briefly with Marceline before he headed to the theater to watch football. I smiled to myself, thinking how Asher's family seemed to fit my definition of a normal family. I snuggled into the blanket a little more and closed my eyes, feeling sleepy with a stomach filled with comfort food.

On Wednesday, things were finally going smooth at work. Asher and I had returned from our wonderful visit to his parents house on Sunday evening, and everything seemed perfect in our lives again. I hadn't looked forward to returning to work, but I was ready. I had taken my assignment with a smile and was ready when my new admission arrived.

The patient was a forty-eight-year old woman being admitted with end-stage liver cancer. Her devoted mother seemed reluctant to leave her side. The patient, born with cerebral palsy, remained her own person, was college educated, and did many things independently. Her mother had been her caregiver her entire life, not trusting anyone else to help with her daughter's care. Despite the many medical challenges the patient had faced, she remained upbeat and positive. Something seemed off with their connection though and as I worked on my admission assessment, the mother answered every question I had, sometimes speaking over the patient.

The patient was kind anytime I asked her to do something for me, but the mother was pushy and aggressive. The mother insisted on watching over my shoulder, and I was quickly becoming frustrated with her being in my way. When the mother stated she didn't plan to leave the patient's bedside, I caught the patient rolling her eyes.

Acting on intuition, I found the social worker and explained my feelings. I couldn't place my finger on it, but I was pretty sure something wasn't right. Together, we agreed on a plan, and she asked the mother to go to her office to sign some paperwork.

"Okay, now that your mom is gone, be real with me. How are things *really* going?"

"Horrible. She won't leave me alone anymore. She used to let me do things without her, but for the last six months or so, she's with me twenty-four seven. I can't stand it. I'm a grown woman!"

"Yeah, that's got to be super frustrating! Do you know why she changed?"

"No idea. When I asked her, she said it's because she's afraid that if she leaves me, I'll get sick and need her. Despite making all of my own decisions, I have needed her help physically, so I didn't have any control over it. It's so stupid though. I have a phone and I can call her if I need her."

"That must be hard."

"Well, when the doctor told me a few days ago that I have end stage cancer, I made the call to hospice when she was in the kitchen getting lunch ready. When the nurse showed up, my mom flipped her lid. Too bad. I told the nurse that I didn't want to die at home and wanted to come here. And the rest is history!" she said triumphantly.

"What are your goals while you're here?" I asked.

"To have a chance to breathe again. To see my friends without my mom in the room. To have privacy! To die on my own terms, not hers." she said.

"Gotcha. So let's create a plan. What are your thoughts?"

"I'd like to have her banned from this facility for a few days," she took a deep breath and continued. "I need a chance to breathe. I want to see the doctor without her here. I'm not going to die tomorrow or anything, so I'd really just love a break from her. Then, we can go from there. Would that be possible?" she asked hopeful.

"Yep. We can make that happen. Let me go talk to the social worker and find out the best way to handle it."

"Good luck. It's not going to go over well. She's been threatening me more and more so be prepared for that too."

"Don't worry, she won't be the first person to threaten me. I've got this, but that's for the heads up!" I said as I closed the door behind me, appreciating the warning.

She was right. I'd pulled the social worker out of her office to explain the situation and then together, we told the mother her daughter's wishes. She went ballistic. She promised to call the police, the mayor, and anyone else who would listen. She said we were violating her parental rights. Every other legal term she could think of, she hurled our direction. Instead of reacting, we escorted her from the building. As we got closer to the door, she seemed to get more and more frantic, aggressive, and combative. Eventually, *we* were the ones who called the police, and they were kind enough to finish her eviction from the building.

Why was she so insistent about being with her daughter around the clock? Bells inside me were triggering, and Munchausen by Proxy was all I could think about. Things just weren't making sense. What was I missing?

I tried to piece together a timeline of her medical history using what I knew and the medical chart, but the reality was becoming clear. Her symptoms weren't all fitting of cerebral palsy or liver cancer. My gut continued to tell me that things weren't adding up. She was smart, beautiful, and fully aware that her mother was up to something. She'd been right to contact a hospice when she received a terminal diagnosis.

Word had gotten around that my patient's mother had gone insane, and the nurses were talking about it as I entered the nursing lounge to gather my stuff at the end of the day. Everyone was throwing out suggestions on the mother's motivation, but the one common idea was clinical insanity. We all agreed the patient was lucky to get out while she still had her wits about her.

Gossip the next day was that her mother had made three attempts to return to the building throughout the evening shift. The police had finally explained that to her that if they were called one more time for her trespassing, she would be taken to jail. That had seemed to do the trick, and she'd given up for the night. The patient had unplugged her phone, and explained to me on morning rounds that she'd had the best night of sleep in her life.

I noticed she was sweating excessively. She hadn't been doing that yesterday. When I called attention to it, she said that it happened regularly, and she barely noticed it anymore. She would get a funny taste in her mouth, start to drool, and sweat like crazy. After a few hours, it would all stop for a while and then pick back up a few hours later. Sometimes, she'd start to vomit or have stomach cramps. Her mother had always freaked out when she started the cycle and used it as an excuse to never leave her.

She didn't have a fever and for the most part, her vital signs were within normal limits for her. Overall, she didn't seem too bothered by these symptoms and didn't want me to do anything about them. She was one of the sweetest people I'd met, and I was really bothered by the unfair hand she'd received at life. I was drawn to her, and I couldn't help it.

Ms. CP, as I'd decided to call her, seemed relaxed and happy without her mother hovering over her. I wanted to do something special for her, so I gathered up her lunch tray and headed for her room. When I presented it to her, she freaked out.

"I can't eat that stuff!" She cried.

"What? What's wrong?"

"That stuff is going to make me sick!"

"What do you mean? Which stuff?"

"All of it. If I eat it, I'm going to be puking within the hour. Not to mention the cramps and reflux before and after."

"Okay. Is there something else we can make you?"

"I'll just drink an Ensure. I seem to tolerate that without problems," she said calming down as I took the tray off her over the bed table.

"Okay. Are you sure that's enough?"

"I've survived on it this long, haven't I?" She laughed nervously. "My mom always gives me Ensure for breakfast and everything is fine. When she serves me lunch, I'm a hot mess. When the explosions have ended, I usually drink another Ensure and life is good. When she brings dinner, I'm a hot mess again. I tried refusing to eat, but she forced me to. Ugh. I'll just take the Ensure. I'm nauseous just thinking about eating."

"Okay. I can handle Ensure," I said out loud, keeping in all of the things I actually wanted to say.

The more I learned about this mother, the more I hated her. Who does something like that to their child? Who forces them to eat when they are sick? Why hadn't she had this problem investigated? Now, I wasn't a mother, but I certainly would have made an appointment with a gastroenterologist if my child puked up every meal I made her.

Internally, I had a battle raging inside me. Would I rather have this type of mother or my own mother who had left? It was like picking the lesser of two evils, either way, there wouldn't be a winner. Trying not to think about it, I headed off to my other patient's room.

"Are you the nurse?" A tall, broad shouldered man asked when I knocked on the door.

"Yes," I said hesitantly.

"Good. My dad is having difficulty breathing and needs some more of that medicine they gave him earlier."

I assessed the resident and his respirations were elevated, I counted thirty-six, with inspiratory wheezing heard. A tall man himself, his feet were touching the footboard as he slid down in bed and his sheets were soaked from sweat. The oxygen cannula remained in place in his nose, but the tubing wasn't connected to anything. The hospital gown he wore had one sleeve unbuttoned and his glasses were on upside down.

"You don't look too comfortable. I'm going to go grab your Duoneb and your pain medicine. I'm also going to see if Marissa is

226

available to come help me get you and your bed cleaned up. I'm guessing you'll feel much better after all that. Where is your nebulizer?" I said as I looked around the room for the compact machine.

"The nebulizer is over by the window," the son said calmly.

"I don't think anything is going to make me comfortable anymore," the patient remarked.

"No? Why do you say that?" I asked.

"Everything I do is uncomfortable. I'm struggling for air all the time and I'm just miserable!" he said breathlessly.

"I'm going to try to make you unmiserable," I said with a smile.

"Ha! Where were you when I picked up that first cigarette? I should have listened to my mother. Mothers always know best," he said with a laugh and eyed his son. I was pretty sure my mother hadn't known best, but really, what did I know about mothers?

"I'm not sure I was born yet when you had your first cigarette," I joked.

"I'm sure you weren't either!" He laughed the best he could and I left to get his meds.

When Marissa and I returned about ten minutes later, the son had left and the patient was laying in bed with his oxygen cannula on the floor, a cigarette in his mouth, and fumbling with a lighter. Marissa and I both made a mad dash for the lighter, yelling "no" as we went. He was quite irritated at being stopped, and made that perfectly clear when he began to fight for the lighter.

"What are you doing?" he said when the lighter was safely in my pocket and out of sight.

"What are *you* doing?" I asked, trying to catch my breath and slow my heart rate back to normal.

"I just wanted a smoke."

"You know that you can't smoke in our building."

"Fine then, take me outside. I don't know why I can't just smoke in here anyway."

"Besides the fire marshall and the State, it's not healthy for you, the staff, visitors, or anyone who would be in this room in the future."

"Screw that. I'm dying. Let a dying man smoke," he pleaded, reaching for my pocket.

"You just told me you regret even starting this habit."

"Yep, but I did and now I have to see it through. Give me back my damn lighter," he demanded as I pushed his hand away from my pocket and took a step back.

"I can't. Do you still want the medicine I brought you?"

"If I can't have my lighter, then I don't want your medicine either. I'll die suffering," he folded his arms across his chest defiantly.

"Okay, if that's what you'd like. Hit your light if you change your mind," I said as I spun around and left the room.

Marissa followed me, shaking her head. We walked back towards the med room together and at the same time saw Ms. CP's mother outside the front door. So much for my day running smoothly, I thought. Rather than dealing with the mother, I called social work and decided to let them handle her. I slipped away to the nursing lounge for a quick bite of lunch before I began my rounds again.

"Is that all you're going to eat?" a voice asked as I pulled my lunch from it's bag.

"Uh, yes," I answered as I looked up and saw Paige. "Why?"

"Oh nothing," she said lazily.

I chose not to engage her and instead picked up my phone and opened Facebook, turning my body away from where she sat in an attempt to avoid her. I could feel her watching me and the more irritated I became, the less appetite I had. Finally, I let her win and packed up what I hadn't eaten and returned my bag to the refrigerator and headed back to the floor. My patients were causing me enough stress today and I didn't need Paige adding to it.

Tenth Month: December

The store shelves were lined with decorations for Christmas and the music was equally as cringe-worthy. I wasn't in the mood for Christmas this year. I should have been feeling holly and jolly, but instead I was a scrooge. Not only were my emotions riding a rollercoaster, my patients had been confusing and mysterious. I was supposed to be excited for the month ahead - excited to be spending the holidays with Asher and his family, but instead, I was exhausted and my body ached.

I pushed through the crowds at the store, found the one item I was looking for, and then tried to wait patiently in line. The scraggly haired woman next to me looked me over head to toe before realizing I was watching her and quickly looking away. Maybe I should have bought a few more things so the one item I had wouldn't have looked so painfully obvious in my hands. A little boy was singing "Jingle Bells", a teenager typed on a cell phone, and a mother tried to shush a baby. All the different noises and the number of people in my close proximity made me feel like I was in a cage, and I felt my anxiety steadily climbing.

My patience had run out by the time I reached the cashier, and I didn't even care when she looked at me with pity. She tried to make small talk, but I wanted to get the hell out of there before my head exploded from the overwhelming stimuli in the store. I just wanted her to put the item in a bag and let me go home. Her cute smile and sing-song like voice was just the icing on the cake and I was trying so very hard to be patient and kind.

I had roughly one hour until Asher would be home from his dinner meeting, and I didn't have precious time to spare. I'd gotten out of work, rushed straight to the store, and then sped home. I couldn't stop thinking about what my patient had said. She had left me confused and all I wanted was to crawl into my bed at home and take a nap.

Everyone called her "Grandma" despite the fact that she had no living relatives. She was nearing one hundred and weighed about the same. She had a good sense of humor and was always the patient I hoped to see on my assignment list. I'd been happy to see her when I walked into her room, but she hadn't had the same spunk she usually did.

"Hey beautiful lady. What's going on?" I asked sympathetically.

"I'm tired today. I think today's going to be the day," she said dramatically as she patted my hand.

"Are you sure?"

She usually told the staff that it was her day to die when she was having a difficult day, but we were usually able to get her laughing within a matter of moments. Today, I hadn't been able to and she had been more tired than she normally was. I had just smiled and tucked her in, kissed her forehead, and opened the blinds to let the light in before I left.

Ms. CP smiled when I entered her room and told me all about her visit with her mother the day before. She'd been cautious, but didn't want to completely shut her mother out. It was then that I noticed her gastrointestinal symptoms had improved since she had admitted to Rolling Hills rather than worsened. Was it a coincidence? In fact, over the last week without her mother, color returned to her cheeks, her vital signs had stabilized, and her stomach cramps had significantly decreased.

"My niece visited yesterday also," she said enthusiastically. "She got accepted into medical school!"

"That's amazing! Where will she go?"

She thought for a moment, then replied, "I can't remember what she said."

"I can't remember what I had for breakfast, let alone something that happened yesterday!" I joked and we both laughed. "You seem to be feeling pretty good lately."

"Yeah, I feel like myself again."

"I'm glad to hear that."

"Have you decided to let your mother visit again?"

"I told her she could visit every few days. I miss her, but I don't want to be overwhelmed again."

"That's understandable."

"I've been thinking. Do you think the doctor here would run some lab tests?"

"It's not something we generally do. Whats up?" I curiously asked.

"Well, I'm feeling so much better than a week ago and want to see what my lab work looks like. To see if it's better, ya know?" she suggested hopefully.

"It never hurts to ask. What will you do if it is better?"

"I'm not sure exactly."

"Any specific tests you want run?" I asked inquisitively.

"A CBC, CMP, and a heavy metal panel," she said as she locked eyes with me.

"A heavy metal panel?"

"A heavy metal panel," she repeated with confidence, her voice strong and steady.

I'd understood her clear as day when she said it the first time, but having her repeat it meant I was absolutely sure of what she'd just said. It was an interesting request and not one I'd encountered before, but I was still so new to nursing. If the results came back positive, what would that mean exactly? Reading the confusion on my face, Ms. CP spoke.

"I've been researching my disease for as long as I can remember and yesterday when I saw my mom again, I realized that some of my symptoms have gotten better or disappeared. I looked into them by themselves and not together with my CP. Honestly, I have more questions than answers at this point."

"I'm not sure what to say, but I'll find out if we can get some lab work done."

"Try to keep it quiet, if you can, because if my mom finds out, all hell will break loose!"

"I will. I saw what happened last time you gave me that warning."

"I know. That's why I told you, and not a nurse yesterday."

I smiled and left her room. My mind was lost in thought for the rest of the shift. When I returned to my sweet elderly lady in the other room just before the end of my shift, she opened one eye and looked at me when I entered. She was laying on her back with her arms folded across her abdomen and a multi-colored crochet throw across her lower body.

"How's it going?" I whispered as I approached her.

With her one eye opened, she smiled and said, "not dead quite yet."

I laughed softly to myself and began to walk to the door when she spoke again, and I turned around to hear her better.

She inhaled deeply and then said, "tell him about the baby" as she exhaled.

"Huh?" I asked, confused.

She didn't answer and she didn't move. In fact, she ceased breathing at all. How could she say something like that and then just die? What did she mean? Tell him about the baby? What baby? Who was the him I was supposed to tell? I grabbed my stethoscope and listened as hard as I could for a heartbeat or a breath. Nothing. I would never have an answer.

Sitting in my car in the parking lot while it warmed up, I continued to think about what my patients had said throughout the day. It was too

233

much to wrap my mind around. A heavy metal panel? Tell him about the baby? Was it a full moon? Was that stuff real? Why did every shift lately leave me feeling physically and emotionally drained?

Just as I turned the key in the ignition, I felt a moment of clarity and a small spark in my brain triggered. It was like finding the last piece to a puzzle you've been working on - pure satisfaction to finally have the answer. That is when I went to the store.

"Ellie? I'm home," Asher called as he set his keys on the table by the door.

"I'm in the bedroom."

Asher appeared in the doorway holding a bouquet of deep wine red roses and a cheesy smile on his face. I laid in bed, under the covers, already dressed in my pajamas. He crawled onto the bed and gently planted a kiss on my lips and handed me the bouquet. The kiss, gentle and sweet, sent a chill down my spine and for a moment, I felt a desire starting to rise inside me. His eyes were bright and his smile was genuine.

"Thank you. They are beautiful! What's up?" I asked, curious.

"I know you haven't been feeling well lately and have been having a hard time at work, so I wanted to bring you something to make you smile. And I have some good news!" He seemed extremely proud of himself.

"I have some news for you too."

"You go first," he said enthusiastically.

"No, let's hear your news first."

"Okay, I'll go first. I got a promotion today!" he said with a return of the big, cheesy smile.

"That's awesome. I'm proud of you!"

"Thanks! What's your news?"

234

"Well, I hope your promotion means more vacation time because I want you to be with me at my OB visits." I waited for him to catch on.

"I'll be with you anywhere you need me to, regardless of a promotion." It had gone over his head.

"That's good. There will be an appointment about once a month for the first few months, and then every 2 weeks, and towards the end it'll be every week." I tried again.

"What kind of visits did you say?"

"OB."

"OB? What's OB?" his confusion was dissolving his cheesy smile.

"Obstetrician."

"Ellie, I'm an engineer, not a nurse. Give it to me straight," he said, clearly annoyed.

"I'm pregnant."

His cheesy smile quickly turned to a jaw drop and back to a cheesy smile. He put his hands over his mouth and took a sharp breath in and slowly exhaled it. Then, he ruffled his hair, all while staying completely silent. I could see him take the sentence in, compute it, and then the words clicked.

Finally, he spoke, "are you serious?"

That weekend, Mary Jane put the last bobby pin into my hair and brushed another layer of blush over my cheekbones. Then, I smoothed my little black dress over my body and slid my feet into my satin pumps. I hooked an earring in each ear and looked in the mirror. I could see Mary Jane smiling behind me.

"Wow" I said quietly as I stared at my reflection.

"I know, right?" Mary Jane asked excitedly. "That LBD looks smokin' hot on your bod."

I shot her a glance. "Who are you?" I asked with a laugh.

"Stella!" she began to laugh. "Clearly I've spent too much time in the carpool with my daughter." I could easily envision her pre-teen daughter, Stella, saying those words.

"I guess so."

With perfect timing, Asher knocked on the door, asking if I was ready. He had been kicked out of the bathroom for the last hour as Mary Jane beautified me for the holiday ball put on by Asher's company. His mouth dropped open the moment he laid eyes on me, and he let out a quiet whistle.

"Wanna skip the ball and stay home?" he asked provocatively while raising his eyebrows.

"Hey! I'm still here, ya know!" Mary Jane protested quickly as she lightly slapped his shoulder.

But, the ball turned out to be a bust. It was held in the ballroom of an older hotel and was too small for all the people that arrived. Dinner included dry chicken, wilted salad, and tough, rubbery green beans. The people who sat at our table were older and talked about muscle aches, Medicare insurance plans, and debated the merits of today's technology compared to "their day and age." I had enough of these talks at work. Needless to say, we were home and in bed by midnight.

By Monday, my energy seemed to have returned to a respectable level, thankfully, and I hit the ground running the moment I walked in the door at work. I barely had time to use the bathroom, let alone take a lunch break. It was becoming quite common to miss my breaks and my body was adapting moderately well.

By the time the end of the shift arrived, I couldn't wait to get home and soak in the bathtub. Instead, Paige caught me just as I was ready to leave and asked to talk with me privately. I dreaded talking to her in public, let alone privately. However, I was curious what she wanted to talk about. Was it just to push my buttons more? I didn't know, but I followed her into a small office and let her close the door behind us.

"I finally figured it out. I've been suspicious for a while now, but I know you're the one granting all these patient's wishes," she said, pointing her finger at me. "You have to stop. I don't know why you're doing it or what you get out of it, but you have to stop. If management finds out it's you, you'll be fired for sure."

"That doesn't make any sense," I said annoyed.

"It doesn't? Well, word is getting out that if you go to Rolling Hills and die, your family will receive big, expensive gifts."

"And that's a bad thing?"

"You aren't getting it, are you?" she said with an obvious eye roll.

"I guess not."

"What about the families that *aren't* getting fancy gifts when their loved one dies?"

"What about them?"

"Oh my God," she said with another eye roll and a shake of her head. "They are going to get pissed off. They are going to be pissed off and aim it right at Rolling Hills. Why didn't *they* get a fancy after-life gift? If the news catches wind of what's been happening, it's going to be a shit show around here!" she said with exasperation.

"What does it have to do with me?" I asked, still pleading the fifth.

"Fuck! When we have the memorial picnic in February and all the families get talking to each other, everyone will know. I'm telling you, it's gonna be big news. And management isn't going to be happy when the families who didn't get anything come after *them*! You can't just pick and choose who to give gifts to! Not to mention, what if people started to come to Rolling Hills *expecting* fancy gifts?" her voice raising, irritated.

"Got it," I said, trying to pacify her and stop her rant.

"Got it? That's all you're going to say? Just admit it. Admit you're the one granting wishes!" Her face turned red with anger.

"No," I said with a steady voice.

"Listen! I'm not playing games. I'll go straight to management and end your games right now," she said through clenched teeth.

"I don't see what management even has to do with this?"

"You're dense, Ellie. People will think it's Rolling Hills footing the bill for the extravagant gifts, not some wannabe superhero nurse. Management will care, trust me."

I didn't answer. I turned myself around, and walked right out of the office. I walked right out the front door and straight to my car. It was either that or slap her across the face. I sat for a few moments in the cold car, waiting for it to warm up, and waiting for my breathing to slow down and my heart rate to return to normal from the rush of adrenaline. What exactly was Paige's point? Once I'd settled down, I had to admit that I could see her point, but how was it her or anyone's business what I did with my money? And was it truly necessary to call me a wannabe superhero?

I was still irritated when I met Asher in the parking lot of the obstetrician's office. I filled out what seemed like a million papers before being led back to a small exam room. After the medical assistant finished with me, the nurse practitioner came in. She talked, asked questions, and then used the doppler to listen for a heartbeat. Asher and I held our breath until that sweet sound brought the doppler to life. All the irritation I felt when we arrived melted away and was replaced with a warm, loving feeling instead.

"Let's keep this to ourselves until we can tell my parents at Christmas, okay?" Asher asked with a smile.

When I awoke the next morning, I was excited for a day of Christmas shopping with Mary Jane. I wasn't sure I'd be able to keep my lips sealed on the whole pregnancy thing. Mary Jane was my best friend and keeping something this big from her was going to be a challenge.

I browsed the stack of advertisements on the kitchen table as I drank my coffee and waited for Mary Jane to arrive. I made myself a list of whom I wanted to buy gifts for and smiled at finally having a list longer than a handful of people as I usually did. My heart hurt a little noticing that not a single person from my own family was on that list. I wasn't sure exactly what to buy for Asher's family, but he had told me to follow my gut and everyone would love it.

Mary Jane and I arrived at the outlet mall mid-morning and already the parking lot held a decent amount of cars. Not deterred, we picked a starting point and intended to move in a well choreographed pattern. We cruised through an appliance shop and a perfume store without buying a single thing. The third store was a children's clothing store and as Mary Jane and I browsed the racks, I picked up a particularly cute ceramic frame for an ultrasound picture. As I carried it, Mary Jane looked at me with complete confusion.

"What are you doing?"

"Shopping?" I said, playing dumb.

"I know *that*. What are you going to do with that frame?" she pointed to the frame in my hands.

"Put a picture in it and give it to Asher's parents for Christmas."

"What picture?"

"My ultrasound picture," I said as I looked at her with a childish grin on my face and she exploded into fits of joy, complete with squeals and hugs. I hadn't lasted very long.

"OMG. We have to celebrate this!" she finally said when she stopped her celebratory dance.

"What do you suggest?"

"Shopping?" We both broke out into more laughter.

239

When we had completed our shopping circuit, the trunk of my car was packed with bags and boxes and wouldn't fit another one if we tried. By all accounts, we had been successful. I had enjoyed spending a day with Mary Jane. It had been therapeutic, like old times.

On our way home, we stopped by Walmart. While Mary Jane went to the pharmacy counter, I snuck over to the layaway counter. I was full of joy and feeling generous. I loved the feeling each time I'd done one of my good deeds at work and I wanted to continue spreading the great fortune I'd been left.

Honestly, I didn't need the millions of dollars I had sitting in an interest bearing account. I'd rather use it for good. If I donated to charity, I couldn't control what it was spent on, so I wanted to continue just randomly doing good deeds when I saw fit. I wanted to do it my way. True to my personality, I wanted everything to be spontaneous.

There were a few people standing behind the blue desk, but no customers were in line or being helped. It was perfect. In just a few quick minutes, I could make someone's Christmas wishes come true. I walked up to the first register and asked to make a payment on an account.

"What's the name?" she asked in a monotone voice.

The cashier had long auburn hair, was probably still in her teens, and wore one of those plastic stretch choker things that were popular in the nineties. Her jeans hugged her full figure frame and her belt was bedazzled. She had what I called "resting bitch face" or a permanent look of irritation. Clearly, she was not pleased I'd interrupted her.

"Um. Can you pick a random account?" The other cashiers stopped what they were doing and began to watch us.

"No, ma'am, I can't. I need a name."

"Smith." I said as the other employees laughed.

"There are twenty-one Smiths in our system. You're going to have to be more specific." Her attitude was bothering me.

"Look, I want to pay off the layaway for complete strangers. Are you going to help me, or do I have to talk to your manager?" I threatened, knowing I didn't have much time until Mary Jane came looking for me.

"Whoa. You don't have to get aggressive, ma'am. I can help you. Like, you want me to just pick a random account?" I was glad she'd surrendered because I didn't really want to pick a fight with this kid.

"Yes, I'd like you to pull up a random account for me, please. I don't have a lot of time," I said with urgency.

"Okay, here's one. Priscilla Parker."

"Okay, how much does she owe?"

"$523.13 is what it shows." I handed her my Visa.

"Now you call them, and have them pick up their items?"

"Yeah, I guess so," she said.

I wasn't convinced she was going to call them. I didn't have time to press her about it though. The recipients would find out eventually, right? I looked over my shoulder, and didn't see Mary Jane.

"Pull up another one."

She did some typing, and then said, "Here's a Robert Small. He owes $301.39 on his account."

Just as she handed me the Visa back with my receipts, I noticed Mary Jane walking near the checkout lanes. I wished the workers a Merry Christmas. With the Walmart teen having sucked out all of my holiday cheer with her bad attitude, Mary Jane and I returned to my house, and I helped her load her packages into her SUV. I didn't even bother to unload the car before I went inside and started a bubble bath.

I was pleased to see Paige wasn't working when I walked into work on Wednesday, and instantly felt a little more energetic as I took report. Being that Christmas was the following week, Rolling Hills had been decorated with holiday spirit and that included a Christmas tree in the nursing lounge. Someone had made little ornaments with each of our names written on them, and small stockings hung along the bottom edge of the dry erase board on the wall.

Marci handed me a twinkly light necklace, and I reluctantly put it around my neck. It made a nice addition to my stethoscope. I looked down at my patient list again and set off to begin my day. In the hall, I heard the familiar sounds of Christmas tunes playing through the speakers and saw that in the one day I'd had off, garland had been hung along every wall. When I stopped to take it all in, I admitted it looked spectacular.

"Isn't it beautiful?" Marci asked as she walked past me.

"Yeah," I called after her as she continued walking.

Just as I put my hand on the door knob of room 20, my phone rang and I stepped back from the doorway to answer it. I was being called to Penny's office and immediately, I felt like a teenager being paged to the principal's office. I began to revisit my steps in my head, trying desperately to think of things I could have done wrong to justify a visit to her office. I don't know why I immediately thought something was wrong, but what else would she call me for?

As I approached her office, I saw two police officers standing outside her door and my stomach began to do somersaults. They followed me into Penny's office, and she introduced them as Officer Perry and Officer Preston.

Penny invited all three of us to have a seat and I wasn't sure if I wanted to cry or vomit. Maybe I wanted to do both. The pregnancy hormones were making me crazy. Despite being the "wild one" as a teenager, I hated getting into trouble and I avoided it at all costs.

"Alright officers, this is the nurse who did the admission on the patient. Now, are we able to discuss what this is about?" Penny asked, looking concerned.

"Sorry to interrupt your day ladies. We appreciate you taking the time to speak with us. Recently, we were contacted, and informed that a heavy metal screening had taken place, and come back suspiciously positive. Social work notified the patient of the results, and we have opened a case regarding a potential poisoning," Officer Preston stated.

"Oh," Penny sighed as if she knew this might be coming.

I shot her a look, as all of this was news to me, "What?"

"Ellie, let me catch you up quick," Penny said, realizing that I was hearing this for the first time. "The heavy metal screening results came back showing an elevated arsenic level. Per her chart, we are unsure where exposure could have happened naturally. As the patient had requested this testing to be done, Connie went in, gave her the results, and asked how she'd like us to proceed. I wasn't aware that Connie contacted the police until just this morning when these officers arrived. Now it makes sense."

"Wow." A wave of relief came over me, realizing that I wasn't in trouble.

"We asked to speak with you, Ellie, to get more information regarding her admission, and interactions with her mother." A light bulb turned on in my brain as Officer Perry spoke. "What were your initial impressions?"

"Well… When they first arrived, as I recall, the mother was very overbearing and domineering. She answered questions for the patient and didn't want to leave her side. The patient expressed that she needed a break from her mother, and asked that we ban her from the facility for a few days. The mother went ballistic and made many attempts to return, and I believe, at one point, the police were contacted."

"Yes, I reviewed that report," Officer Preston said as he flipped through a notepad.

"A few days later, she… the patient… told me that she had noticed her symptoms had gotten better since she'd arrived. She told me she'd done some research and that's when she asked for a heavy metal screening to be done. I contacted Penny."

"Did the mother make any statements that may have seemed... out of place?" Officer Perry asked, poised to write in her notepad.

"Nothing specific. I got a weird vibe from her, but I don't remember anything she *said* that set off warning bells. It was just the way she acted that caused me to become concerned," I replied.

"What type of behaviors?" Officer Perry asked.

"Like I said before, refusing to leave the patient's side, answering questions for her, the way she watched over my shoulder as I did my assessment. Then, the way the patient acted relieved when her mother wasn't in the room anymore. It was just suspicious."

"May we speak with the patient?" Officer Preston asked, looking at Penny and then at me.

"Of course," Penny replied without hesitating.

"Is that all you need from me?" I asked.

"Yeah, I think so. If not, we'll find you," Officer Preston said with a small laugh.

I headed back towards room 20 to begin my day, but I couldn't help thinking about what had just happened. Poisoned? If she really was poisoned by her mother, then I was right about Munchausen by Proxy syndrome. The worst part would be that no one caught on before she ended up with liver cancer. I felt a range of emotions, but pushed them aside so that I could focus on my patients for the day.

The nursing lounge was full of chatter at lunchtime as everyone gossiped about the police showing up and the potential poisoning. Rather than participate, I ate my lunch quickly and then found an empty room to make some phone calls. When I finished and emerged from the empty room, the hallway was filled with Christmas carolers singing "Deck the Halls" so I headed in the opposite direction and walked the long way around the building to my patient's rooms. I wasn't in the mood to be "merry and bright."

Towards the end of the shift, when I was sure most staff members would be charting or finishing tasks, I slipped into the nursing lounge and was relieved to find it empty. I had planned on doing something special for Christmas for everyone, but had been waiting for the right moment. With Christmas only two days away, I was running out of time. I dug in my bag and found a stack of Christmas cards and began to quickly place them into staff mailboxes. I wanted to be as discreet as possible so that hopefully no one would know the cards were from me. When they started talking about it later, I'd suggest it was a Secret Santa or something.

I was sure Paige would assume it was me from the get-go, but I didn't let that stop me. Despite my level of distaste for the woman, even she got a card with $500 in it, just as everyone else did. Had she not gotten a card, I'd have stooped to her level, and she'd have won. Instead, I was going to kill her with kindness and include her in my secret giving. I finished before anyone entered the lounge and I quickly left, and returned to my computer to finish my own charting.

On Christmas morning, I woke up feeling depressed and found a tray filled with breakfast and coffee on a little table next to my bed. Off to the side was a note from Asher wishing me a Merry Christmas. No matter how amazing Asher was and would be, I missed my dad and there was no way around it. This was the first Christmas without him and despite the fact that we were driving to Asher's parents in the afternoon, no one could replace the hole I felt in my heart.

When I finally decided to get out of bed and make my way into the living room, Asher was already showered and dressed and the car was loaded to the brim. He wrapped me in his arms, gave me a kiss on the forehead, grabbed my hand, and led me to the couch. Per my wishes, we hadn't decorated the house for Christmas, and therefore, didn't have a Christmas tree. Asher had been reluctant to go without one, but had relented when I promised we would next year.

He picked up a package wrapped in shiny blue snowflake paper with a red satin bow and handed it to me. His face reminded me of the boy in "A Christmas Story" when he thought about the BB gun. I carefully unwrapped the package and found another wrapped box. When I unwrapped the second box, I saw a Littmann stethoscope. When I opened the box, there was a beautiful plum colored stethoscope with my future name engraved on it.

"Oh, Ash! I love it!"

"Is it the right one?" he asked hesitantly.

"Yes! And you put my name on it."

"Sure did," he said proudly.

"Thank you. It's perfect."

I set the stethoscope down, gave him a hug, and kissed him passionately. I then felt him twist me around so that I was laying on the couch, and he was laying half of his weight on top of me. I knew exactly where this was leading and I didn't stop it. I wanted him as much as he wanted me.

We were finally on the road an hour later than planned, but neither of us cared. We would get there when we got there. The roads were pretty clear of traffic, and we were making good time until I was reminded that I was pregnant. Suddenly and without warning, I would have to pee, and Asher would have to quickly find a rest stop. By the third emergency stop, I could see I was testing his patience, but I didn't have a choice.

Overall, we arrived at his parent's house three hours later than expected, and by the time we knocked on the front door, his mother was in a near panic state. We had answered all of her many phone calls as we traveled, but that just wasn't enough. About the fourth call, she told

Asher that she wouldn't relax until he was in her living room. He had rolled his eyes and assured her we were on our way. Then, at the end of each call, she would remind him not to speed. He would hang up the phone and laugh each time, but I secretly knew he enjoyed her many calls. Having lost both of my own parents, *I* was enjoying her many calls just as much as Asher.

Our bags were left by the door, and Marceline ushered us straight into the living room when we arrived. It was late and the kids had already opened their gifts, and the remnants lay scattered across the floor as they ran in and out of the room with their new toys. The adults sat around the room sipping champagne and watching "A Christmas Story" on the television. Asher had warned me that it was a family tradition to watch Christmas movies together on Christmas. The following day would be spent watching college football.

The living room was decorated impressively with a large evergreen tree decorated in gold and maroon as the centerpiece of the big picture window. Atop the tree sat an elegant angel with golden, sparkly wings. Stockings were lined by the fireplace and the pictures on the walls had been replaced with winter scenes instead of the garden ones that hung there the rest of the year. I noted my name embroidered on one of the stockings. It was heartwarming, and I was thankful to be accepted into such a loving family. The mantle held a nativity scene made of what appeared to be carved ivory. Marceline noted that it was a family heirloom when she caught me looking at it.

Andrea jumped up and took a small green package from under the tree and handed it to Asher, insisting that he open it. Inside was a wallet and he faked excitement. He then went to the tree and selected a red bag and handed it to his father. It continued on like this until all the presents from under the tree had been opened.

"Wait!" Asher exclaimed. "We have a few more. Ellie, will you go grab them from our bags?"

Everyone had a look of confusion on their faces as I ran to grab the other three gifts from our bags by the door. When I returned, I handed them to the appropriate people, and returned to my seat next to Asher. As they tore off the wrapping paper and opened the boxes, our secret was revealed.

"What is this?" Asher's father asked as he looked at the picture in the frame.

"It's an ultrasound picture, Dad," Asher responded.

Andrea, Benedict, and Marceline knew immediately what it meant, and they began to congratulate me when the realization finally hit Asher's father. He crossed the room with two steps and gave Asher a tight embrace. Once the congratulations settled down and everyone's questions had been answered, Andrea escaped to the kitchen and returned with a tray of snacks. It was nearing midnight at this point and all I wanted was to climb into the plush bed upstairs and fall asleep. Instead, I stayed in the living room and fell asleep with my head on Asher's lap while everyone watched Christmas movies.

When I woke up at the end of the movie, I noticed the stockings had all been filled. Everyone was picking up the room and heading for bed. A glance at the clock showed it was around two in the morning. Asher held my hand as we made our way upstairs to our bedroom.

Once nestled under the covers, I looked up into his eyes and said, "Merry Christmas."

The next morning, breakfast was interrupted by a loud bang from another room followed by a scream. Andrea jumped up and rushed from the room without hesitation. Asher rolled his eyes and ate another slice of bacon. I toasted him with my cup of coffee and took a sip of the steaming hot dark roast Albert had made.

Andrea returned to the breakfast nook carrying a crying child with blood dripping from his chin. He had run into something, still to be determined, and his teeth had cut into his bottom lip. Andrea, of course,

248

panicked and ready to drive him to the emergency room when Benedict had reminded her that I was a nurse.

I quickly calmed Max down, applied some pressure to the cut, and did a quick assessment. He would need a few stitches, but nothing an urgent care couldn't handle. Relieved, Andrea went upstairs to get dressed while Benedict got Max situated in the car. Asher and I agreed to watch Molly while they were gone.

"That was cool what you did," Asher said as he returned to his breakfast.

"What?"

"Ya know, calmed my sister down. I saw it really helped Max relax a little too."

"Just another day in the life of a nurse," I said with a giggle.

Four days later, Asher and I said our goodbyes, drove ourselves back to the airport near our house, and flew straight to New York City. I waited in the lobby of the hotel while Asher went to check us in. I sat down on an expensive circular couch that stretched around a large tree that reached at least two stories high. As I glanced around and watched the people moving about, I noticed a man standing near a window watching his cell phone intently. At this distance, it looked like Mystery Man, but I wasn't entirely confident.

I stood and began walking in his direction slowly, watching his every move so that I wouldn't lose sight of him. Just as I got near enough to get a clear look, a bellhop with a large luggage rack crossed in front of me and when it had passed, the man was gone. I quickly walked to where he had been and frantically looked around. He was gone. Had I imagined the entire thing?

I returned to the circle couch just as Asher reached it and handed me a credit card shaped room key. I glanced at the window one final time before following Asher toward a column of elevators. I wasn't sure if my mind had been playing tricks on me or if I had actually seen Mystery Man. I pushed all thoughts of Mystery Man aside, deciding I was paranoid.

We spent the next two days doing all the touristy things, such as watching a Broadway show, exploring Times Square, and ice skating near the Rockefeller Center. The atmosphere changed when New Year's Eve arrived and the barriers began to line the streets. I was excited to spend our first New Year's Eve together as well as my first in New York City.

I stepped out of the bathroom wearing a long, red sequined gown with a sweetheart neckline and did a twirl for Asher. He helped secure my necklace, and I tightened his tie before we headed off for our dinner reservations. I wrapped my shawl around me tighter when I was blasted with cold air as we exited the hotel, but the restaurant was only a short walk away, so I didn't complain.

Everywhere I looked, there were people, but Asher held my hand tightly as he navigated through the mass. I had never been one to mind crowds, but I was feeling slightly claustrophobic as I looked around. Finally, we reached our destination, and made our way inside.

The restaurant had live music when the dinner service was completed and televisions were brought in to show the programming from all the big networks. Our table sat near a bank of windows, and we had the perfect view to watch the ball drop from inside the cozy restaurant. As midnight neared, the restaurant offered free champagne and everyone began to push toward us as the countdown began.

10.. 9.. 8.. 7.. 6.. 5.. 4.. 3.. 2.. 1

Eleventh Month: January

(Part I)

Asher pulled me close, kissing me as "Auld Lang Syne" played from every speaker in the city and confetti flew from every direction. The sound inside the restaurant was deafening and the energy was palpable. When a man standing next to me attempted to kiss me during the celebration, I shoved him and leaned closer to Asher.

By 02:00 a.m., I was naked in Asher's arms back in our hotel room. I had no problems falling asleep a short time later, and slept until nearly 09:00 a.m. when Asher woke me so we could check out on time. While I enjoyed the experience of a New Year's Eve in Times Square, I was looking forward to getting back to our own home. I love being spontaneous, but there was never a bed quite like my own.

I stood in the bathroom mirror looking at my stomach from both the front and side. I could see the start of a small bump, but nothing that anyone else would notice. I thought about all the times my friends had gotten pregnant and how their lives had changed once the baby was born. My hormones were in full swing when I finally detached myself from the bathroom mirror.

"Asher, I want to fly to Las Vegas and get married right now," I announced as I stepped out of the bathroom.

"What?" Asher looked shocked.

"I want to fly to Las Vegas right now and get married," I repeated confidently.

"Uh… Have you been drinking?" he joked.

"No, sir. I have not."

"What brought this on?"

"Hormones," I said with a laugh.

"Ellie, I'll marry you any day of the week. If you're sure that's what you want, I'll get the tickets changed."

"I'm sure. We can always do a reception later. I don't have many family and friends to invite to some big wedding and this would take away all the pressure, don't you think? Not to mention, my father isn't here to walk me down the aisle. I can just see your mother forcing us into some elaborate show put on for her friends. And I'd be a fat duck waddling down the aisle."

"You make a valid point. About my mom, that is. You won't ever be a fat duck."

"We haven't gotten far enough into this pregnancy to accurately say never," I chided.

One minute I had been looking forward to getting back to our normal routine and settling back down and the next, I was yearning for something spontaneous again. An elopement was certainly spontaneous! But as we boarded the plane for Las Vegas instead of home, I thought more about it. The more I thought about it, the more confident I was that it was exactly what I wanted to do. I didn't want some southern plantation wedding. I wanted a quick wedding chapel in the middle of the desert, just the two of us. Or three.

When the plane landed and we'd reached our hotel room, we asked the concierge for a wedding chapel recommendation. He not only made a recommendation, he arranged transportation to the chapel, had potential wedding dresses sent to our room to be tried on, and had ordered flowers. I'd picked out a plain white sundress that hid the growing bump that only I noticed. I had no problems getting to sleep that night as I lay in bed with Asher's arm wrapped around my waist.

Eloping always had seemed like something I'd do. When I'd envisioned my wedding day as a little girl, it had always been a small

252

affair. As I got older, I thought about a destination wedding or something. I had even thought about just visiting the courthouse. I'd never enjoyed being the center of attention like that. I knew that by the time I'd invited everyone my dad would insist we had to, it would be a wedding with over five hundred guests on my side alone.

Then there was the fact that I had literally spent my youth flying by the seat of my pants and planning nothing. Once I'd settled down as an adult, life had become too boring at times. The thrill of making a decision and just acting on it right then and there felt exhilarating. A part of me felt like the old me again.

In the morning, we enjoyed a breakfast delivered by room service and took our time primping for the "best day of our lives." We met the driver in the lobby at eleven sharp and were headed to the wedding chapel for our appointment. As I looked up at the building, it glowed in the sunlight and the front window was covered in hearts of varying shades of red. It was definitely a stereotypical wedding chapel.

When the marriage license had been signed and we were officially husband and wife, we stepped from the chapel into the desert sun. Once my eyes adjusted to the sunlight, I noticed a man running down the sidewalk towards us. Asher and I watched, waiting to see what was happening. In his hand, he carried what looked to be a handgun. Noticing this, Asher stepped in front of me just in case it was, in fact, a real handgun.

A man wearing a suit appeared from the side of the chapel and tackled the running man when he was about twenty yards from us. Startled, I jumped back. The man in the suit flipped the runner onto his stomach and placed his knee into his back, holding him in place. The runner screamed to be freed as the man in the suit placed handcuffs on him and spoke into some sort of microphone.

Within moments, the local police arrived and took custody of the prisoner. Neither Asher nor I knew exactly what to say or do, so we stood there looking like tourists, frozen in place. Once the man in the suit finished talking to the police officer, he began to walk in our direction. It was then that I noticed it wasn't just any man, but the mystery man who had been showing up everywhere I was!

"Who the hell are you?" I shouted as he approached. "And why are you following me?"

"As I told you before, I am Jennings," he said as reached us.

"And why are you following me?"

"What do you mean?"

"I mean, why are you following me?"

"I guess I'm confused," he said.

"You're confused? Oh great," I said in disbelief.

"Well, I'm not *that* confused. I'm your security," he said, as if I should have known this already.

"What do you mean by that? I don't have any security. I don't *need* security."

"On the contrary, my dear..."

I cut him off before he could explain further, "Don't you call me dear! You don't know me."

"Ellie, my name is Jennings. I have been your personal security for nearly a year now. Before that, I was your father's personal security for almost twenty years!"

"What?" I thought about that for a moment. "Why?"

"Your dad has some pretty important contracts and had received threats on occasion. After someone made an attempt to hurt him, he hired me."

"What does that have to do with me? I'm not my father."

"Well, by extension, you are. The day your father passed away, I became *your* security. My job is to simply be in the same places that you are so that I can assess for threats and intervene, if possible, before a situation occurs. Just by being the owner of your father's company, you are at risk. You are the one with the contracts now."

"The owner?" Asher turned to me with a look of confusion.

"So who in the hell was that guy?" I pointed to the man he had been tackled, now in the back of a police car, and ignored Asher's question.

"Well… A few months back I got some intel from a trusted source that someone might attempt to kidnap you in exchange for information found within one of the contracts. I know it sounds completely crazy and like something from a movie, but I stepped up my detail at that point just in case."

"Wait a minute. Your father *owned* his company?" Asher continued looking for answers.

"I see. So you just follow me around?" I ignored Asher again.

"My goal is to simply always be in the background. Not seen and not heard. You've caught me a few times, but I really try hard to stay out of your sight." He scratched his head. "That was always important to your father. He didn't want to feel as thought he had a security detail. Instead, he just wanted to know that I was there."

"How long does all this security business last?"

"Well, I suppose it will continue until I retire or you fire me."

"When was someone going to tell me?" I demanded.

"I thought someone *had*," he admitted.

"How much am I paying you for all this special security?"

"Well, that's confidential."

"Confidential?"

"Another thing your father never wanted to know — how much the security was costing him," he laughed.

Asher continued to stand as he looked from me to Jennings and back again. Several times it looked like he had a question, but he never spoke. I sat down on the bench outside the chapel and tried to process all of this new information. I practically had my own secret service agent and I never even knew. That meant he was exceptionally skilled at his job, or I was exceptionally blind to the world around me. I thought back to the last twenty years and couldn't recall a single time my dad mentioned it or acted differently. Was I really that oblivious?

"Alright, Jennings. Here's the new deal," I said at last. "I'd like to know when you're around me. I want to be able to see you so I don't feel spied on. You don't have to sit directly next to me or anything. No hovering like an actual security guard, but it would be nice to be able to have you in my eyesight. Perhaps I would feel a little safer. You can keep how much money you make to yourself - I'll let you have that one."

"Ma'am, you have a deal! That will actually make my job a hell of a lot easier if I don't have to work so hard trying to hide in plain sight."

"I'm still confused," Asher pipped up.

"So what else do you know about me, Jennings?" I asked curiously.

"Uh... That's confidential, Ma'am." Jennings gave an apologetic shrug and a small laugh, but I nodded acceptance.

"One last question."

"Anything."

"Do you.. or did you.. drive a white SUV?" The pieces of a lost puzzle began to click in my head.

He shifted his balance awkwardly and looked down at his feet. "I'd rather not say."

"You hit me?" I spoke barely above a whisper. "But why?"

"I fell asleep at the wheel." He said, looking ashamed.

I was flabbergasted and angry. He could have killed me. But he just disappeared instead and let everyone think I was crazy. I decided this would be a conversation for another time. I wanted to enjoy my day and I didn't want to let something I had no control over have control of me.

When we returned to the hotel room, I was ready to take a nap. It had been a busy day thus far and the excitement from our marriage and with the discovery of Jennings, I was mentally drained. Asher had given up trying to get answers from me. I hadn't exactly lied to him, but I had certainly left out the information about my father *owning* the company. I knew that I should have confessed *all* my secrets to him, but the longer time went on, the harder it became until now, when it was impossible.

When we returned home the following day, I felt nothing but jet lag. It had been a wonderful vacation, but I was ready to sleep in my own bed. It had been so rejuvenating to fly by the seat of my pants again, but this time I was eager to come home to my own bed and return to a routine. Clearly, I had matured and accepted adulthood. When Asher asked why I even went to work anymore, considering my great wealth, I explained that I didn't do it for the money. I did it because it was something I had a passion for and it fulfilled my purpose in life.

"You just work so you can fund your other lifestyle, right?" he joked.

"Is that the one in which I own a motorhome or the one where I have my own personal secret-service-type security?"

"Hmm… Let me think about it," he flashed his pearly whites at me and tackled me onto the couch. Somehow he had come to terms with everything and had forgiven me.

When I returned to work a few days later, all the decorations had been removed from the hallways. The building was back to looking the way it had before the holidays started. I noticed the whiteboard had many new names signifying we'd lost many of our patients while I had been away. It was one of the things I didn't like about working at the hospice facility. Sometimes I wish I had more time to get to know the patients and truly understand their needs. Instead, I felt I spent all my time focusing on symptom management and ensuring that when they passed away they were as peaceful as possible.

As I took my seat in the nursing lounge, Paige walked in and sat down next to me. The smirk on her face read trouble, but I tried my best to ignore her. She talked animatedly to the other nurses and did her best to ignore *me*. I was completely fine with this. The less attention she paid to me, the better! When someone asked me a question and I answered, she pretended to notice me for the first time.

After she finished looking me over, she told me that it appeared I'd had too many cookies over my vacation as I'd gained some weight around the middle. I was flabbergasted that she would say something so rude. Feeling vicious, I looked her right in the eyes and told her I was pregnant.

From a girls night long ago, I knew that Paige and her husband had tried getting pregnant for many years but had failed. It was a low blow to tell her I was pregnant the way I did, but it had been equally horrifying for her to tell me I was getting fat. It had worked, and she hadn't said another word to me until report was done.

"You're going to hell, you know that?" Her face turned red with boiling anger.

"You'll be right there beside me."

I might have tolerated her bullshit when I was Ellie Arthur, but I wasn't going to tolerate it now that I was Ellie Grant. Something had come over me the moment she walked in and had taken a seat next to me. I didn't want to let her bully me anymore. I hadn't done anything wrong. I had simply stated the truth. I *had* gained weight around my middle section, but it wasn't from too many cookies. If she felt victimized from my response, that was her problem. Like it or not, my abdomen was going to continue growing.

"Did I hear you tell Paige that you're pregnant?" Jan leaned towards me and asked.

"Yep." I glowed when she said that word — pregnant.

As the day began to wind down, I had completed my charting and was ready to run out the door the moment I finished report. I had a date with Mary Jane at the restaurant down the street that I loved. Instead, I heard a loud crash as I walked down the hall and quickly changed directions, heading toward the noise. Laying on the floor in a pool of blood was a patient. Why did stuff like this always happen when you wanted to leave the most? I rushed to her side as I used my phone to call for help.

The laceration on her forehead was shaped like a moon and blood was pouring out of it. Another nurse appeared with a towel and some gloves. We applied pressure to her forehead and began assessing for other injuries. Situations like this always left us in a tricky spot since being sent to the emergency room wasn't something we did for hospice patients, but this woman needed stitches and there was no way around it.

By the time we had her loaded into the ambulance and finished charting, I had worked an hour past my scheduled time. Mary Jane had replied to my message that she was starving and still wanted to meet for dinner. Relieved, I didn't waste any time getting out of the building and into my car. My own belly was growling and a bowl of garlic parmesan was just what I was craving.

It was the following Tuesday when things started to unravel. The last few weeks had been a whirlwind of excitement and joy, leaving me living in the clouds. I knew sooner or later I'd have to crash back to Earth, but I hadn't expected it quite so soon. I had married the man of

259

my dreams and was carrying our child. Not to mention, I had been able to shut Paige down, ensuring that I could continue providing the wishes for my patient's families in secret.

But as I stood talking to Ms. CP, my gut told me things were not going to end well. I'd always been one to trust my gut. I assumed that this time it was telling me not to get close to Ms. CP. Maybe it was predicting her death sooner than we imagined? I wasn't exactly sure but for the first time, I didn't want to listen to it. I didn't want things to go wrong. My gut just had to be wrong this time, didn't it?

"Have you got a discharge date yet?"

"What do you mean?"

"Well, I thought that you would be able to return home or go to assisted living now that you're not taking poison on a daily basis."

"Oh. No, I don't want to go anywhere," she stated happily.

"You don't?" I was completely confused.

"No." Her eyes darted around the room, and then she leaned towards me and whispered, "I've heard rumors that if you die here, someone carries out your final wish for your family!"

I was silent. What was I supposed to say to that? My brain couldn't think fast enough to come up with an answer before she continued talking. I wasn't prepared for what she would say.

"Look, my niece is starting medical school soon and I'd love nothing more than to see her start a career without student loans. Wouldn't that be amazing? I can't change the fact that I have liver cancer even though I've stopped taking the poison, so I figured I'd just stay here until I die. At least then something good would come from this whole thing, right?"

"What are you talking about?"

My gut was contracting and spasming. Something wasn't right. Everything about this seemed completely wrong. What was she talking about. Was she saying what I thought she was? Could it be true?

260

Eleventh Month: January

(Part II)

"Well, I want to die here so my final wish can be granted. That's what happens when you die at Rolling Hills, you know? At least that's what I've heard," she said with a shrug of her shoulders.

"Who told you that?" I tried to hide my anger at the situation.

"Paige."

I knew my face was probably doing all the talking for me in the absence of my vocal abilities. I couldn't believe what I had just heard come from Ms. CP's mouth. Had Paige really told her that someone was granting wishes at Rolling Hills? Was it Paige's way to get back at me after all? I felt rage boiling inside me, and I was trying my best to remain calm while I was in the patient's room.

"I wouldn't believe everything you hear from her," I said evenly.

"Well, to be honest, I heard it in my support group a few months before I came here, and then Paige confirmed it when I asked her about it."

A support group? What had I done? What had I gotten myself into? I had wanted to do something kind for others. I wanted to share my wealth with people who needed it. Instead, I felt taken advantage of. This was an over-the-top sick game, and I was just some pawn. Suddenly, my anger was replaced by the need to vomit. Had this woman really come here just so I could pay for her niece's medical school when she died?

"Be honest with me. Did your mom really poison you?" I needed the truth.

She lowered her head and looked at her hands as they fiddled with each other. "Not exactly," she said barely above a whisper. "It was part of the plan."

I couldn't believe my ears. A flurry of emotions blew through me as my brain tried to think. In essence, my generosity had led someone to practically commit suicide in an elaborate scheme to get medical school paid for. Not only that, her mother was currently sitting in jail for a crime she hadn't committed. This couldn't be real life. This was a Hallmark movie.

"I'm so confused. If this was all some plan, why did you have her banned from the facility? Why did you ask for the heavy metal screen? Why did you let them arrest her?" I asked as I tried to stay calm but found my voice rising with each question anyway.

"I don't know."

"Really?"

"When I got here, I wanted a chance to process everything, so I had her banned. She was so insistent on watching everything so the plan wouldn't unravel. When I finally let her visit, she threatened me and I broke." She wiped at a tear forming in the corner of her eye. Fake tear, I'm sure. "I knew I'd been drinking arsenic in my Ensure for a while. I got scared, so I asked for the blood work. Then things just started to happen."

"You realize you have liver cancer from all that arsenic and there is no going back?"

"Yeah," she said quietly. "Things escalated quickly."

"I think I'm going to be sick," I said as I ran from the room.

I went straight to Penny's office and informed her that I was sick. I was physically and emotionally sick. I was disgusted with Ms. CP but I was also disgusted with myself. The worst part was that I had absolutely zero people I could talk to about it. It was time to come clean to Asher about everything. About what I had been secretly doing. I was disappointed in myself for keeping it from him this long. What kind of start was this to our marriage?

I sat on the couch and patiently waited for Asher to arrive home that evening. I'd made dinner and had it on the table for the last thirty minutes when he finally arrived. Surprised to see me, he admitted he'd stopped at McDonald's and had a cheeseburger. Once he'd confessed this, I didn't have any further words to say. I'd simply gotten up, cleared the dishes, and gone to bed without saying a word. All the good deeds I did seemed to end in disaster.

At first, he had tried to talk to me, but I'd pretended he was invisible. He hadn't understood *why* what he'd done had been so wrong. Honest, he hadn't done anything wrong, but between the pregnancy hormones and my racing mind, I couldn't talk. I'd learned a very long time ago from Thumper that if I couldn't say nothin' nice, I shouldn't say anything at all. And so I hadn't.

Around eleven, I heard him quietly crawl into his side of the bed. I hadn't been asleep. I couldn't sleep. I couldn't get comfortable and I couldn't shut off my brain. I cycled between anger, crying, confusion, and irritation. To top it off, I was having intermittent cramps. I'd google'd the cramps hours ago to find that it could be caused from pretty much anything.

Without warning, I felt a trickle of liquid on my leg. Assuming I'd peed myself, I was irritated to be awoken after finally having fallen asleep. I threw off the covers and made my way to the bathroom. By the time I reached the door, I was more alarmed since the liquid had continued. One would think that if I were peeing myself, I'd have gotten control of it when I had woken up.

"Asher!" I screamed with a blood curdling cry.

From the bathroom, I heard the click of the bedside lamp turning on and shuffling before Asher presented himself at the door of the bathroom. Normally, I would have found his shirtless body a turn on, but I was in panic mode. Asher rubbed at his eyes, trying to get them to focus. Finally, his eyes adjusted, and he looked at me.

"Shit!" He had seen the trail of blood on the ceramic tile floor.

"I need to go to the hospital. Now," I said, feeling quite afraid.

"What is happening?" His medical knowledge was extremely limited and all he knew was blood equaled bad.

"I'm not exactly sure, but I might be having a miscarriage."

"A miscarriage? I thought we had passed that point?" His face read confusion as he pulled on pajama bottoms and a white t-shirt that had been hanging on the back of the door.

"I mean, I thought we had too. I know things can happen at any point thought. We just need to get to the ER," I said as I tried to hold back tears.

Ten minutes later, we were in the car and headed towards McKinley Hospital Emergency Room. I had padded my underwear with multiple pads and prayed that everything would be okay. In my heart, I wasn't nearly as confident that things would be. Neither of us spoke a word as Asher drove. The gut feeling I had at the beginning of the day turned out right, just as it always had.

Hours later when we emerged from the emergency room, we returned home completely deflated. My fear had been confirmed. The life inside me was no longer alive. I would meet with my obstetrician the next day to discuss how we would proceed, but the bottom line remained the same. Emotionally, and now physically, I was empty inside.

I took two weeks off of work to recover physically. I wasn't sure I'd ever recover emotionally. The first week, I laid in bed, and ignored most of the world. The second week, I pulled myself together and began a few projects around the house. I wasn't weak and I would fight to get back into the swing of things, but it was so hard. "Devastated" didn't describe my feelings enough.

Asher and I had grieved together. It had been an entirely new side of him, and I liked it. He was compassionate, understanding, and thoughtful. He had been strong and had been the one to inform his family both of the wedding and the miscarriage. I could hear his mother through the phone from the other side of the couch. First she was angry that we'd gotten married without anyone, but she'd softened when he told her of the miscarriage.

Finally, I felt that the best thing to do was to return to work. I needed to get out of the house and back into a routine. Asher had encouraged me to take my time and go at my own pace. I hadn't had the chance to tell him what had happened at work with Ms. CP and at this point, I didn't want to tell him. I wanted to just let everything settled down. I wanted life to return to the way it had been. I wanted to pretend it had never happened.

My stomach churned as I pulled into the parking lot of Rolling Hills. I took a long, deep breath and pulled on my big girl panties. As I looked at the dry erase board, I noticed that Ms. CP was no longer a patient. I wondered how that had ended, but was too afraid to ask. I was also thankful that Paige wasn't working. I was in no mood to be threatened again. I accepted my assignment, and chose to clear my head and focus on my work.

However, my first patient was an ass, plain and simple. Rude, unpleasant, foul-mouthed, grumpy, aggressive, sarcastic, racist.... Every negative adjective to describe a person would apply to him. After meeting him for the first time, I'd wondered what could have happened to him to cause him to be this way. What awful things must he have been through to make him this awful of a person? It was almost a punishment to be assigned his room, but I had the luck of the draw on this particular day.

Faking it would be how I would make it through the day. Fake it until you make it. At least that's what my dad used to tell me when he didn't know what he was doing but had to make it appear he did. I would fake a smile and make it through this. I inhaled deeply and walked in the room with my shoulders back and my head held high.

"What do you want?" He croaked at the sight of me.

I wanted to reply with "nothing, you asshole" but I knew that wasn't an option, so I just ignored his greeting completely, and approached him as he sat in his recliner doing a crossword puzzle. He watched my every move over the top of his half moon reading glasses. He had been admitted for congestive heart failure, but he didn't seem to have a heart or else the one he did have had already failed him. Feeling particularly irritable this morning, I knew I was making the wrong choice, but I went for it anyway.

"How many years have you smoked?" My lip turned up in a mischievous smile.

"What?" he asked confused.

"I was just wondering how many years you've been a smoker, that's all." I stood patiently waiting for an answer.

"That's none of your damn business," he said as he pulled his crossword closer to him as if I were trying to read what he was doing.

"You sound like you've been coughing and I thought maybe it was because you've been a smoker. It must just be extra fluid on your heart causing the cough," I said, lying out of my teeth.

He gritted his teeth and replied, "one pack a day for nearly sixty years."

"Ah, that makes more sense," I said feeling proud and ashamed that I'd been able to get under his skin.

"What makes more sense?" he asked with irritation.

"Your cough," I stated confidently as I checked his liter flow on the oxygen.

"I don't have a cough," he said and then spat excess saliva into a cup on his over the bed table.

"Oh. My mistake," I said politely as jammed my fingers into each of his legs looking for edema. "You should really keep these elevated."

"Listen, dummy, don't tell me what to do," he said through gritted teeth.

"Listen, sir, there is no need to call me names. I'm just doing my job," I said with a satisfied smile that doubled for a customer service smile.

"Don't give me that 'I'm just doing my job' bullshit. I know everyone around here thinks I'm an ass and says shit just to piss me off." My head snapped in his direction, impressed that he was finally understanding reality.

"Are you?" I asked, pushing my luck even further.

"Am I what?"

"An ass?"

"What do you think?" It felt like we were playing a dangerous game of chess, and he had just placed an attack on my queen. It was now my turn to get the queen out of danger or surrender her with an equally daring move.

"I think you already know the answer to that." Checkmate.

"You win," he said with a smirk.

I wasn't sure if he was irritated that I had played his own game or if he was proud of me. I just hoped that the nastiness would end for the day so we could get business taken care of and both live to see the next. My gut told me, however, that the battle was just beginning.

"Are you having any pain?"

"No."

"Shortness of breath?"

"Always."

"I noticed your legs are swollen. Do they hurt?"

"I said no pain."

"Hungry?"

"I could go for a small sandwich," he said with a suspicious side eye glance.

"Any trouble urinating?"

"Are you serious?" His face turned a deeper shade of red. "Why the hell do you have so many Goddamn questions this morning. Can't you just let a man die in peace? Shit. Get out of my room," he said pointing toward the door and throwing his pen in my general direction.

"Okay. I'll be back in a little while. If you need anything, just call," I said using the most pleasant voice I could muster while still hiding my laugh. I picked up the pen on my way out of the room and shoved it in my pocket.

"You bitch! Give that…" I heard as I walked off down the hall. I hadn't stayed to hear the rest of his verbal assault.

As I left the shit show from one room, I walked into a shit show of another kind in the next one. The patient was attempting to stand herself up with the assistance of a walker, but was struggling to lift herself from a sitting position to standing. Understanding that she had to use the bathroom, I helped her to the standing position. As she took the first step, I heard the small, wet noise escape from her. She either hadn't heard it or felt it or was choosing to pretend it didn't happen. I was used to patients passing gas while I was helping them so it hadn't phased me.

As she took the second step, the smell blasted me in the face and took my breath away. What had she eaten? She smelled like she had died inside. I tried to hold my breath or breathe through my mouth. Third step. Fourth step and another, louder, noise escaped. It was on the fifth step that I saw a small, black blob drop to the floor.

"Ooooohhhh nooooo. Ooooohhhh noooo. I didn't make it. I didn't make it. Ooooooohhhhh nooooo," she repeated over and over as she continued to inch closer and closer to the bathroom.

Like a trail of breadcrumbs in "Hansel and Gretel", black, sticky mounds led from the middle of the room to the bathroom. Sitting safely on the toilet, she released what she had been trying to hold in and I excused myself to give her privacy. In reality, I excused myself to find fresh air, but she didn't need to know that. Finding a housekeeper, I asked for assistance and together we donned gloves and began the arduous task of cleaning the stool from the floor.

Finishing the last pile, I heard the patient moan from the bathroom and knocked on the door, asking if she needed assistance. Another moan. Taking a deep breath of semi-fresh air, I cracked the door open and peeked in the bathroom. She sat slouched on the toilet, her chin to her chest, grasping the grab bars with white knuckles with one hand while the other clucked at her abdomen. She moaned again.

"Are you okay?" I asked seriously.

Another moan.

"Does your stomach hurt?"

No answer. I called her name but all she did was grunt in reply. I looked into the toilet behind her and saw it was coated in black, coffee ground stool with specks of fresh blood throughout. Using my fingers, I grabbed at her wrist and found a pulse. Tachycardia. I grabbed my phone and called for assistance from the aide and together we supported her, got her cleaned up, and back in her bed. Finally opening her eyes, she looked up at me and the corner of her mouth pulled to a slight smile.

"Call my husband?" she asked meekly.

"Yep." I said as I stepped away to make the phone call.

When I returned a few minutes later, her eyes were closed, and she looked like a peaceful angel. I pulled the blanket over her and let her rest. Before I reached her door, I heard yelling from the hallway and pulled the door shut behind me as I hurried to see who was out there.

Mr. Grump stood in the middle of the hallway, hospital gown flapping behind him, yelling at a woman as she walked by.

"Where's my damn nurse?" he barked after her.

"I'm right here."

He whirled around so fast that he nearly fell over. He stared at me as if he were trying to focus and make sure I wasn't lying to him, that I was, in fact, his nurse. Drawing his finger in the air, he charged toward me with his finger aimed in my direction. He stopped with his finger a few inches from my face and his face contorted into a look of evil, his eyes large and round.

"Where the hell have you been?"

"Were you looking for me?" I pressed my luck again.

"I shouldn't have to look for you. You're here to tend to me, don't you know?"

"Sir, I was assisting another patient of mine. I am here now. What can I do for you?" I said using a pleasant, calm, and even tone that was sure to only push his buttons further.

"What can you do for me? What can *you* do for *me*?" His words grew louder. "You can give me some Goddamn pain medicine is what you can do for me! Fuck! You aren't good for anything, are you?"

Steadying myself, "Where is your pain at?"

"Just give me the medicine already, bitch."

Not wanting to play nice nor push him any further, I picked up my phone and called for assistance, but did not move from my spot. I had made up my mind that if I kept pushing my sweet, innocent tone with him, he was going to snap and potentially hurt me. Eventually, I decided I had other things to deal with than being treated this way. A swarm of staff members rounded the corner and came to my aid. Needless to say, I wouldn't be granting anything from his wish list.

Our director of maintenance was able to convince him that "these bitches" weren't worth his energy and to return to his room. Penny instructed me to document my interactions with him for the day and to reassess his pain in half an hour. She didn't get an argument from me. I wanted to check on my other patients instead of fighting with Mr. Grump.

The patient in room 13, a lonely woman in her sixties, had called my phone just then and asked if her neighbor could bring in her dogs from home for a visit. Per our policy, this was allowed, and they had arrived in what seemed like moments after she'd called the neighbor with the news. The four dachshunds were friendly and wasted no time loving on their mother. All of them miniature with long hair, their fur was a variety of browns and blacks and one with a mixture of both. Admittedly, I wasn't a dog person, but they had jumped up to greet me when I'd entered the room and I had softened slightly.

"Aren't they precious?" Mrs. Dog Lover asked when I reached her bedside.

"They are beautiful. What are their names?" I lied as I reach to pet one that was eagerly begging to be caressed.

"Jasmine, Tammy, Sadie, and Patricia," she said proudly.

"Nice to meet you ladies," I directed toward the pooches.

Two of the dogs continued to lay close to Mrs. Dog Lover's side and didn't acknowledge me. The other two graciously accepted my hands atop their heads. Mrs. Dog Lover appeared pleased that someone else was showing her precious babies love. The neighbor sat unenthused on the couch, typing away at a laptop and ignoring the entire exchange.

"What can I do for you?" I asked once the greetings to the dogs had been finished.

"Is there any chance I could get a bowl of water for the girls?" she asked, petting one curled up near her armpit.

"Yes, of course." I said annoyed that she'd interrupted my lunch for this.

"Thanks a million."

When I returned with a bowl of water, three of the dogs jumped from the bed and ran to the bowl and began to drink, water sloshing all over the floor. A dog person would have known that was going to happen and placed a towel down first, but that just wasn't me. We hadn't had pets growing up and I had zero desire to have one now. I like that I could come and go as I please.

"Is there anything else I can get for you?" I asked, hiding my irritation.

"Can you help me sit up a little more?" she asked.

"Of course I can."

When the task was completed, I said goodbye to the dogs and slipped from the room. I headed back to Mr. Grump, and he had calmed down slightly and refrained from swearing at me as he told me about his chest pain and gave it a score of three out of ten. I gave him some Tylenol, which made him angry because he was hoping I would give him morphine. He then demanded a cigarette and I told him we didn't have any. He kicked me out of his room again at that point and I gladly obliged.

Retracing my steps, I gazed into Mrs. GI Bleed's room and saw her chatting with her husband. Her snow-white hair surrounded her pale face and highlighted her sky blue eyes. Her husband didn't have any hair on his head, but did have a nicely managed snow-white beard. If I'd have seen them at a quick glance, I may have thought they were Santa and Mrs. Claus. I smiled to myself and kept going.

Back in Mrs. Dog Lover's room, her precious girls had gone home with the neighbor, and she was softly crying. I pulled up a chair next to her bed, sat down, and asked how I could help. She shook her head, but she didn't speak.

"Is it the girls?" I asked quietly.

She nodded.

"I'm going to miss them," she said.

"I know you are. They will miss you too." I tried to comfort her.

"I just wish I knew they would be okay. I adopted them from the shelter a few years back, ya know?"

It was my turn to nod my head. I didn't know what I was supposed to say to that. I'd never even set foot in an animal shelter, let alone taken a pet home from there. There was zero chance I could understand the heartache she felt.

"They were so skinny. I had to take them all home with me. I know they are in good hands with the neighbor. He works from home, so that's good. I spent many years working at the shelter and never felt I had to take any of the animals home until I met my girls. I just wish I could do more for them. Do more for all the animals..." she trailed off and covered her face.

I sat quietly, not knowing what to say exactly. Instead, I just rubbed my hand up and down her arm and attempted to comfort her. After a few moments, she pulled her hands away from her face and thanked me for letting her vent. I stood up, gave her a little hug, and told her to call if she needed anything as I headed out of her room. I paused at the door, looked back at her and smiled. It was finally lunchtime.

I'd just finished gulping down some moderately warm soup when the phone rang yet again.

Twelfth Month: February

The air was freezing and snow covered the ground a foot deep. Asher's mother had picked a fine time to have a baby, I thought as I waited for my car to warm up. Since he was the first to have a birthday since getting married, I was determined to find a way to make it special. The problem had been coming up with ideas. I'd finally settled on something and kept it a surprise. Clearly, I was good at keeping things a secret.

When Asher's birthday arrived, he was excited to unwrap the small box that had been sitting on the coffee table for three whole days. It was like keeping a child from their presents at Christmas. He woke up early that morning and eagerly began asking when he could open up the delicately wrapped present.

"Fine, you may open it," I said, pretending to give in.

He tore the paper off, opened the box, and began to read the small card inside the box. Excited, he kissed me. We had an hour to get ready before we needed to leave for the birthday surprise. He had been ready in fifteen minutes.

We arrived at the airport, but instead of driving towards the departures terminal, we drove to an entrance at the back of the building. A large sign guided us towards a hanger nestled between several medium-sized trees. Inside, a helicopter sat parked. Eyeing the flying machine, Asher's excitement grew.

The helicopter tour of the city only lasted an hour, but had spectacular views of both the city and the countryside. Even Asher admitted it had been romantic. When we landed, Asher had kissed me before exiting the helicopter, and sincerely thanked me. I was glad he had enjoyed it as much as I had. We both needed something like that in our lives at the moment.

That evening, Asher's parents flew into town and we had dinner at a local restaurant before driving them to their hotel. Asher's parents had made his birthday an annual trip to visit him for the last ten years. It was the first time we had seen them since we'd eloped. I had been worried that things might have been awkward, but Marceline had cleared the air the moment they arrived. They had declined the invitation to stay at our house citing not wanting to intrude. That was bogus because they would always be welcome at our house.

After a week of touring the city, fancy dinners that Asher and I hated, and a visit to a nearby winery, his parents were dropped off at the airport, and it was just the two of us once more. Back at home, I finished laundry while he finished the dishes. We climbed into bed early and mentally prepared ourselves for the work week ahead.

"I had a great birthday week, Ellie," he said as he laid his head next to mine on my pillow.

"I'm glad you enjoyed it. I loved getting to spend time with you and your parents."

"*Our* parents," he corrected.

"Our parents."

It still sounded weird saying that. Not only was I not used to saying *our*, I wasn't used to the pleural of the word parent. I hadn't had parent*s* in like thirty years. Despite it feeling weird to use those words, I absolutely loved it.

"Happy birthday." I planted a kiss on his lips.

Not breaking from the kiss, he rolled over onto me, and kissed me passionately. I didn't fight. It would be the first time we'd made love in a long time and the first since our miscarriage. I was more than ready. I missed this part of him. I missed this part of *us*.

When my alarm went off the next morning, I threw it across the room. Unfortunately, it hadn't made the annoying sound coming from it stop. I had no choice but to get out of bed and fetch the damn thing. Once I'd done that, I forced myself to accept the fact that it was time to get up and made my way to the shower.

The patient smiled as I introduced myself. His hair had been gone for many years, and he had wrinkles around his eyes. His hands had age spots and calluses from ninety-two years of hard work. He didn't carry any extra weight around the middle, and I could clearly see his collar bones through his skin. Despite these obvious signs of aging, his eyes remained a vivid blue color and when he looked at me, they smiled. His skin was pale from attempting to beat leukemia and having failed.

"How are you this morning?" I asked with an upbeat tone.

"Tired," he replied with a recognizable German accent.

"That's understandable. Are you having any pain?"

"Nein."

"Ah, German. Very nice."

He smiled. "Have you been?"

"I have, in fact, but it was many years ago. Are you from Germany?"

"Ya. I grew up in Mönchengladbach, outside of Düsseldorf. I moved here in my early teens with my family."

"Wow. There was a lot going on in Germany when you were born and raised. Moving to the States must have been a very big change for your family."

"Yes it was. It took time to get acclimated, but eventually we did. My father was a member of the Nazi party and at the end of the war, he felt it was better if we fled. We came home from school one day to all our belongings packed up, and we left." He looked down at his hands. "I can't say that things were much better here because being a Nazi was

276

a terrible crime, but my father lied and said we were running from Nazi Germany. I always wonder if our lives would have been easier if we'd have gone to East instead."

I didn't say a word. How was I supposed to respond to that? When I mentioned Germany, I hadn't expected a full confession of sorts. Instead of speaking, I busied myself around the room. I didn't know what I should or shouldn't say.

"Are you mad at me?" he asked quietly as I returned to his bedside.

Caught off guard, I responded, "Of course not. Why would I be mad at you?"

"I don't know. You didn't say anything. I thought maybe I shouldn't have told you."

"I'm not mad at you. In fact, I'm glad you told me. I just didn't know what to say."

"Yeah, that happens too."

"Do you want to talk about it?"

"It's not that I *want* to talk about it, but I wish my kids could understand what it was like when I grew up. You know? See where I lived and understand what my childhood was like. It was a happy childhood, despite a war starting. I wish I'd been able to take them back. To help them see."

"Have you talked to them about it?"

"I always talked to them about it. Mönchengladbach is a beautiful city full of beautiful people. The German people are very kind and welcoming. I needed them to grow up with a different mind that I did, so I spent many hours telling them my stories."

"Then I don't think you'll have to worry too much."

"I suppose. Can I ask you a favor?"

"Of course. No promises though," I teased.

"Can I have some toast?" he asked with a laugh.

"Oh, that I can do!" I said as I headed towards the door.

"Thank you," he called after me.

I knew what I wanted to do, and I knew that I shouldn't. The reality was that the decision was mine, and mine alone, to make. I knew the consequences. I toyed back and forth, made a decision, and stuck with it. I couldn't let one bad experience stop me from all the good ones.

The final week of February meant the annual Hospice Memorial Gathering at Rolling Hills. Families of all the patients we had lost over the previous year were invited to join us in remembering their loved ones. It first started out as a small gathering when a nurse invited a few families that had grown close to her. Afterward, the families stated how much they had loved it, and a tradition was born.

Tables and chairs were set up under a white wedding style tent on the front lawn, a cake had been bought, and beautiful arrangements of flowers were everywhere. A heater off to one corner helped keep the space toasty warm. By two o'clock, the tent was bustling with staff and their families, eagerly waiting to greet the patient's families as they arrived. I was excited to see some families and there were a few I was dreading. I pulled Asher a little closer when the tent door opened and the first guests began to arrive.

A podium had been set up along the longest wall, but no one currently stood at it. Behind the podium were small handcrafted floral arrangements attached to the tent wall with patient's names on them. Several children playing a game of tag ran by us. I noticed it was loud in the enclosed space, but the mood was upbeat and everyone seemed to be enjoying themselves. I saw a few faces with tears, but mostly smiles.

I wasn't sure how these events went since it was my first one, so Asher and I stood towards a far wall and just observed everyone mingling. I kept looking for Ben, Ramona, and Lily, but didn't see them. I hadn't talked to any of them in a while, so I wasn't sure if they were even planning to come.

I hadn't gone to my mother's funeral. I felt guilty right then for not having kept in contact, but snapped out of it when I reminded myself that contact is a two-way street. Ben could have contacted *me*. I'd sent a card with a generous gift, and never even received so much as a "Thank You". I don't know where the relationship broke down at, but I didn't want to play games. As horrible as I felt thinking it, I didn't want to fight for it.

Eventually, I saw Penny step up to the podium and tap on the microphone. I jumped, not realizing a speaker was directly behind us. Penny asked for everyone to find a seat so that she could begin a presentation. Asher and I found two empty seats a short distance away, sitting next to a woman I didn't recognize.

"First, want to thank everyone for coming today. It's such an honor that we can gather together and remember those that we have lost over the last year. For some, the wounds are still fresh and for others, the healing has already begun. Our hope is that through our fellowship today, no one will face their loss alone."

Everyone clapped.

"This year, we celebrate the lives of the men and women we have loved and lost. Each of these individuals has made a difference in the life of someone in this room. It has been an honor to care for your loved ones and from all of us here at Rolling Hills, thank you for trusting us with the care of your loved one. We are glad you could make it today to join us for fellowship.

"At this time, I'd like to open the mic up to anyone wishing to share how they were impacted by their loved one," Penny said, smiling, as she stepped aside.

Several people stood and moved towards the podium, forming a line. A man stepped up to the microphone first, and introduced himself as Mike Sharma. Mike spoke about the sacrifices his mother made to ensure he and his siblings had a quality education. Next, a woman I recognized as the wife of an old man I had cared for, came to the microphone. Dressed in a pastel floral sundress with a cropped cardigan, she looked younger than I remembered her.

"My husband and I enjoyed traveling from the time we were married until he became too ill to leave the house. He taught me to enjoy each day as if it were my last, to enjoy the birds and fresh mountain air, and to look at each sunset as a promise of a new start the following day. At his funeral, the funeral director brought me a card with my name on it. It was a plain white envelope with a single rose on it. Inside was a note from my husband telling me that I was to finish our bucket list rather than sit around the house missing him. At the bottom of the note was a phone number, and directions to call it."

She pulled a tissue from her purse and dabbed her eyes. The daughter standing next to her gave her hand a squeeze. She took a few deep breaths, looked around the room, and then continued.

"When I called, I was informed that my husband had bought me an RV, and I could pick it up at my convenience. I was shocked at first because I don't know where he got the money, but I've spent this time doing just what he asked of me — traveling the world. Let me tell you, I know a piece of him is with me everywhere I go. It was the best gift I've ever received."

She pulled another tissue from her purse and dabbed her eyes again. She was immediately pulled into a hug from her daughter, and they stepped back from the microphone and returned to their seats. Alice, the daughter I helped to unite with her birth mother, stepped up to the microphone and pulled out a lined sheet of notebook paper from her pocket to read from.

"I had the opportunity to meet my birth mother and my sisters because of the kindness shown by the nurses here. Specifically, Ellie," she said as she looked through the tent trying to see me. "I got a chance to spend a single day with her, and I am forever grateful that the staff here listened to her and cared enough to help her, not just with her physical needs, but the emotional ones as well. I will forever cherish that one day I spent meeting my birth mother. Thank you."

The sisters standing off to the side embraced her in a hug, and they walked back to their seats as a few more family members approached the microphone, and discussed the impact of their loved ones. I didn't recognize everyone as both families from those who had lived at the facility and those who had been cared for at home were invited.

I didn't want public recognition when I began granting the wishes of my dying patients, and I still didn't. I just wanted to know that their families would have something, a part of those lost, long after they had passed away. Hearing the impact statements in person, I was filled with satisfaction, and an overall good feeling. But did it outweigh what Ms. CP and her mother did?

Out of the corner of my eye, I noticed Paige whispering in Penny's ear, and my gut told me exactly what she was doing. But Penny didn't have an angry face when Paige finished. Penny was smiling. What did her smile mean? Was it good? Was it bad? Instead of worrying about what was going to happen, I returned my focus on the speakers giving impact statements. I would worry about Paige later. I recognized another family member stepping up to the microphone.

"My son died at a young age from Amyotrophic lateral sclerosis, more commonly known as ALS or Lou Gehrig's disease. During his time at home, he endured great challenges physically and emotionally. Throughout those challenges, he continued to protect his children and do everything in his power to ensure they had a better quality of life. When he came to Rolling Hills, the staff embraced him. They truly loved him. They helped him die with dignity and in comfort. Honestly, they protected him and his children when he no longer could. Before he passed away, I took custody of his children, and I was approached by a family lawyer who said he had been paid to help my husband and I seek adoption rights for our grandchildren. We had been anxious about how we would make it happen financially, but this angel appeared and told us everything was already arranged and paid for. I feel comfort knowing that my son continues to make miracles happen for his children, even after his passing."

As if lightning had struck, Asher snapped his head in my direction, and began to stare at me. Without so much as a glance, I knew exactly what was happening in Asher's head at that moment. He was putting the puzzle together. I kept my eyes forward, locked in on the podium. My secret was out. More families I recognized stood in line to give their impact statements.

"My name is Delilah. I lost my dad earlier this summer. He was someone who liked to fix things. If you had a problem, you called my dad, and he would drop everything and help fix it. He promised my son, Jonah, the classic car they had rebuilt together for graduation, but the car had to be sold at auction to pay for the medical bills that had piled up. My dad managed to fix that too. Jonah received the keys to the car at his graduation party. There is an angel among us. There are no words to describe the lasting impact that car has had on my son and will have on him in the future. Anytime he sits in that driver's seat, he feels his grandfather's presence. Each time I see Jonah smile, I see my father. I miss him, but this makes losing him hurt a little less."

She finished with a smile. She then stepped aside while another person took the podium. I didn't recognize her, but everything became familiar when she began to speak.

"My mother passed away just a few months ago. She was my best friend. Not a day goes by that I don't think about her, try to call her, or think of things I didn't get the chance to say to her. The most important one being thank you. The one thing she wished for more than anything was for grandchildren. My husband and I were unable to give her that. I watched her play with my cousin's children and my heart always broke. At her funeral, I got a card from her telling me to call the fertility center and when I did, I cried. I am nine weeks pregnant today with twins because of her. Despite not being here on earth, I know she will be with them every step of the way. Her impact will extend beyond me directly to the next generation. And she will finally have her wish."

I noticed people whispering to each other and dabbing at their eyes. I tried to see where Paige had gone, but I didn't find her anywhere in the crowd. Penny continued to sit at the table near the podium with a smile on her face, attentively listening to the impact statements.

"Uh, hello. I'm not much for public speaking really. I just wanted to thank everyone here for taking good care of my mom. We came to Rolling Hills after a storm damaged our roof. Let me tell ya, she was pissed at me for cancellin' that insurance. I kept saying it would be okay, but she was spittin' mad at me.

"My mom hated hospitals. However, she has a fairy godmother or somethin' because the next day a contractor showed up at our house and told us everything had been paid for! They fixed the roof right away. My mom was able to go home a few days later. It was amazing. Being home is all she wished for. Uh... That's all." He stepped down from the podium.

I recognized the two men took the podium next. Their dad had been one of my favorite patients to date, and I was eager to hear them talk.

"My name is Bobby, and this is my brother Billy. Our dad was quite the character, and always keep us on our toes. Man, I know when he was here, he... uh... kept finding new ways to try to escape." The audience laughed. "He was a good escape artist too, let me tell ya. A real Houdini if you ask me. Anyway, he always dreamed of escaping to bigger places. After he escaped Rolling Hills and went to Heaven, Billy and I got a card from him with everything we needed to escape to Iceland to scatter his ashes. Ha. We won't forget that trip, that's for sure. We miss him, but memories like this keep us smiling." Billy hugged him, and they went back to their seats.

"My sister passed away recently and when she would call me at night, she always told me how great everyone was to her. You all let her bring her dogs up here. She loved those dogs so much. I wasn't able to get back to see her before she passed away or anything, but I got a card from the local shelter where she had worked years ago a short time after she passed thanking me for the donation of dog food from Jasmine, Sadie, Tammy, and Patricia. Those were her girls! My sister sure is a sneaky one! What she wouldn't do for those dogs." The woman returned to her seat, laughing and shaking her head.

"My dad passed away two weeks ago. It's still pretty fresh for me to talk about, but one thing he really struggled with throughout our lives was with his German heritage. Our grandfather had been a Nazi. My dad learned a long time ago, after coming to the U.S., what being a Nazi *really* meant and vowed to make sure that my brothers and sisters and I loved *all* people for who they are. He would tell us stories about where he grew up and *how* he grew up, and I'm so thankful that he didn't shield us from that. Last week at his funeral, we got a card with the phone number of a travel agent. When I called, the woman told me he had paid for us kids to visit his hometown in Germany, to meet with extended family members, and see where he grew up. This is something we cherish and appreciate so much. I know he had always wished we would take this trip and I'm glad he made it happen for us," she said with a smile. She motioned for the next person to take the microphone.

"My name is Steven and my siblings and I lost our mother awhile back to gastric cancer. I want to say thank you to everyone for taking care of her. She was always taking care of us and I'm glad she had such excellent care at the end of her life. After she passed away, she left us a card with an address on it. Her final wish was for us to continue spending time together as a family. To allow our children to grow up knowing their cousins. She sure had great memories with her own cousins, we had great relationships with our cousins, and she wanted us to give that to our kids as well. The address was a lake house with room for all of us that is apparently ours as long as we vacation as a family at least once a year. Her legacy is impacting not only my siblings and I, but our future generations as well. Family was everything to her." He hugged his sister and they took their seats.

Several more impact statements were read from families I didn't know before the last person approached the microphone. He was the young husband to a woman I had cared for. I was glad to see he was doing decently well. He was trying to keep himself from crying, I could see that, as he finally took his turn.

"My wife was my world. I was so scared when she was diagnosed with cancer, and we had many talks about what would happen when she was gone. She hated the thought of leaving me, but we both knew she didn't have a choice. She taught me the true definition of love, in every way. She encouraged me to keep my life moving and to always remember her. When I was sorting everything out after she passed away, I called the bank to have our mortgage fixed and learned that we didn't have one anymore. It was paid it off," he paused, clearly choked up, and shook his head, looking at the desk part of the podium, "My wife did that. I love her so much," he said as a steady stream of tears overtook him, and he practically ran back to his seat.

Seeing no more family members in line, Penny stood to continue with the presentation or make closing statements. I wasn't sure. As I looked around at the faces in the crowd, I saw happiness. We were a part of that. The staff weren't just caring for patients, we were caring for families. We weren't just a part of their lives for a few days, we were a part of their lives forever. We were their last memories with their loved ones.

I didn't hear what Penny was saying as Asher leaned over to me and began whispering into my ear.

"Are. You. Serious?"

I turned and locked eyes with him. "I'm serious."

"Do they know?" he whispered.

"As far as I know, they have no clue. As far as they know, their loved ones planned it all along," I whispered back.

"You're a beautiful person," he said as he kissed me.

"Thank you for trusting me when I told you I couldn't tell you my secret, but that you'd know at some point."

"Of course. I love you, Ellie Grant. More than you could possibly know."

He planted a firm kiss on my lips and squeezed my hands. I felt butterflies fluttering in my stomach. Was this was what pure joy and happiness felt like? My good deeds had impacted *generations* without that even being my intention. I had just wanted to help fulfill the last wishes of people that crossed my path. I wanted to use my good fortune to give back to others.

Truth be told, I wasn't going to stop. Paige could kiss my ass. It wasn't my fault that the entire situation with Ms. CP had taken place. I had no control over that. It wasn't fair for someone to dictate how I spent my money. I went into nursing to make a difference and to take care of people. I was doing just that. Nursing is and always had been about taking care of *all* the needs of patients. That includes physical *and* emotional.

Maybe I wouldn't stay at Rolling Hills. Maybe I would move on. I didn't know the future, but I did know that my future was looking bright as long as I had Asher and my nursing career.

Finally, the event had wound down, and I was exhausted. My feet ached from wearing pumps. I grabbed Asher's hand and led him towards the front of the tent. Paige stood a few feet from the entrance and her eyes were locked on me.

"Nice work, Ellie," she said sarcastically as we approached the front door.

"Go to hell, Paige," Asher said as he led me past her.

I was incredibly impressed and turned on hearing him stick up for me like that. We said goodbye to a few more people standing by the door, and headed towards the car in the parking lot. Calling my name, Delilah ran up to me. As I turned around, she handed me an envelope with a smile plastered on her face.

"You forgot to sign this," she smiled with a mischievous grin.

"What?" I replied, interested in the envelope.

I tore it open and as I read it, my cheeks began to flush. How long had she known the truth? Inside was a single piece of thick cream paper folded into thirds. Unfolded, the paper contained official looking blue embossed print. It was the title for a 1964 Corvette Sting Ray.

"I'll keep your secret," she whispered as she handed me a ballpoint pen.

What Did You Think of The Wish Lists?

First of all, thank you for purchasing The Wish Lists. I know you could have picked any number of books to read, but you picked my book, and for that I am extremely grateful.

If you enjoyed this book, I'd like to hear from you! I hope that you could take some time to post a review on Amazon, and share with your family and friends by posting to Facebook, Twitter, or Instagram.

I want you, the reader, to know that your review is very important and so, if you'd like to leave a review, all you have to do is visit:

https://www.amazon.com/dp/1694114090

Love always, JM Spade

Made in the
USA
Middletown, DE